THE SCAM

EVIE HUNTER

Boldwood

First published in Great Britain in 2022 by Boldwood Books Ltd.

Copyright © Evie Hunter, 2022

Cover Photography Depositphotos and iStock

Every effort has been made to obtain the necessary permissions with reference to copyright material, both illustrative and quoted. We apologise for any omissions in this respect and will be pleased to make the appropriate acknowledgements in any future edition.

A CIP catalogue record for this book is available from the British Library.

Paperback ISBN 978-1-80280-282-5

Large Print ISBN 978-1-80280-281-8

Hardback ISBN 978-1-80280-280-1

Ebook ISBN 978-1-80280-284-9

Kindle ISBN 978-1-80280-283-2

Audio CD ISBN 978-1-80280-275-7

MP3 CD ISBN 978-1-80280-276-4

Digital audio download ISBN 978-1-80280-278-8

Boldwood Books Ltd
23 Bowerdean Street
London SW6 3TN
www.boldwoodbooks.com

With grateful thanks to my sister-in-law, Monette Benedict, for her unstinting support during a very difficult time. I love you. x

1

In Saint-Tropez in villa overlooking the sea.
In hot tub with hotter man. The stars are putting on a display just for us. Need to pinch myself. Is this really happening to me? xx

Skylar Kennedy grinned as she pressed send, imagining the WhatsApp message winging its way through cyberspace and landing in Nancy's inbox with a soft thud. She would be less than human if she didn't pause to envisage the envy on her friend's face, Sky decided, since ordinarily she wasn't the one who got the man. Well, not the fit one anyway. It was cold and wet in the UK right now, which only added to Sky's smug feeling of satisfaction as she soaked up the sunshine during the day and was wined and dined in five-star luxury at night because... well because things like this simply didn't happen to Sky and she was supposed to enjoy the attention, wasn't she?

Nancy was the girl who had it all – looks, confidence, a figure to die for and a game plan mapped out for the rest of her life. Sky had always been her bag-carrier, overlooked or disregarded as insignificant by the beautiful people drawn to Nancy like moths to the proverbial. Sky hated the limelight so that situation suited her perfectly. She was out several nights a week, whenever Nancy needed support, which allowed Sky to convince herself that she wasn't being reclusive. She had a social life, of sorts, and lived vicariously on exaggerated tales of Nancy's various romantic conquests.

That was more than enough for Sky.

Or had been, until Karim Amin came into her life, at which point her lack of enthusiasm for the dating game made sense. She had subconsciously been waiting for that moment, she realised and was now getting her reward.

She and Nancy had been in a club together when they first noticed Karim. Well, it hadn't been just the two of them who'd noticed him walk in with his retinue as though he owned the place. Every female head in the place had turned to stare in open admiration. Later Sky learned that he *did* own the place. Well, he had a controlling share in the consortium that had transformed Alexandria into the happening joint that it had rapidly become. His flair and vision were responsible for that, Sky now knew, even though Karim was too modest to make the admission himself.

Clichéd though it might sound, their eyes had clashed across the crowded room and Sky had felt her insides lurch. It seemed downright ridiculous to confess, even to Nancy, that she'd felt an instant connection. It was as though she had been marking time, waiting for the moment that would align her stars and make sense of her existence.

Oblivious to the turn that Sky's thoughts had taken, it was Nancy who'd had the confidence to approach Karim. Nothing fazed Nancy. Sky still recalled the seductive sway of her hips as she approached his table, secure in the knowledge that she wouldn't be rejected. Karim's gaze had roamed over her generous curves with a provocative half-smile, and had then landed on Sky, who stood rooted to the spot a few paces behind her friend. It was at her that he flashed an uncontrived smile; her whom he'd invited to have a drink with him. Nancy, to her credit, had shrugged off her only failure in living memory and told Sky to have fun.

But she hadn't intended her to have *this* much fun, Sky knew. Nancy had advised against accepting Karim's invitation to spend the weekend in Saint-Tropez, pointing out that Sky barely knew the man and that he could be an axe murderer, or worse. Sky found it hard to imagine anything worse and tried not to take offence because Nancy clearly thought Karim had an ulterior motive in seeking Sky out. Besides, they'd been dating sporadically for two months, the unscheduled nature of their relationship down to the fact that Karim travelled so much.

'It's not as though he's taking me to some dark and distant land,' Sky pointed out impatiently. 'We're going to the South of France, that's all. You're the one who's always telling me to get out more.'

'Just be careful and make sure you send me regular messages so that I know you're safe.'

They hugged. Nancy's brief moment of jealousy, if that's what it had been, was a thing of the past and their friendship was solid again.

Sky had kept her promise and sent regular updates. Nancy was probably sick of them by now but Sky simply couldn't help showing off, just a little. It wasn't as though they'd met on a questionable dating site or that Karim was a scammer. Nancy had verified his ownership online of Alexandria before grudgingly agreeing that he appeared to be the genuine article. Anyway, Sky would never register on a dating site, despite Nancy's insistence that they were safe if you were cautious and that it was the way everyone hooked up nowadays. She wasn't born yesterday and wouldn't concede all her worldly wealth to a good-looking parasite even if she had been tempted to dig her toes into that particular shark-infested pond. Besides, her trusty sixth sense had assured her it wouldn't be necessary. She just had to exercise patience and the man of her dreams would eventually come along and sweep her off her feet.

Karim had proven to be that man.

So far, everything had been beyond fabulous. Karim was amusing and attentive; a thoughtful and unselfish lover who was accustomed to the best of everything. A nagging little voice at the back of Sky's mind wondered, in that case, why he had settled for her. A man with his looks, charm, intelligence and wealth could have anyone he wanted and Sky was well aware that she fell far short of perfection.

He had left her alone in the hot tub whilst he took a business call. There had been any number of them during the two-day break. He always apologised profusely but Sky went out of her way to assure him that she didn't mind. Of course, a man as successful as he clearly was could never be completely off duty. He had actually confessed that he was a bit of a control freak and never entirely trusted anyone else to get the job done, even though he paid his people handsomely and employed only the best and brightest minds. That, Sky assumed, was the key to his success.

She heard his footsteps on the boarded deck as he returned to the hot tub and she hastily hid her phone beneath her towel. She didn't want him to think that she was boasting to Nancy, even though she had been.

'Hey.' Karim flashed the sexy smile that turned Sky's insides to mulch, dropping the towel that he'd draped casually around his waist as he climbed back into the hot tub. Water splashed over its edge as he sat beside her and slipped an arm around her shoulders. 'Sorry about that. Sometimes I wonder why I employ so many people when they don't seem to be able to tie their own shoelaces without me holding their hands.' He sighed but Sky knew from what he'd already told her that he wouldn't have it any other way. 'Now, where were we? Hey,' he added, frowning, 'your glass is empty. Can't have that.'

He reached behind her, extracted a half full bottle of Krug from the chiller and refilled both of their glasses. He handed hers to her and raised his own in a toast.

'To you,' he said, smiling into her eyes. 'And to my good fortune in having met you. If I had not gone to the club that night, then...'

Flustered by the compliment, Sky took a sip of the ruinously expensive champagne and it slipped smoothly down her throat. A little too smoothly. This was their second bottle and she had a horrible feeling that she'd drunk a lot more of it than he had. Every time his phone rang he filled her glass before leaving the tub to answer it. And although Sky had been full of good intentions to sip delicately while she waited for him to come back, she always seemed to drain her glass. Drunk on euphoria, she told herself as bubbles went up her nose, causing her to sneeze somewhat inelegantly.

She touched her flute to his and the ring of crystal on crystal echoed through the night.

'I still don't understand what it is that you do,' Sky said, wanting to know everything there was to know about this oh-so-fascinating entrepreneur, wanting to leave him in no doubt that she was interested.

She was still convinced that he must be married, or have a significant other waiting patiently for his return in one of his many properties scattered across Europe and beyond. Much as she liked him, she would not be his bit on the side.

That was the question she most wanted to ask: did he have children? And where were Karim's parents, his siblings? Nancy's online sleuthing had revealed that he was a self-made man and philanthropist who'd been born in Alexandria, Egypt and was thirty-five years old. There were pictures of him at various swanky charity dos, always with a different woman. He seldom gave interviews and seemed to actively discourage publicity.

'I make money and give it away,' he said with a self-deprecating shrug.

'Why? How?' She turned to face him, frowning. 'I don't understand.'

'Ah, my sweet girl, you think I should keep it all and forget about those less fortunate than me?'

'No, no, of course not!' Sky's head swam and she felt her cheeks warm. Damn it, she had been so careful not to appear too enthusiastic, to take this weekend in her stride and pretend it was the type of thing she was accustomed to, but the excessive amounts of champagne had loosened her tongue. 'That isn't what I mean at all.' She reached up to touch his face. 'I admire your altruistic character, really I do, but you must admit that most wealthy men dedicate themselves to increasing that wealth and jealously guarding what they have amassed.'

'I, my sweet, am not most men.' He stared up at the sky, a faraway look on his face, and she knew he was no longer thinking about her.

'Tell me,' she said, in a softly persuasive tone. 'I want to know everything there is to know about you.' *Especially the stuff you'll never admit to.*

He was silent for so long that at first she thought he wouldn't answer her. 'My parents and siblings were all wiped out in a car bomb attack when I was a child.' His voice, when he finally spoke, was low and lacked emotion.

'No!' Appalled, Sky abruptly sat up, causing a mini tidal wave to splash over the edge of the tub. 'That's terrible.'

'I was the only survivor. I was just nine at the time and at school, which saved me.'

'I hope you weren't the one to find them.'

'No, my darling. I love your empathy,' he added, turning to look at her again and doubtless observing the tears pouring down her face. 'Someone came to the school and herded us children together. Mine was not the only family wiped out that day.'

'I am so sorry.' She leaned the side of her face against his shoulder, conscious of his accelerated heartrate. 'How do you get over something like that?'

'You don't. It stays with you always. You develop survivor's guilt which destroys you slowly, if you allow it to.' The shoulder that she was using as a pillow stiffened beneath her cheek. 'I was alone, lonely and life seemed pointless. As I grew older I became more resentful and decided that none of it was my fault. I had the capacity to fight back.' He waved a hand. 'Not with bombs and bullets, but with my brains. So I made it my mission to help people like me who had been displaced, their lives torn apart for a senseless cause. I started a small importing and exporting business, using grass roots knowledge of my native Egypt to understand what people needed, and it grew from there.'

'You are remarkable. You make it all sound so easy.'

'No, my love, there is nothing special about me.' He kissed her brow. 'I am a survivor, nothing more.'

'Didn't you feel a burning desire for revenge? I know I would.'

'Of course. That is why so much of my work is clandestine.'

'Clandestine? What do you mean?'

He smiled at her but said nothing, presumably waiting for her to join the dots.

'You work for your government?' she asked.

He smiled down at her. 'I cannot tell you precisely what I do, or for whom. Suffice it to say that my efforts bring their own reward. But there is a downside, too. I make a lot of enemies. There is a target on my back, which is why I am not married and why I don't have children of my own, much as I would like them.'

Sky was ashamed at the relief that washed over her at this admission. The man had settled for a lonely existence because he was so deeply scared and she was selfishly glad that he didn't have a wife waiting in the wings. She was truly a terrible person, it seemed.

Karim went on, 'Those who wish me harm would seize on any such weakness and I couldn't stand the loss of someone dear to me; not for a second time.'

Sky nodded her understanding, impressed by his selflessness, his steely determination to avenge his lost family. 'You are always looking over your shoulder,' she said in a voice laced with sympathy.

He shrugged. 'I am well protected.'

Sky knew that was true. She found the rotation of never less than four men patrolling the property a little intrusive, although she understood better now the need for their presence, and for all the high-tech security inside the villa itself.

'Besides,' he added, 'my business interests, and other occupations, take me all over the world. As you know from my inability to plan our dates very far in advance, I am never in the same place for long.'

'You own this property?'

'Nothing is in my name. I don't come here often but meeting you...' He looked down at her and the grip of winter left his eyes, to be replaced with an expression of soft admiration. 'Meeting you unlocked something inside me and I wanted to share a few precious days with you.'

'Oh, Karim.' Fresh tears swamped her eyes. 'I feel the same way but never dreamed that you would want me.'

'So little self-confidence,' he said, smiling as he shook his head and tutted. 'That is one of the things I adore about you.'

'With good reason. I am not Nancy.'

'I barely noticed Nancy. Beautiful women like her abound the world over but are high-maintenance.'

'Yes,' she said, nodding because it was true. Nancy did need a lot of attention. 'I understand.'

The soft touch of his hand on her forearm prevented Sky from feeling peeved that he hadn't included her in that category. She was glad that he had not, she told herself, especially now that she knew something about the heavy burden he bore on a daily basis. She wanted him to take her seriously, not look upon her as a glamourous plaything in need of constant nurturing. Besides, the truth could never hurt – not really. She wasn't in Nancy's league, had never been high-maintenance in her life and was content simply to have caught the attention of such a charming and charismatic man.

How long his interest would last before he grew tired of her, or because she was not his priority, she preferred not to think about. All that mattered was that they were here together and he was plying her with attention, as well as revealing aspects of his life that she suspected he seldom talked about. That was more than enough to satisfy Sky. She would simply attempt to commit every word, every gesture, every nuance to memory and if it all fell apart tomorrow, at least she would be able to look back on this blissful moment played out beneath a blanket of stars.

'In my situation it would be suicidal to take up with someone like your friend.'

Before Sky could think of an intelligent response his phone rang again. He cursed, excused himself and clambered elegantly from the tub. Sky enjoyed the sight of his tight naked butt as he walked away from her, phone pressed to his ear. She noticed one of his bodyguards lurking in the shadows, out of earshot but able to see Sky in all her nakedness if she herself got out of the tub.

'Not happening,' she muttered, resubmerging herself beneath the warm bubbles and sighing with contentment.

'I am sorry, my darling.' Sky had almost dropped off to sleep and started violently at the sound of Karim's voice close to her ear. 'We will have to cut this trip short, I'm afraid.'

A small gasp of disappointment slipped past Sky's guard. 'That's a shame,' she said, trying not to pout. 'But we were due to go home tomorrow anyway and I am grateful for the time that we have spent together.'

'You make it sound as though we won't be doing it again.'

'Well, after what you just said about commitments, I did think...'

'That I was letting you down gently?' He smiled and shook his head. 'You don't get away that easily. My men will put you on a flight back to London but I have to go immediately.'

'Oh.' This time she was unable to hide her dismay. The way his men looked at her gave her the creeps. 'I thought you would—'

'Alas, I must go to Egypt. Now. Tonight.' He took her hand and helped her from the tub. She forgot about his men, lurking nearby, no doubt ogling her, and instead allowed Karim to take her in his arms. 'But I will be back in England within the week and we will pick up where we left off. I am not about to let another man get anywhere near what's mine. You can count on that.'

He kissed her and Sky's head swirled. Not because of the champagne this time but because he had sounded so possessive.

And because he was determined to see her again, regardless of the danger. That, after all, had been her ultimate goal.

2

Ryan Callahan sat at the back of the departure lounge. Just like everyone else, he scrolled through his phone, giving the appearance of being totally engrossed. Unlike everyone else though, he kept Skylar Kennedy in his sights. She looked distracted. Perhaps she'd been crying. It was hard to tell given that she was wearing shades that covered half her face. She kept her gaze focused on the phone in her hands, as though willing it to ring, and never once turned in his direction.

Business-class passengers were invited to board and Sky got up with the privileged few to make her way to the gate. She didn't push herself forward with the passengers who moved with purpose and authority. She looked unsure of herself, as though she expected to be turned back at any moment, or have her right to board with the elite challenged.

This woman was unaccustomed to travelling in style, it would appear, which made Ryan highly suspicious about Amin's interest in her. She was most definitely not Amin's usual type – could Ryan somehow exploit the fact that she'd gotten herself in above her head, even if she didn't yet realise it? Amin must have a reason for involving himself with this latest conquest. He didn't ordinarily take his women abroad with him so he obviously had a particular interest in this one, and Ryan doubted whether that interest was purely amatory. Amin used people the way that most men used credit cards.

Ryan waited until his row at the front of economy was called and smiled at Sky as he passed her aisle seat at the rear of the business cabin. She was still wearing her dark glasses and it was impossible for Ryan to judge if she was even looking his way. Something, or someone, had clearly upset her and it didn't take the brain of a rocket scientist to figure out who that someone had to be.

With an aisle seat himself just behind Sky but on the opposite side of the aisle and with the curtains that divided business from the hoi polloi pulled back pending take off, Ryan still had her clearly in his sights. The guy beside her in the window seat tried to engage her in conversation, but Sky appeared to answer him in monosyllables. When that failed to deter him, she snatched the safety card from the seat pocket in front of her and studied it intently, not appearing to notice that she was holding it upside down.

The flight was bumpy but uneventful. When they landed, Ryan loitered, letting everyone else disembark before him. As he left the plane he smiled at the flight attendant who had been flirting with him for the entire journey and sauntered through the terminal to passport control. Once clear, he made his way to the baggage hall, standing well back from the carousel where the luggage from their flight were being delivered. Ryan didn't have a bag himself but watched as Sky struggled to grab hers from the conveyer. A guy helped her with it. She thanked him and wheeled her case through the green channel.

Ryan followed. He knew her name and absolutely nothing else about her, except for the fact that she'd spent the weekend with Karim Amin – a weekend that had been cut short, presumably because Amin had received a better offer. Perhaps that was what had upset Sky so badly. Women of all ages appeared to fall for the bastard, swallowing his lies without seeming to question them. Ryan hoped Sky was not that gullible. The turn his thoughts had taken brought him up short as he followed her into the train station. He had a job to do, Sky had unexpectedly fallen into his lap and was a means to an end. You couldn't make an omelette without cracking a few eggs. Besides, when she found out what really made Amin tick, she'd thank Ryan for saving her hide.

She was clearly waiting for the London train and Ryan took up a position a little further down the platform. He very much doubted whether she would recognise him from the plane but it wouldn't do to blow it now by getting too close.

First of all he needed to find out where she lived; and with whom. Ryan was curious about her, partly because she wasn't the statuesque model-type that Amin usually went for. This one was shy, self-effacing and unused to the glamorous life, as evidenced by her choice of transportation. Ryan had assumed she would head for the taxi rank and was pleasantly surprised when she didn't, making it that much easier to follow her. The tracker he had surreptitiously attached to the underside of her case when she moved away from the carousel and pushed her way through the crowds would probably not be called into play.

He was going off the grid on this one, he knew, as he boarded the train at the opposite end of the carriage to the one she occupied. Once again she took an aisle seat, making it easier for Ryan to keep her in his sights. She sat there, staring into space, not reaching for reading material. She had her phone in her hand and checked it constantly. Ryan was willing to bet that she was hoping for a message from Amin.

She left the train at Clapham Junction. Grateful for the crowds in the cosmopolitan suburb, Ryan was able to follow pretty close without much possibility of her noticing him. She paused outside a terraced house divided into flats a few streets back from Clapham Common and rummaged in her handbag. Producing a set of keys, she opened the door, dragged her case in behind her and slammed the door shut again. Ryan leapt on to the porch and peered through the frosted glass, just about able to make her out dragging her bag up the stairs. He glanced at the doorbells, two to each floor. He knew she didn't live on the ground floor so he had a one in four chance of guessing right.

Standing back, he watched the upper floors for signs of sudden activity. It was a dull afternoon and anyone arriving home would naturally snap a light on.

Nothing moved.

'Shit!'

There were no names on the bells. People had stopped advertising who they were in that way, even if they were prepared to plaster the most intimate details of their private lives all over social media, for fear of drawing unwanted attention to themselves. The irony was not lost on Ryan.

Aware that he would be able to discover the names of the occupants easily enough, Ryan was on the point of leaving when a figure appeared in the first-floor window, hugging a white cat close to her body and staring directly down at him.

It was Sky.

She had removed her shades and Ryan was too far away to make out her features. There was no mistaking the waterfall of dark hair that hung over one shoulder in a thick riot of curls, though. He could see her shoulders shaking and sensed that she must be crying.

'Don't cry for that arsehole,' Ryan muttered. 'He ain't worth it.'

He was sorely tempted to ring her bell and try to... To what, precisely? He wasn't authorised to involve anyone else in a highly sensitive operation. Hell, he wasn't even supposed to be keeping tabs on Amin. That duty fell to others, but Ryan's reason was highly personal and he'd done it on his own time. Since he'd been in the South of France anyway, he'd stopped by the place Amin used in Saint-Tropez on a whim, having bumped into him, almost literally, in the market, his arm draped around Sky, oblivious to Ryan's presence, two ostentatious heavies trailing behind him. They weren't especially vigilant since neither of them had noticed Ryan.

Something was definitely off about Amin's behaviour, and it could just be the opportunity that Ryan and his colleagues had been waiting for. So he'd followed Sky to the airport, discovering her name when he heard her give it to the woman on the British Airways desk, claiming that a ticket had been left for her. That implied to Ryan that she was returning to London unexpectedly because Amin had received a call to arms, so Ryan had purchased a ticket for himself on the same flight and here he was.

Sky was still at her window, absently stroking the cat and staring out, but Ryan was no longer convinced that she was looking at him. She was away with the fairies, most likely, completely taken in by Amin's seduction technique. The spell was broken when another woman stepped up to Sky and gave her a hug. The cat got squashed between them and extricated itself with an indignant swish of its tail.

That decided it as far as Ryan was concerned. Ringing Sky's bell had always been a risk; she was bound to run to Amin with tales of Ryan's accusations. Even so, his habitual common sense and professionalism had flown out the window at the sight of Sky's shaking shoulders and if it wasn't for the presence of the other woman he might well have followed his instincts and tried to talk to her.

'Another time,' he said aloud, as he scrolled through his contacts and dialled a number.

* * *

'Come on then, give.' Nancy released Sky from a fierce hug. Perdita took exception to being squashed between them, gave an indignant howl and leapt from Sky's arms as Nancy stood back to examine Sky's face, ignoring the cat that now wound herself around Nancy's legs, hoping no doubt to be fed. Nancy scowled at whatever she read from Sky's expression, an expression that Sky couldn't seem to moderate. Not that she needed to, not with Nancy. They had few secrets from one another. Only one massive one, as it happened, and Sky had perfected the art of protecting it.

'What did the bastard do to you? Why are you back early? Why have you been crying? If he's hurt you, I'm going to kill him, slowly and painfully.'

'No, he didn't hurt me, Nancy.' Sky shook her head. 'Quite the opposite. We had a whale of a time. Beyond my wildest imaginings. Everything was... well, perfect, five-star. Nothing was too much trouble for him. I felt truly cherished.'

'Well, then, why the long face? What are you looking at, come to that?' Nancy asked.

Sky stared intently out of the window, squinting at the figure standing across the street staring directly up at her. 'That man over there, the one on his phone looking up at us. I'm absolutely sure he was on the same flight as me.'

'Impossible!' Nancy laughed. 'You've clearly had too much sex and not nearly enough sleep. You're imagining things.'

'Perhaps.'

But Sky didn't think so. Karim had warned her about the possibility of being followed. She remembered what he had said about forming close and lasting friendships for fear of those friends being used to get to him. Sky was motivated to prove that she was loyal and trustworthy and that no one would ever manipulate her into giving up Karim's secrets. Not that she knew anything much, not yet at least, but that was beside the point. And no matter what Nancy said, no matter how far away she was from the guy in the street, she was absolutely sure that she had seen him on the flight home.

He was hard to overlook.

The man walked away, phone pressed to his ear, and Sky turned to face Nancy, a smile breaking through her unease.

'Come on then, girl, give.' Nancy clapped her hands. 'I want all the gory details and don't you dare leave anything out.'

They sat on the sofa. Nancy had already cracked open a bottle of wine and Sky did it justice as she talked non-stop about the wonders of Saint-Tropez in general and Karim in particular.

'You're glowing, lit up from the inside,' Nancy said, squeezing Sky's hand. 'I'm glad. You're long overdue a little fun after all you've been through. But tell me, if it was all so wonderful, what are you doing home again a day early?'

Sky screwed up her features. 'He got an emergency call and had to scurry back to Egypt.'

Nancy frowned. 'It couldn't wait another day, until your weekend was done?'

'He's driven. A self-confessed control freak. That's what's makes him so successful.' Sky giggled. 'He's very hands-on.'

Nancy grinned but the gesture lacked humour and smacked of suspicion.

'I'll bet he is. Just be careful, darling. I don't want to see you get hurt.'

'Can't you just be happy for me?' Sky asked.

'You know I am.' Nancy topped up their glasses. 'I realise this isn't Krug and you're not drinking it in a hot tub with a hunk. Instead, it's supermarket plonk and you're here with me when you'd much prefer to be elsewhere. But still, you know what they say, better to be a has been than a never was. Cheers!'

Nancy raised her glass and clinked it against Sky's. It made a dull thunk, a million times removed from the high-pitched ringing sound produced by Karim's crystal. When did Sky come to be so judgemental about inconsequential stuff, or to care about it at all, for that matter? Part of her wondered if she was changing her perceptions in order to fit into Karim's world. She hoped she wasn't that shallow. Sky was her own woman and wasn't about to change for anyone.

Not even Karim.

Sky declined Nancy's offer of food, claiming to have eaten on the plane, which was untrue and almost the first time that she hadn't been completely honest with her oldest friend. The truth was that Sky had barely touched a morsel since leaving Karim. She was too wound up to eat and the wine she'd just drunk was threatening to give her indigestion. She cried off from accompanying Nancy to some club or other, wondering how her friend could even imagine that she'd put herself out there when she was 'in a relationship' with every girl's wildest fantasy.

Instead, she took a long shower and went to bed early, even though she knew she wouldn't sleep. She tried not to check her phone every two minutes, hoping for a message from Karim. He had promised to text when he landed but had warned her that it might not be possible. He had more important things to do, she knew, but her insecurities had surfaced the moment he'd kissed her goodbye and despite all his promises she now worried that he had forgotten all about her.

'Where are you?' she cried impatiently.

No call came and Sky eventually fell asleep, feeling bereft. And hungry. Common sense told her that she wasn't Karim's priority but her heart was having none of it. How long did it take to bang out a one-line text? she wondered. Images of him dead or dying in a ditch flooded her mind.

God, she was a mess!

She drifted into the kitchen after ten o'clock the following morning. Having not slept all night, or so it had felt, she'd actually fallen into a heavy sleep as dawn seeped round the gap in her bedroom curtains. Fortunately, she worked from home and set her own hours. Then she remembered it was Sunday.

'You should have given me a shout,' Sky said, yawning behind her hand and simultaneously tucking a tangled strand of hair behind her ear.

'I did try but you were dead to the world.' Nancy looked up from her computer. A graphic designer in great demand, Nancy's decision to go self-employed was starting to pay off and Sky was delighted that her friend's talent was now getting the recognition it deserved. 'Thought you might have wanted to go for a run with me.'

'You've been out already and are now working, on a Sunday.' Sky raised a brow. 'I'm impressed, especially since you probably didn't get in until the early hours.'

'No such thing as a Sunday off when you work for yourself. And I was home and tucked up in bed, all alone, by midnight.'

'Goodness. Are you feeling quite well?'

Nancy laughed. 'You can have too much of a good thing. All the straight single guys are *sooo* boring.'

Sky nodded, thinking of Karim as she poured water into the coffee machine, filled the coffee filter, placed a cup under the spout and pressed the button to set the machine whirling.

'You look terrible,' Nancy said, concern etched in her features when Sky sat at the table across from her, blowing impatiently on her coffee so that she could have a much-needed infusion of java.

'Yeah well...'

'What is it?' Nancy cocked her head to one side as she examined Sky. 'You've not heard from him, I take it.'

Sky shook her head, trying to behave casually, aware that her friend knew her too well to be deceived by the display but was kind enough to pretend. 'I can't help worrying,' she said lamely, telling herself that Karim would definitely be in touch. He was simply playing a waiting game, hoping to make her nervous. Well, he was succeeding.

'Why? He's a big boy and has a lot of commitments. You said so yourself last night; several times, if memory serves.' Nancy rested her chin on her hand. 'You're worried, I suppose, that he has another woman waiting in the wings.'

'Well, wouldn't you be? I mean, you've seen what he looks like and the standard of living he takes for granted.' Sky glanced down at her tatty robe. She hadn't even showered or brushed her hair, and was instead wallowing in self-pity. 'He can do a ton better than me.' She tried a smile on for size. 'But still, at least I had a fabulous weekend – well, almost a complete weekend – that I will never forget.'

'You're selling yourself short, Sky.' Nancy expelled a long-suffering sigh. 'How many more times do I have to tell you?'

'Easy for you to say. You have self-confidence, a lovely face and a killer body; I don't.'

'What did Karim tell you about himself? Come on, give.' Nancy leaned forward. 'You must know more about him now than you did before you went away. Or were you so busy screwing one another's brains out that there was no time for talk?' Her eyes glistened with amusement. 'In which case, I'll forgive you. I mean, priorities and all that.'

'His entire family were wiped out by a car bomb.' Sky dashed a tear aside. 'Can you imagine anything worse.'

'In Egypt?'

'Yes.' Sky blinked. 'I assume so. I didn't actually ask.'

'I didn't think suicide bombings were such a big thing in Egypt.'

'Good point. He was deeply emotional when he told me about it, that's all I know. I don't think he talks about it much.' Sky yawned behind her hand. 'Anyway, I think he's still suffering from survivor's guilt; I know I would be which explains why... well, why he does so much good with his money.'

'What good does he do?' Nancy asked, a sceptical edge to her voice.

'He gives a lot to charity.' Sky sounded deliberately vague, aware that she'd already said more than she should have. Karim trusted her and she had too much invested in their fledgling relationship to blow it by betraying that trust, even though she knew she could depend upon Nancy's discretion.

'So do most men in his position.' Nancy shrugged. 'It's tax deductible.'

'Don't be so cynical!'

Nancy chuckled. 'He's a businessman, darling. He will think that way and if he doesn't you can be sure that his accountants will point him in the appropriate direction. Making donations is a good look for men in his position.'

'If they shout about it,' Sky shot back, wondering why Nancy was being so negative. 'Karim doesn't.'

'Well, we know that, don't we? There was suspiciously little to be found about him online.'

Sky hated that she was unable to put Nancy straight about such a principled man's... well, principles. Karim was haunted by his demons and would likely never know inner peace ever again. *Join the club!* She still recalled his distant, desolate expression when he talked about his dead family. Whatever else he might be into, he couldn't fake that sort of emotional turmoil.

'He likes to keep a low profile and let his actions talk for him.'

'*Okay.*'

'Really, Nancy, why are you so suspicious? Just because he's good-looking and it was me he went for—'

'Sky, I'm happy for you, really I am. But I still can't understand what could be so urgent that it couldn't have waited another day until your weekend was over and done with.'

Sky knew it wasn't that simple but wasn't about to say. She was happy with the progress she'd made with Karim and that was all that mattered.

Her phone beeped with an incoming message at that precise moment and Sky pounced on it like a parched woman reaching for water. Nancy chuckled, but not unkindly.

'Atagirl!' she said. 'Play it cool.'

'It's him!'

Hi. All well. Back to UK in two days. Miss you already. Xx

'Well?' Nancy's eyes gleamed with curiosity. 'Still in one piece, I take it.'

Sky bit her lower lip to stop herself from crying with relief. 'He'll be back in a couple of days.'

'Good. I take it he will be wining and dining you in the manner you deserve.'

'I expect so,' Sky replied vaguely, conscious of the fact that Karim hadn't asked her to keep the time free for him. But he'd contacted her, hadn't he, when he had other, more pressing, priorities? Sky suddenly felt capable of conquering the world.

Nancy had returned her attention to her computer screen but she was scowling and Sky could sense her biting back the remarks she wanted to make. Sky simply didn't care. Karim was coming back to London, he was still alive and still thinking about her.

She was back on track.

She got up from her place at the table and danced across the kitchen, deciding to skip breakfast. She'd put on a few pounds and didn't want Karim to think she didn't care about her appearance.

'I'm going for a power walk around the common,' she told Nancy. 'Then a long hot soak in the bath and general pampering will be in order.'

Nancy smiled and waved her off. Engrossed with whatever she was doing online, she didn't even look up.

3

Sunday afternoon and Karim luxuriated in the Saint-Tropez hot tub, a curvy blonde's head nestled against his shoulder as his hands lazily explored the curves in question. Poor little Sky, he thought, chuckling. She'd read his deliberately delayed message the moment he sent it. She'd probably had her phone in her hand the entire time, wondering where he was, who he was with, waiting for him to get in touch. She was well and truly hooked. All he had to do was reel her in. He had always believed that the moment he separated her from her streetwise, overly suspicious friend she would be ripe for exploitation. Even so, he still needed to play her carefully; the carrot and stick approach.

He had almost passed her over when he realised just how closely her friend protected her. There were plenty of other targets and he didn't need that sort of aggravation, or attention. He intended to run Sky for his own purposes and so it wasn't only her friend that he had to take into consideration. If word got back that he was making a bid for freedom...

Karim shuddered. The consequences didn't bear thinking about. But what other choice did he have? When a wounded animal was backed into a corner, it was a case of fight or flight. Karim had always been a street fighter. Even if the rough edges had been smoothed out, his self-interest was as sharp as ever.

The friend was one hot babe, the type he'd ordinarily go for, Karim accepted, and he'd seen the look of surprise on her face when he'd ignored her in favour of Sky. Her pride was injured – a woman scorned and all that – so he'd known that he would need to divide in order to conquer. How hard would it be to win the trust of a meek little thing like Sky? The challenge had fired his determination, given him a purpose and fresh impetus. Now it was game on.

His minders were all gone, hired by the hour simply to intimidate Sky. Karim knew that first impressions moulded mindsets. Obsessed people saw only what they expected to see and seldom asked probing questions. Sky had toddled back to London with a head full of images of a cutting-edge entrepreneur whose life was perpetually in danger. He chuckled, thinking that was true but not for the reasons she supposed.

With the terrace to himself he fucked the blonde hard and quickly right there in the tub, carelessly sploshing water over its edge. Images of Sky filled his head and it was her name that he called out when he came. What the fuck was that all about? He wondered afterwards. The blonde, he knew, hadn't been close to climax but he really didn't give a toss. This wasn't about her and she was damned lucky to have caught his attention. What more could she possibly expect?

His phone hadn't rung once since Sky had left him. All the pre-arranged 'business' calls had stopped when there was no further need to make an impression and Karim's time was now his own; no pretence necessary. So why did part of him wish that Sky was still sharing the hot tub with him? He shook his head, thinking he must be going soft, or that his diet was deficient, or... well, something.

Karim was a strictly love-'em-and-leave-'em type of guy. His one golden rule was never to get emotionally involved. It would never be permitted by his lord and master, even if he felt so inclined. But he did not. You couldn't tie a free spirit down, he reasoned. Besides, why settle for domestic boredom when there was a whole exotic field just waiting to be ploughed? He didn't possess a conscience either so the fact that he was playing Sky couldn't possibly account for the fact that he was still thinking about her with affection, could it?

Nah! He dismissed the possibility with a splashy flip of a wrist beneath the water. It was her naiveté, her inexperience, her anxiousness to please that had temporarily appealed to him. But sophisticated women like the one currently leaning against his shoulder were more to his taste, he reminded himself. Sky was simply a means to an end.

His current squeeze was clearly peeved at his preoccupation and set to work with her hand beneath the water, attempting to recapture his attention. Karim closed his eyes, leaned his head back against the cushioned side of the tub and let her do her worst. He was on the point of climax when his other phone rang. It wasn't a number he gave out to anyone – certainly not his women.

Only one person could be calling him.

His erection withered and a surge of anger clouded his brain as he pushed the girl's hand roughly aside, feeling like a recalcitrant child being called to account for his actions. He reminded himself that his caller couldn't possibly know about Sky and even if he did, he was his own man and could entertain whoever he liked in his down time.

Thus reassured, he climbed from the tub, squared his shoulders and answered the call.

'Yes,' he said when he was out of the girl's earshot, his voice stopping just sort of deferential. Karim might fear the guy on the other end of the line, and need him to think he was toeing the line – at least for now – but he didn't defer to anyone.

'Where are you?'

Karim knew better than to lie. The man never asked a question that he didn't know the answer to. 'Saint-Tropez.'

'Get your arse back to London. Call me as soon as you arrive. I expect to hear from you later today.'

Karim opened his mouth to protest but his contact had already rung off. He swore profusely, aware that he had no choice but to catch the last flight back to London or live with the consequences. Choosing the second alternative would bring unwanted attention on him at a time when his own plans for independence were creeping closer to fruition.

'Hold that thought,' he muttered, aware that when the boss summoned a minion, the minion obeyed the call to arms.

'You'll have to go,' he said abruptly to the woman in the hot tub, who had turned to look at him with big, soulful eyes and a come-on expression. 'Business.'

'Aw, baby!'

'Out! Now.'

He slapped her backside when she stood up, dripping water, and turned back to the house to dress and grab the essentials. Karim was used to moving around at short notice and had refined the concept of travelling light to an art form. He rang the airline and got himself a ticket on the late BA flight, then called a taxi, which he bundled the still protesting woman into the moment it arrived. He climbed into it after her, telling the driver to take him to the airport and to be quick about it. He could drop the woman off at her flat after that and she could pay the fucking fare. She had done sod all else for him that night.

The flight was half-empty and Karim slept for its short duration, wondering about the sudden requirement for his presence in England. His father had sounded on edge, causing Karim to wonder what he'd done to earn parental disapproval on this occasion. Equally resigned to the fact that he would not be left in ignorance for long. Hoping against hope that the old man couldn't read minds. He wouldn't put it past him.

* * *

Ryan reported for duty at the offices of Fenchurch Associates early Sunday morning, having resisted the urge to return to his post outside Sky's flat. He would be of more use at a computer, finding out all he could about her and trying to figure out why she had attracted Amin's interest. Amin's departure from the norm was highly suspicious and could well be the 'in' on his operation that they'd consistently failed to find. Ryan suspected that his boss though, who had tunnel vision and was obliged anyway to obey orders from recognised government agencies, would not agree. Better to find some sort of definite link between Sky and Amin, or better yet a crack in Amin's organisation, and then go to them with what he knew.

Although never completely empty, the unremarkable, at least from the outside, office premises that he shared with his fellow investigators was relatively quiet that morning. Only the hum of state-of-the-art computer equipment and other high-tech gizmos greeted him. He saw one or two heads bent over screens but received only brief acknowledgements as he made his way to his own cubbyhole and fired up his computer.

He took a sip of the coffee he'd purchased at the station as he waited for the machine to run through its encryption process. Once it had done so he would be free to surf in total anonymity. He'd resisted the urge to delve into Sky's background from home the previous night. If he did anything even remotely connected to his top-secret work for various government agencies from anywhere other than the office it was grounds for instant dismissal. No excuses.

No exceptions.

The first thing Ryan did was to type Sky's address into the land registry, assuming that she rented the flat she lived in. Clapham rental prices had skyrocketed over recent years as central London spilled out deeper into the suburbs, making the suburbs in question fashionable. He wondered how many people shared this particular dwelling in order to make the rent.

'Holy shit!'

'Problem?' A head appeared over the partition, making Ryan realise that he had spoken louder than he'd intended.

'Nope. Sorry about that.'

His colleague's head disappeared again and Ryan leaned back in his chair, tapping a pencil against his teeth as he absorbed what he had just learned. Skylar Kennedy had bought a two-bedroomed flat for three-quarters of a million quid outright. Where the fuck had she found that sort of money? Was she involved in Amin's dirty work rather than a victim? Were they an official item?

Ryan's chosen profession had hardened him to the fact that people were seldom what they appeared to be on the surface and so he couldn't discount the possibility. He was paid to be suspicious. Sky had been crying but perhaps that was because she and Amin had argued. Perhaps he'd dumped her, accounting for her abrupt return to the UK. That possibility improved Ryan's mood. He was well aware of the capabilities of women scorned and could put a case to Steve to recruit her to their cause. That way he could run her and protect her from the inevitable blowback. Whatever Sky had got herself involved with, he didn't want to think of her as being quite as corrupt as her hopefully former boyfriend.

'Discipline, Callahan,' Ryan muttered, aware from bitter experience that personal involvement in any of their investigations seldom ended well. Feeling mildly protective towards a woman he knew absolutely nothing about was highly unprofessional and could result in Ryan being thrown out of a job that challenged his intellect and satisfied his need to keep the world a slightly safer place.

He continued to surf the net, eager to find out all he could about Skylar Kennedy, looking for clues to account for Amin's interest in her. Born in Wiltshire, she was the only child of a surveyor and his estate agent wife. She appeared to have lived an idyllic life, attending private school and then Manchester University, from which establishment she graduated with a decent degree in economics.

Economics?

Ryan sat a little straighter, thinking that if she was involved with Amin then she could well have been recruited for that reason. Someone had to launder their ill-gotten gains.

'Damn!' he muttered, but more quietly this time, aware that his colleagues would not appreciate more interruptions. He wondered why he felt both surprised and vaguely disappointed when he'd found the possible connection he'd set out to look for.

He pressed a few buttons and focused his attention on the results that flashed up, providing a plethora of information on private individuals not available to the general public. Whoever believed that big brother was alive and as intrusive as ever was right on the money but access to the information in question was jealously guarded, available only to those who needed to know.

The majority of the population most definitely didn't need to.

Sky's world had imploded when her mother died of cancer five years previously. Two years later her father was dead too. He had driven his car into a tree in broad daylight on a sunny day and died at the scene. There was no other vehicle involved and Kennedy's car wasn't defective, so suicide was suspected. But it couldn't be proven and Sky had inherited the family home as well as a hefty pay-out on the life insurance.

That would explain her ability to purchase the flat in Clapham but significantly failed to explain why she would risk getting involved with money laundering. She certainly didn't need to; unless she was either an adrenalin junkie, in it for the thrill, or she had gone completely off the rails since the death of her father. Ryan had uncovered several pictures of them together and it was clear from her expression that they had been devoted to each other, casting doubt on the suicide theory. Would a man who adored his only child be selfish enough to kill himself?

Grief, Ryan knew, did odd things to people and made them act out of character.

'You're on the Amin case?'

Beth, one of the geeks, had come up to Ryan's desk without him hearing her.

'I am, kinda. What you got?'

'Karim Amin's on the move. He raised a flag on our system when he booked a seat on the last flight out of Saint-Tropez tonight,' she said. 'Thought you'd want to know.'

Ryan glanced at his watch, not surprised that he'd got carried away with his legitimate work, as well as trying to find out more about Sky's involvement with Amin and that it was now late afternoon. His stomach gave an embarrassing rumble, reminding him that he hadn't eaten all day. 'Thanks.'

Ryan smiled at Beth. She never wasted an opportunity to visit Ryan's desk in person rather than communicating via the office's encrypted messaging system. Ryan didn't mix business with pleasure, not ever, not any more, so Beth was wasting her time.

'No biggie,' she replied, sauntering away again.

'Oh, Beth?'

She turned back. 'Yeah.'

'When did Amin leave the country? No one told me that he had.'

'You were in France on the Boswell case so someone else would have picked up his trail. Amin flew into Saint-Tropez with a woman but left without her. That's all I know. It's not really my assignment. I just happened to see the name flash up on the system and thought you'd want to know.'

'Appreciate it.'

Ryan returned his attention to his screen. He'd been distracted by leads on another case for several hours but now returned his attention to Sky, determined to learn all he could about her. She was twenty-seven, had never been married and he couldn't find her name linked to any man who had come to his agency's attention. She worked from her Clapham flat as a freelance economist and according to her website she helped 'a steadily growing band of clients to examine historical economic trends in relation to modern-day supply and demand', whatever the hell that meant. The testimonials on the site were glowing. Of course they were. She would hardly publicise anything negative. But there were independent accolades heaped upon her by satisfied customers too. *Gotta love the current demand for feedback on absolutely everything,* Ryan thought, aware that it often made his work a little easier.

He looked into her financials next and gave a low whistle when he discovered that her overall wealth amounted to almost two million quid. Daddy had clearly done well for himself. She had sold the family home for over a million. Savings and the insurance pay-out left a healthy balance, even after she'd paid cash for the Clapham flat.

Ryan accepted that if Karim had done his homework and was targeting Sky for her money, then he'd done a bang-up job. Even so, her willingness to allow herself to be exploited irritated Ryan. She might be a first-rate economist but she didn't seem to shine in social situations, he discovered. He checked her social media pages. The photos all showed her with a friend, probably the one who shared her flat but Ryan couldn't be sure because he hadn't seen her face. Anyway, the friend appeared to be the life and soul. She was astoundingly pretty and clearly had the confidence to back up her looks. Sky tended to hang back in pictures, looking uncomfortable to be caught on camara. Ryan couldn't have said why but he was willing to guess that she went out because it was what people did but would prefer to be at home, curled up with a good book.

When he had learned everything the system could tell him about Sky, Ryan sat back and pondered his discoveries. It was too good a lead to pass up, at least in his mind, but he was pretty sure that his boss would think otherwise. Perhaps he should run Sky off the books, in the same way he'd pursued Amin in his own time? But he dismissed the possibility before it took too firm a hold. If Sky's name had flashed up on Beth's screen along with Amin's when they'd left England together then she would already be on the agency's radar. He wanted to find out if she'd be willing to help the agency, but not at any cost.

And definitely not at the cost of a job that he loved and was good at.

Ryan's cogitations were brought to an abrupt halt by the arrival of Steve Wingate, his boss.

'Hey, Steve. What got you here on a Sunday?' Ryan asked. 'I thought only us drones were required to put in an appearance.'

'No rest for the wicked,' Steve replied, his expression sombre. 'Team meeting in five minutes.'

The heads of his co-workers appeared over the partitions, looking equally surprised. They had team meetings on the fly; it was the nature of their secretive work which was too delicate to entrust even to their highly encrypted messaging system. But those meetings seldom happened on a Sunday, which was when Steve put off the mantle of responsibility for twenty-four hours, attempting to perfect his golf game, about which he was passionate.

Something untoward had to have happened and Ryan knew from the significant look that Steve had bestowed upon him that it had to do with the Amin investigation. Ryan was lead investigator. It wasn't his only case and others were deployed to rotate with him as and when. Ryan had his own reasons for wanting to bring Amin and those he worked for to justice. It was the most sensitive and potentially explosive undercover operation that had ever come their agency's way. It was testament, Ryan reckoned, to the government's desperation. Something of this nature would ordinarily be handled by the security services, and was being... up to a point. As usual, their organisation was doing the heavy lifting and taking all the risks simply because they didn't officially exist. Hollywood would doubtless label them as black-ops, whatever the hell that meant. Ryan, not a great one for labels, only knew that it gave him and his colleagues a level of freedom to get the job done, little or no red tape to negotiate.

No wonder Steve looked like his ulcer was playing him up, Ryan thought, sparing a moment's sympathy for his boss and good friend.

Ryan picked up his phone and was the first to join Steve in his office.

'What's up?' he asked.

Steve, busy reading through his messages, waved the question aside. 'Haven't seen your report from France yet,' he said instead.

'That's because I haven't written it yet.'

Steve finally looked up, but he wasn't smiling. 'Is there something you need to tell me?' he asked.

Ryan was left with the uneasy feeling that Steve already knew he'd been following Sky Kennedy. Not much got past him. He had sources that he jealously guarded, a lot of them in low places. Ryan's reluctance to tell him about her, at least yet, surprised him. But then again, Steve and Ryan had their disagreements about the direction of this investigation to the point that Steve had threatened to remove Ryan from it.

Ryan was equally determined not to let that happen.

The rest of the team, three people, shuffled into the room and everyone took a chair around the conference table. Not all of them were directly involved with the Amin case but Steve believed that everyone in his carefully chosen team should be kept up to speed with all their investigations.

'Operation Sphinx,' Steve said, referring to the unimaginative name given to the Amin case. 'There are developments.'

Ryan was conscious of Steve's gaze focused on him as he spoke and wondered just how much he already knew, or guessed, about Ryan's extracurricular investigation.

'They're upping their game,' Steve continued, 'but then we already knew that. A lorry was stopped at Dover yesterday morning with a dozen undocumented men, women and children hidden inside, barely alive, and ten kilos of Afghanistan's finest. It's a major capture for us.'

'Can it be traced back to the organisation that interests us?' someone asked.

'We think so.' But Steve didn't sound too sure. 'The police are running checks. We have to keep a low profile, as always, and let the authorities be seen to be doing something. We'll be the last to know what's found out, as always, unless there's dirty work to be done, of course. Anyway, a reliable source tipped Gerry off,' he added, referring to one of their absent colleagues, 'which is how we were able to alert border forces. Problem is, that source has gone to ground.'

'Gone to ground or gone into it?' Ryan asked, aware that the ruthless individuals making a profit from the misery of others were... well, ruthless.

'That is what we are attempting to discover.'

'What about the lorry driver?' Beth asked. 'An innocent dupe, I imagine.'

'You imagine right. He knows nothing but he's being held and grilled by our friends in MI5.' Steve tapped his fingers on the surface of the conference table. 'Our problem is, we're still no closer to identifying the guy at the top of the food chain.'

'We know enough of his lieutenants,' someone pointed out.

'And we also know that if we haul any of them in, Mr Big will just bury himself deeper under a blanket of respectability and layers of protection, calling in favours from friends in high places to keep his identity under wraps.'

'We know about Karim Amin,' someone else said. 'He's up to his grubby little neck in the business and quite high up too.'

'And too canny to be caught. He knows we suspect him,' Steve said, allowing his frustration to show. 'You were on him in France, Bill. What do you have to report?'

'Lost him in Paris last Thursday.' Bill, Steve's second in command, looked sheepish. 'Sorry, boss. I'm pretty sure he didn't clock me but we all know he works on the assumption that he's always under surveillance and gives us the slip only when he needs to. He came back to England a few hours after I lost him. He was tracked through Heathrow.'

'And went out again to Saint-Tropez the next day,' Beth added. She glanced at Ryan, who gave an infinitesimal shake of his head, preventing her from mentioning that Amin had not been travelling alone. Ryan wasn't sure why but all his instincts screamed at him to keep what he knew about Sky to himself; at least for the time being. He didn't want her dragged into this dangerous morass if she really was an innocent bystander. Besides, if her affair with Amin was still ongoing, she was bound to run to him with tales of Ryan's approach.

The situation was simply too volatile to take that risk.

Ryan, as a head-hunted member of Steve's elite organisation enjoyed a degree of freedom that was not available to his official colleagues in MI5. They had to abide by the rules, after a fashion, but everything that Steve's team did was deniable. Ryan knew very well that if any of them screwed up they would be thrown to the wolves but Ryan, who had been a member of the team for two years, had always thrived on the pressure. He enjoyed pitting his wits against some of the most ruthless criminals and terrorists to grace the UK's shores, free from the restrictions placed upon the police, where the balance appeared to have swung in favour of the accused.

And, of course, every conniving scrote worthy of the name knew his rights better than the arresting officers. No wonder morale within the police service was running at an all-time low, Ryan often thought.

'What are our instructions?' Bill asked.

'We're upping the ante,' Steve replied. 'These people have got to be stopped.'

What Steve meant, Ryan assumed, was that they needed to put more pressure on their informants. Drugs flooding the country and undocumented people abandoned in flimsy boats to die or be rescued by chance wouldn't have got Whitehall's knickers in this much of a twist, Ryan knew, as he glanced at the stress etched into Steve's features. Their brief was to discover what the intentions of those at the top of Amin's organisation actually were. Intelligence pointed to a terror campaign in the planning that had the powers that be wetting themselves in fear. The would-be terrorists were well organised, patient and exceedingly well funded. The people smuggling, to say nothing of the lucrative drug business, would ensure a healthy bank balance, paid for by the misery of others.

Steve gave instructions to ramp up surveillance, both physical and virtual, and the meeting broke up. At a gesture from Steve, Ryan remained behind, closing the door behind Beth, who had taken her time gathering up her possessions before leaving. She sent Ryan a what-the-hell look, aware that she had held vital information back from the rest of the meeting and no doubt wondering why Ryan had been so reluctant to share.

'Okay, Ryan, give.' Steve perched his backside on the edge of his desk, his expression severe. 'What aren't you telling me?'

'Amin is our way in,' Ryan replied with authority, keeping his voice even.

Steve appeared to conduct a struggle with himself not to roll his eyes. A struggle that he eventually lost. 'Not that again,' he said, sighing. 'Don't make this personal. How many more times do I have to spell it out for you? Sarah's gone,' he added, in a more moderate tone. 'And nothing will bring her back. Let it go.'

Ryan inhaled sharply at the mention of Sarah's name. The love of his life for whose death he would always feel responsible. 'Tell me something I don't know,' he said sharply.

'Bearing grudges never achieved anything. Take it from one who knows.'

Easy for you to say. 'I finished the operation in Saint-Tropez and ran past Amin's hidey-hole on my way to the airport, more out of habit than expectation.' Ryan paused. 'He was there, with a woman.'

'Nothing new about that. We know he's a serial womaniser and suspect that he uses the presence of those women to hide his other activities.'

'Not the type of woman he was with this time. And he sent her back to London early and alone.'

Steve looked up from his phone and sat forward. 'Go on.'

'I've delved into her background. She's well off and unless I miss my guess, totally bowled over by the attention she's getting.'

Steve gave Ryan his full attention as he reiterated what he'd learned about Sky, clearly drawing the same conclusion as Ryan himself had. 'We've always supposed that he's a high-up in the chain of command but have never been able to catch him with those who pull the strings. Nor have the service been able to haul him in for questioning. He's too damned wily for that. If he gave Bill the slip in Paris then he has to be craftier than a fox.'

'He would have met with someone important,' Ryan agreed, 'and needed to be sure that he wasn't followed. And yet, I could see him on the terrace of that Saint-Tropez house, in the hot tub with Sky, as clear as you like.'

'He wanted to be seen?'

'That's my view. Not sure if he knew I was there but, like Bill said, he always assumes he's being watched.' Ryan growled with frustration. 'It was like he was taunting me.'

Steve fixed Ryan with a considering look, making Ryan wonder about his need to pull this particular civilian into the grubby world of counter-espionage. He hadn't been able to save Sarah and there was something about Sky that reminded him of her and his burning need to get revenge. Then his professionalism kicked in. He would do whatever it took to keep the country safe and put his personal feelings aside; it was as simple and straightforward as that.

'So Amin could, just possibly, be setting himself up with a wealthy patsy in order to break free, take over command...' Steve spread his hands. 'What the hell and why didn't you share what you know with the team?'

'Too sensitive,' Ryan replied. 'From what I can find out online about the girl, I'm as sure as I can be that she's an innocent. She certainly hasn't come to our attention before now. But she will need to be handled with kid gloves. I reckon she's besotted with Amin and will run to him if we try to convince her he's not worth knowing. Amin's booked on a flight back to the UK tonight. It will be interesting to see how quickly he gets in touch with her. If he does.'

'Even more reason to involve the team...'

'Steve!' Ryan paused, choosing his words with care. 'I trust them all and yet don't trust anyone. It's the nature of the game. You know that.'

'Doesn't mean I have to like it.' Steve threw himself into the chair behind his desk, causing the springs to protest with a loud squeak. 'Do what you need to do. Make contact with the girl and keep me in the loop. This is time-sensitive, Ryan. I reckon the service has got it right and there really is something big in the offing. If we're the ones to blow the lid on it then our funding will be secure for the foreseeable.'

'I thought we'd made ourselves indispensable. I didn't know our funding was under threat.'

Steve waved an arm in an expansive arc. 'It always is. We're expendable in the eyes of government, mainly because we're invisible and don't get any credit for the legwork and intelligence we supply.'

'Wouldn't have it any other way,' Ryan said, chuckling as he headed for the door.

4

Karim was in a foul temper by the time his flight landed, delayed by over an hour, at a crowded and inhospitable Heathrow. He took a cab into central London, eschewing all the cabbie's attempts to strike up a conversation. Instead, his mind dwelt on the difficult meeting that lay ahead of him with his father.

A father who Sky – indeed, the whole world – believed had died in a terrorist attack. Karim wished on a daily basis that he had, then his life would have taken a very different direction. He himself didn't give a flying fuck about the old man's extreme beliefs. In fact, he rather enjoyed the liberal excesses of the decadent West. So did his father, but that didn't prevent him from getting embroiled in plans to attack the infidels.

The hypocrisy of his father's stance wasn't lost on Karim but he knew better than to voice his opinion on the subject. He had to toe the family line or risk having his credit curtailed, a threat that his father frequently made. He really would cut him off, too, if he felt he was being disrespected and that simply didn't bear thinking about.

Despite the fact that he had no choice, Karim was still smarting at being ordered home like a recalcitrant schoolboy expected to answer for youthful indiscretions, aware that his father enjoyed reinforcing his control simply because he could. He was a grown man, damn it! A man who had killed without a second thought in his father's service. And as a means of self-preservation – but that was beside the point.

He wouldn't need to protect himself if his life had gone the way he'd intended; if he'd been left in peace to take over his father's legitimate business.

Sighing, Karim paid off the cab in central London and took two more in order to reach his father's Islington abode. Satisfied that he hadn't been followed, he knocked and was admitted by one of his father's body-guards. It smarted that he wasn't permitted to have a key, despite the fact that he had his own suite of rooms here. He preferred to spend as little time as possible with his father but that was something else that was beside the point. It was demeaning to have to knock and wait to be admitted. Just as well there was no tradesman's entrance, otherwise he wouldn't have been surprised to be redirected to it.

He walked purposefully past the beefy guard without bothering to acknowledge him, shrugged out of his coat and threw it at another of his father's minions. Without breaking stride, he headed for the study at the end of a long corridor. A third guard, stationed outside, opened the door for him.

'What kept you?' His father was seated in front of a roaring fire. It was a warm evening and the fire wasn't necessary. Karim assumed he was making another of his obscure points with his excess.

'French air-traffic controllers playing silly buggers.' Karim took the chair across from his father, refusing to wait for an invitation to sit, or any sort of affectionate greeting. The old man looked upon emotion as a weakness.

Karim took his time settling into his chair as he studied the man who had given him life and endeavoured to influence his thinking about... well, everything. At least he had his father to thank for his looks, with his waterfall of thick white hair and clear, intelligent eyes. Fahad Amin, he knew, was still a magnet for women of all ages, and not only because he flaunted his wealth in a refined sort of way. He had an abundance of charm, when he chose to deploy it, and could be exceedingly generous. The women he dated never got to see even a glimpse of his cruel, ruthless character – a man with tunnel vision bent on vengeance at any cost.

'What's so urgent?' Karim asked, yawning ostentatiously behind his hand.

'We are moving the agenda forward,' his father replied casually, as though they were discussing a change in the weather.

'Why?'

'We must adapt according to the political landscape. You are well aware of that so why must you always question everything I tell you?'

'Because you expect me to do the heavy lifting, *Al'ab*. I prefer to know the full particulars of my mission, if it's all the same to you.'

His father frowned at the cynical note in Karim's voice. Karim didn't have the energy to care. He was tired and annoyed that his weekend had been brought to a premature close. Equally, he was relieved that he hadn't been summoned to account for his association with Sky. His father frowned upon Karim doing what he himself did on a regular basis. *Don't do as I do...*

'There is an international trade delegation coming to this country in two weeks' time.'

'What of it?' Karim lifted one shoulder in a negligent shrug. 'We have known about that for months.'

'What we did not know is that the newly appointed US president plans to fly in and put his considerable weight behind the talks. Pushing for something to do with corn, I think.' His father flashed a rare smile that owed little to humour. 'Kansas has to be good for something.'

Karim's heart sank. He was well aware that the only regime his father hated more than those of Western Europe collectively, was America's. He despised everything that the capitalists stood for, even if that didn't prevent him from enjoying the freedoms of the West himself. *Hypocrisy, keep thy faith.*

'Holy fuck!' Karim half-rose from his chair, too shocked to curb language that he knew would annoy his father. 'Surely you don't expect me to assassinate the most powerful man in the world.'

'A man who was responsible for the death of your mother and sisters,' his father replied, his tone harsh, unforgiving. 'Never lose sight of that fact.'

'Not him.'

'Bah, one of his predecessors.' The older man flapped a wrist in a gesture of indifference. 'What does it matter?'

Karim knew it would be a waste of breath to point out that his family had been killed by one of their own; a homegrown car bomber in training who had got it horribly wrong. His father maintained the view that the accident would not have occurred had it not been for interference by the West in Middle Eastern affairs and to his mind that made retaliation necessary.

To this day, Karim still did not know who the man who killed his family actually was, although he had his suspicions. About that and many other aspects of a fatality that Karim had been too young to properly understand, or question, at the time. A subject that he would not dare to question his father about now. His father was tight-lipped about a situation that he had used to reinvent himself, having the means and influence to make it happen.

'That's as may be, but he will be better protected than the crown jewels during his visit. It will be suicide for anyone to try to take him out.' Karim stood up completely this time and turned his back to the fire, his fingers laced behind him as he squared his shoulders. 'Or could it be,' he asked, eyeing his father with icy disdain, 'that you are disappointed in your only remaining child and want rid of him? A martyr in a holy war. Now that would be a cause worthy of the Amin name.' *In your eyes.*

'Don't be so ridiculous, Karim.' His father's voice was laced with impatience. 'You have been overindulged and enjoy your pleasures a little too much, but for all that you are a good boy.'

Boy? 'I am relieved to hear it. In which case, why aim so high? Our previous plan would have had just as much impact.'

'Rubbish! The man is the president of the supposedly greatest yet most corrupt power in the world. His death will make headlines and the perpetrators' names will go down in history, Allah be praised.'

Karim sighed. His father's religious beliefs were... well, spasmodic. Convenient. Karim had come to the conclusion that he used Allah as an excuse to bully and intimidate and no one dared to call him on it for fear of enduring the harsh punishments that would be sure to follow. Not even Karim.

'Where will the president be staying?'

'At the American embassy for the one night he remains on English soil and even I know that it will be impossible to get to him there. But he is having talks with the British prime minister at Chequers.' Karim's father's eyes burned with fervour. 'Only imagine killing two birds with one bomb.'

Karim would much prefer not to. Apart from anything else, Chequers would be as well guarded as the US Embassy, what with the terrorist threat remaining so high. But because it was in the countryside his father seemed to think that its defences would be penetrable. His father didn't get embroiled with detail; he didn't need to. He wasn't the one taking the risks. All those that did were expendable to the cause in his eyes, even Karim.

What to do? How to make him see sense? Karim paced the length of the room, conscious of his father's determination as he remained silent, fully expecting Karim to acquiesce. All the time he did so he enjoyed the freedom to spend the old man's money and live the high life.

But that was the point. All the money in the world would be no good to him if he was dead. And even if by some miracle he was able to pull the assassination off, no stone would remain unturned in the hunt for the perpetrators. Tempting rewards for information would be offered and someone would eventually leak his name.

'Go upstairs and get some rest.' His father flapped a hand in casual dismissal. As far as he was concerned, the matter was settled. Karim's objections would not be taken into account. 'You look terrible. I have called a meeting for tomorrow afternoon. Hopefully, by then, you will have some worthwhile contributions to make.' Karim's father returned his attention to the newspaper he had been reading when Karim had entered the room.

He left without saying a word and slowly climbed the stairs, wondering how the hell to get out of this one.

There was only one thing for it, he decided, as he stripped off and jumped in the shower. He would just have to bring his plans for Sky forward. He had been intending to play her slowly, win her complete trust and give her something to remember whilst he was at it. It seemed only fair, given that she was about to demonstrate exceptional generosity, even though she wasn't aware of the fact.

But his hand had been forced and there was now no time to play nice.

* * *

As the new week got underway Sky tried hard to concentrate on her growing workload and put Karim firmly to the back of her mind. He was safe in Egypt, she knew at least that much from the one message he had sent her.

'Nothing from lover boy?' Nancy asked, not unkindly, when she came across Sky in the kitchen, toying with a slice of toast she had no appetite for.

Sky stroked Perdita when she leapt lightly on to her knee. At least the stress had killed her usually voracious appetite, Sky conceded with a wry smile, thinking that not all clouds heralded the onset of rain.

'It was just a fling,' Sky replied, not sounding the least bit convincing, perhaps because it had not been. Not from Sky's perspective. She didn't do flings and didn't sleep around. It just wasn't her style.

'Flings are a trip to the local Indian, a few drinks and a quick shag,' Nancy replied, cheerfully. 'Take it from one who knows. Men who take their dates to private villas in the South of France are not looking for flings.' She gave Sky's shoulders a squeeze. 'You'll hear from him soon. Trust me on this. The man has got it bad for you, which shows very good taste on his part, but if he hurts you I shall poke his eyes out with a sharp stick and you can tell him so from me.'

Sky smiled, but it felt strained. 'Thanks, but I don't think he intends to hurt me.'

'Perhaps not but I don't entirely trust him and won't until he proves himself to be a worthy recipient of your affections.' Nancy filled the kettle and flipped the switch. 'I know men.'

That much was certainly true but at that precise moment Sky doubted her own name. She had scoured the internet for any mention of Karim, even though she was aware that he didn't court publicity. His part-ownership of the club where they had met was a fragment of the picture he'd taken pains to build up of a London-based entrepreneur, he had told her. An excellent cover for his true agenda.

A rich playboy with more money than sense. He backed that impression up on the club's website, where he was pictured with a variety of beautiful women draped all over him. Confusion curdled Sky's insides whenever she viewed the pictures, which she did frequently. She couldn't compete with any of them, which is why she didn't share Nancy's opinion that he would come running back to her. Why would he? What did she have to offer that the others didn't have in more abundance – looks, bodies to die for and innate self-confidence by the mile – the sole preserve of the truly beautiful.

Hell, she didn't even like nightclubs very much. She hated club music and had found the courage to make that admission to Karim. He was so easy to talk to and wanted to know everything there was to know about her, so it had just sort of slipped out. She thought it would make her appear gauche, off-trend. Instead, he'd smiled and told her he agreed but had to keep up appearances. It was all a part of his cover.

Sky sighed, abandoned her toast, tipped a protesting Perdita from her knee and tried to prepare her mind for the day ahead. She had a ton of work to do but her heart wasn't in it. Work had saved her sanity since her father's death and she had thrown herself into it, building up her client base through referrals and a growing reputation for integrity. More often than not, Nancy had to drag her away from her computer and force her to socialise.

Now, all she could think about was Karim and when she could reasonably expect to hear from him. When she would see him again. *If* she would. Finally she was getting somewhere and work had never seemed less important. She told herself repeatedly that he wasn't in a position to send her messages. His priorities would be focused on outwitting his enemies and staying alive.

Her brain got the message but her heart was having none of it. Surely there had to be a way? The worry caused her to be inattentive and she made several basic errors with her current project. Cursing, she deleted her recommendations and started again, adjuring herself to concentrate.

A headache, the consequence of not sleeping well, pummelled her temples from the inside. Sighing, Sky gave up on her work and decided to get some fresh air. It might help to clear the fug from her brain.

Anything was possible.

The weather was fine and Clapham Common was awash with people of all ages taking advantage of the open space in the heart of the cosmopolitan suburb. Children ran everywhere, chased by harried parents. Enthusiasts flew kites. Joggers, bikers and skateboarders dodged through the crowds. Youths slouched against trees – smoking, swigging beer from cans and attempting to look cool in their baggy jeans hanging down round their hips, the names of branded underwear blazoned in visible elastic around their waists. Sky ignored their jeers and catcalls as she walked swiftly past, her mind in another stratosphere.

On her second circuit she saw a man whom she'd vaguely noticed the first time around. He would be hard to miss – he was your stereotypical tall, dark and handsome type. Not in Amin's league but still pretty hot.

He was leaning against the same tree as before, his eyes covered by dark glasses, making it impossible for her to read his expression. Dressed casually in jeans and a T-shirt, he wasn't attempting to read from his phone and wasn't enjoying the weather either. Perhaps he was waiting for someone, Sky reasoned, but he showed no indication of scanning the crowd, looking for his friend. Why her attention had been drawn to him and she now found it hard to dismiss him from her mind she was unable to say. She didn't feel threatened but did think there was something familiar about him.

When he was still there on her third circuit, she felt creeped out. Had her weekend with Karim come to the attention of his enemies? Her heartrate accelerated as that possibility took a firmer hold. Were they attempting to get to him through her?

'Don't be ridiculous!' she muttered, increasing her pace and deciding to return to the relative safety of her flat. 'Not everything is about you.'

But it felt that way. She had managed to convince herself it was the same man who'd been watching her flat after she got back from the airport. Not that she'd seen his face, but there was something about this guy's muscular build that struck a chord.

Perdita wound herself round Sky's legs when she returned to the flat, seeming to think that she ought to be fed.

'I'm being watched.' She bent to scoop the cat into her arms and the purring intensified. 'But you don't care, do you?' She kissed Perdita's nose, returned her to the floor and obliged with the food.

'What to do?' Sky wondered aloud, aware that her options were limited. Unless... until she heard from Karim, there was nothing she could do. And perhaps not even then. He might think she was being paranoid, seeing shadows on a cloudy day, and want nothing more to do with such a neurotic woman.

Attempting to put the unsettling incident behind her, Sky returned to her computer with fresh determination to finish her current assignment, *sans* errors. Even so, she got up from her desk after just five minutes and peered out the window. It wasn't possible to see the common, there were too many buildings in her way, but at least the man hadn't followed her back to this road. Well, if he had, there was no sign of him now.

She breathed a little more easily and returned to her computer, still a bundle of nerves. She had barely sat down before her phone rang. She glanced at the display and her heart stuttered when Karim's name flashed up.

'You're home!' she cried, taking the call and sounding far more enthusiastic than she probably should have. Nancy, an authority on such matters, would have advised her to play it cool.

'*Habibi*, did you miss me?' Karim's deep, arresting voice echoed down the line. He was back, he was alive and, significantly, he was calling her. Nothing else mattered. She had no idea what the endearment meant but it sounded exotic.

'You're alive. I was so worried.'

He chuckled. 'You are so sweet. Don't worry about me, I am indestructible – but best not to discuss these things on an open line. Anyone could be listening.'

Sky nodded, even though he couldn't see the gesture, berating herself for being so careless. Instinctively she walked to the window with her phone, anxious to see if the man from the common had appeared. Thankfully, he had not.

'Sorry,' she said contritely. 'I'm new to this. The last thing I want to do is endanger you.'

'No apology necessary, my love. It is I who am sorry for dragging you into my world but I saw you in the club that night and something clicked in my soul.'

Sky swallowed. 'Your soul?' *Really?*

'My soul. I simply couldn't help myself.' Sky felt the full force of a compliment that sounded sincere. 'When can I see you?'

Now! 'Whenever you would like to. Come to the flat. I'll cook for you.'

'No, best not draw attention to our friendship.'

Friendship. Is that all it is to him? 'No, of course not,' Sky said hastily, reminding herself of the danger he lived with on a daily basis.

'I am at the Bayswater Boutique Hotel. Do you know it?'

Did she know it? It was *the* trendiest new boutique hotel in London, accessible only to the very rich, known for its discretion.

'I am registered as Mr Jenkins. I have a suite on the top floor. Can you come here, my darling? I will order room service.'

Could she come? Sky had been waiting a long time for this moment and felt as though she could fly there. 'Of course.' She forced herself to keep her voice casual. 'What time would you like me there?'

'Come early. Six o'clock. I cannot wait to see you. I will tell them at reception to expect you. But now, I have to go. I will count the hours.'

So too would Sky. 'Alright, Mr Jenkins,' she said, smiling at the thought of such a mundane name being attached to such an exotic man. 'I will be there at six.'

'My darling,' he replied softly.

They said goodbye and Sky rushed to her room, scrabbling through her wardrobe for something elegant yet casual to wear. Something that wouldn't make it look as though she hadn't spent the intervening hours between now and when she would actually see him preparing herself.

5

Ryan felt convinced that Sky had recognised him. Was that why he'd made himself so obvious, he wondered. Had he wanted to force a confrontation? He berated himself for his lack of professionalism. He was part of an elite organisation that could have written the book on covert surveillance. Ryan excelled at what he did, which made his stubborn determination to keep Sky Kennedy within his sights – to protect her interests despite the fact that she was consorting with a dangerous man, an enemy of the state – that much harder to fathom.

Even if Amin was back in the country, the rational side of Ryan's brain told him in no uncertain terms that he wouldn't meet Sky anywhere as public as the common. Unless, of course, his intentions were driven solely by lust – but what were the chances of him taking the risk? He seldom consorted with his dates in public places, making a target of himself. Ryan spared a moment's thought for Sky's curvaceous figure and decided that it was possible Amin's priorities had changed.

Ryan moved towards the Tube station, scowling as he tried to make sense of a senseless situation. His instincts were usually on the money, he reasoned, and he felt increasingly convinced that Sky would lead Ryan and his team to the holy grail – the man pulling Amin's strings. There was so very little known about the group's objectives; suspiciously little. What they did know had come from several reliable sources; none of whom knew the entire picture, but whose information was sufficiently credible to have rung alarm bells within governmental corridors.

'No pressure, then,' Ryan muttered.

All they knew was that the cell existed, they were planning something outrageous and that Amin was up to his neck in it. Ryan wondered if Amin was a red herring. It seemed highly suspicious that his name constantly came to their attention, thanks to the narks on their payroll, and yet they knew absolutely nothing about his paymasters, their target... diddly squat.

It was damned frustrating. He felt justified in running down whatever leads came his way, no matter how tenuous. He was seriously considering installing listening devices in Sky's flat, to protect her as much as to gain information, or so he chose to believe. He didn't need clearance; that was one of the up sides of working for a security contractor. They were free to do as they pleased in the national interest, just so long as they didn't expect to be bailed out by officialdom in the event of being caught with their fingers in the cookie jar.

Ryan's mobile chirped in his pocket as he unlocked the reinforced door to his basic flat in Brixton and disengaged the alarm.

'The US president is gracing us with his presence at the trade talks,' Steve told him with a heavy sigh.

'Christ, that's all we need.' Ryan's mind went into overdrive, ever-increasing possibilities fighting for supremacy. 'And we're finding out about this now?'

'Word just came through. The media will have it later today. Seems to me that Amin's group might be planning something.'

'Surely you don't think they'd be quite that ambitious?' Ryan threw his keys into the pot on the hall stand and went into his small living room, frowning at his phone. 'Besides, if it's only just been confirmed...'

'He's the ultimate target. The one that every terrorist with a grudge most wants to have a pop at, or take the credit for targeting. Propaganda is king. It would account for so little intel having reached us. Tenuous, I know, but we can't afford to dismiss the possibility out of hand.'

'The idiot's giving them the opportunity to get their ducks in a row.

The talks are two weeks away. Why make the announcement so far in advance and give them time to make their plans?' Ryan rubbed his chin. 'We knew something big was in the offing but this is above my paygrade. I don't intend to be a scapegoat if it all goes pear-shaped.'

'Every agency with a fancy set of initials is on the case.' Steve's chuckle owed little to humour, Ryan assumed, well aware of the additional strain this visit would place on Steve's already overburdened shoulders. 'As usual, we'll be working off the books. I'll give you more men if you need them, Ryan, but we need to up the surveillance on all our suspects, especially Amin. He came back into the country, as you know.'

'Yeah, Beth told us he'd booked a ticket on the last flight out of Saint-Tropez on Sunday.'

'Unfortunately we found out too late to pick him up this end.'

'Sounds like he was called back in a hurry. Perhaps when his handler heard about the presidential visit. His communication lines are probably better than ours.'

Steve's grunt reverberated down the line. 'That's my guess.'

'I need to think of another way to find him.' And he already had a plan formulating. 'Leave it with me.'

'Don't go rogue on me, Ryan. This is the big one.'

'Me? Rogue?' Ryan grinned. 'When do I ever?'

Steve chuckled and cut the connection without saying goodbye.

'Game on,' Ryan muttered, putting in a call to Ed, the head of the small team who worked surveillance on his cases. 'Have a job for you,' he said when Ed answered the call. 'I need you to tail a woman twenty-four/seven.' Ryan reeled off Sky's name and address. 'I want to know if she so much as coughs.'

'Okay.'

'She works from home. Let me know if she goes anywhere unusual.'

'Will do.'

'Good man.' Ryan ended the call and headed for the shower.

* * *

Sky had changed her mind four times thus far about what to wear for her date with Karim, well aware of the importance of appearing confident, independent and capable. She had no intention of clinging to Karim in the way that the sleek models on his website appeared to. She was not that shallow.

Nancy arrived home, took one glance at the pile of clothes discarded on Sky's bed and took control.

'You've heard from him, I take it,' she said smiling.

Sky's smile felt too wide for her face. Even Nancy sounded impressed when she told her where he was staying.

'Doesn't he have a home here in London?' she asked. 'I mean, he spends a lot of his time here and hotels are expensive.'

Sky didn't want to admit that she didn't know. 'I don't think money is any object,' she said vaguely.

'Try this.' Nancy handed Sky a favoured maxi skirt.

'It doesn't fit.' Sky shook her head sadly. 'I haven't been able to get into it for months.'

'You've dropped a few pounds so you might now.'

Sky knew there was no arguing with Nancy when she made up her mind so dutifully stepped into the skirt.

'Eureka!' she cried triumphantly when it zipped up at the first try. The flimsy material floated round her legs like a whispered promise and made her feel feminine to her fingertips. She teamed it with a pink top that sculpted her body, emphasising her breasts – arguably her best feature. She brushed her hair until it rippled down her back in a disorderly riot of curls and applied light make-up.

Examining her appearance critically in Nancy's full-length glass – something she seldom bothered to do – Sky decided there was definitely something different about her. Her skin glowed and there was a wicked little glint in her eyes that made them sparkle.

'Well,' she told Nancy and an uninterested Perdita, who had taken up residence on Nancy's bed, intent upon her ablutions, 'perhaps you were right all along, Nancy, and I should have put myself out there years ago.'

She collected up a light jacket, her phone, bag and keys, and squared her shoulders. *I can do this,* she repeatedly told herself as nerves threatened to overwhelm her. *At last, my time has come.*

'Anyway, don't forget that I'm off first thing,' Nancy said, pulling a suitcase from her wardrobe.

'Of course. I had forgotten. Two weeks of sun, sea, sand and... whatever, with the new dream guy you met the other week and said you didn't like.'

'I said I hadn't made my mind about him. He improves with acquaintance.'

Sky smiled. 'Has he told you where he's taking you yet?'

'Nope. Only to pack for warmer climes,' Nancy said, grinning as she dithered over two bikinis and finished up throwing them both in her case.

'Well, I'll be back before you go.'

'Have fun in the meantime and don't do anything I wouldn't do.'

Sky laughed. 'That gives me plenty of scope,' she said, kissing Nancy and leaving the flat.

She appreciated the one or two admiring glances sent her way as she caught the Tube. That hadn't happened before and boosted her self-confidence. Ordinarily, Sky was easy to overlook in a crowd and that was just the way she liked it. But today she was out to make a statement and tossed her head with newfound confidence, sending her curls rippling over her shoulders.

Her high spirits took a nose dive when she reached her destination and was confronted by that most terrifying of creatures: a uniformed doorman who would doubtless assume his duties included ejecting anyone he didn't think belonged in his hotel. She felt obliged to explain herself but the words stalled on her tongue. The doorman surprised her when he offered her a smart salute and the suggestion of a most unprofessional wink before opening the door, granting her access to the hallowed reception hall. Sky thanked him as she stepped through the door he held open for her.

'I am here to see Mr Jenkins,' she told the young man behind the desk.

'You are Miss Kennedy, no? Mr Jenkins is expecting you.' He ticked off a name – presumably hers – on a handwritten list. Sky vaguely wondered why it wasn't computerised. 'Please take the lift to the second floor. Suite A.'

She felt the man's gaze boring into her back as she walked away. Eschewing the lift, Sky headed for the stairs. She disliked confined spaces and since she would only have to negotiate two floors, she ran up the thickly carpeted stairs instead. Taking a calming breath when she reached the ornate double doors to Suite A, she did her level best to quell the horde of butterflies that had taken to the wing in her belly and tapped at the door.

It swung open almost immediately, before Sky had had a proper opportunity to prepare herself to face the man who invaded her dreams. Her every waking moment. A man who was dangerously close to becoming an obsession.

'*Chérie!* You are a vision.' He opened his arms wide and after a fractional hesitation, she flung herself into them.

Karim swung her from her feet and into the room, kicking the door closed behind him. Much as she enjoyed the flamboyant gesture, her first thought was for his bodyguards. She was damned if she'd have them intruding on this moment, no doubt sniggering behind their stony expressions and wondering at Karim's questionable taste. To her relief, a quick glance confirmed that they were alone.

Karim put her down again but kept her in his arms and kissed her long and deep. Sky's insides curdled as she wrapped her arms around his neck and returned his kiss, fully invested in the moment. They were both breathing heavily when Karim finally released her.

'My love, I have missed you so much.'

'I was so worried about you,' she said at the same time.

'You are adorable.'

He took her hand and led her through a room so opulent that she gasped aloud. But Karim clearly took it in his stride and didn't see anything untoward in her reaction. Sky attempted to copy his nonchalance, think how gauche she must seem to such a sophisticated man. Unlike her, he oozed confidence and felt no need to play a part.

They sat on a U-sharped sofa that offered a good view over the nearby park and Karim slipped his arm around her shoulders.

'I want to know everything you have done since we were last together,' he insisted.

That's easy. I've been preparing for this moment. 'I've been busy, catching up with work. Boring stuff; not like you.'

He chuckled. 'Where are my manners?' He leapt athletically to his feet. 'We must celebrate.'

Sky noticed a bottle of champagne in a cooler, sitting beside two crystal flutes. He popped the cork without spilling a drop and poured the liquid into the glasses.

'To you,' he said, handing her a glass and clicking his against it.

Sky took a sip and sneezed when the bubbles went up her nose. 'What are we celebrating?' she asked.

'Being with you is cause enough for celebration. I have not stopped thinking about you.'

She widened her eyes. 'Really?'

'Yes, really.' He took her free hand and kissed the back of it. 'Why do you find it so hard to believe?'

'Where are your bodyguards?' she asked, unable to think of a way to answer his question that wouldn't highlight her inexperience with men.

'I do not have them around me here. It draws unnecessary attention. Besides, I wanted you to myself.'

He squeezed her hand, let it go and then topped up her almost empty glass. Sky didn't recall drinking its contents quite so fast, preferring to think that the dizziness she felt was another form of intoxication.

He talked, mostly about himself, and she listened. He didn't tell her where he had been and what he had done but presumably he wasn't permitted to. It didn't matter to Sky if he talked about the bubonic plague, just so long as she held his full attention. That, after all, was the entire point. His compliments flowed and could so easily have turned her head, if she let them. But she was too pragmatic to lose her grip on reality. She knew very well that she wasn't beautiful, or witty, or captivating – none of the things that he implied. She was simply Skylar Kennedy – shy, introverted and not very worldly.

'Come,' he said, taking her hand and pulling her to her feet when they had drunk the last of the champagne. 'I want you. Now. I cannot wait.'

He led her into an equally opulent bedroom, undressed her slowly, his eyes full of appreciation as he stripped away the flimsy layers, and set about proving the extent of his desire. Sky froze momentarily, swallowed repeatedly and followed his lead, telling herself this was what she wanted. She could do this.

'You are so very beautiful.' He leaned on one elbow afterwards and lazily traced a finger down the centre of her torso. 'Absolutely perfect.'

'What are you plans, Karim?' she asked. 'How long will you be in England?'

'Ha, I never know these things – but a few weeks, I hope. I want to get to know everything there is to know about you.'

Only weeks? 'There is little for you to learn. You know where I live and that my parents are dead and that I share my flat with my best friend.'

'You work from home, no?'

'Yes, but I go out to see clients sometimes. I have to go down to Sussex tomorrow to interview a new referral.'

'Then I am sure they will adore you.' His voice dropped to a provocative whisper. 'But not as much as I do.'

Sky smiled but couldn't disguise a yawn that refused to remain hidden behind her hand.

'My darling, you are exhausted.' He slipped an arm around her and drew her head to rest on his shoulder. 'Sleep. We will eat later.'

Sky's eyelids dutifully fluttered to a close and she welcomed the temporary respite.

* * *

She woke with a jolt, unsure how long she had slept for, and felt a moment's panic when she realised that she was in the bed alone. A loud, angry voice coming from the next room had woken her. A voice that was quickly hushed.

'What on earth...'

Rubbing sleep from her eyes, she pushed back the duvet, grabbed a towelling robe from the bathroom and crept to the door; curious to know what the argument was about. Terrified that one of Karim's enemies had found him. Even more worried that she might unwittingly have drawn that person here. Her heart palpitated as her mind briefly dwelt upon the man she had seen on the common – a man whom she had convinced herself really had been watching her.

'Idiot!' Karim whisper-shouted the word with enough venom to reach Sky's ears and make her shiver. Where was the kind, considerate, softly spoken lover who had just quit their bed? she wondered. She had never heard him talk so aggressively and it frightened her. This, presumably, was the voice of the man who risked his life on a daily basis in an effort to make the world a safer place. 'What on earth did you come here for? You will lead the chase to my door, you fool.'

'There was nowhere else to go. I panicked.'

Sky didn't recognise the responding voice. There was no deference in it, merely defiance. Sky was furious. He was distracting Karim and could spoil everything.

'You cannot stay here. I have company.' Karim's voice had dropped to a threatening whisper but by pressing her ear to the door, Sky could just about make out the words.

'Ha! When do you not?'

'Keep your voice down!' Karim hissed. 'You will wake her and I don't want to have to explain this.'

'Give her something to knock her out. I need to lie low for a few hours. I missed a camera and they have my face.'

'Fool! You should know better.'

'The order was given in a hurry.' The man's voice was a nasal whine. 'There was no time to reconnoitre and I had to take what I was told about cameras in good faith.'

'Who gave the kill order?' Karim asked.

Kill?

'Your father, of course. Who else?'

Father? Sky fell back on to the bed in a daze. This made no sense. Karim's father was dead, killed by a bomb attack initiated by terrorists.

What the hell was going on? Who was Karim? She realised then that she only knew what he'd chosen to tell her about himself and had no way to verify what she thought she knew.

'Go in the other bedroom and don't make a sound,' Karim said curtly. 'I will deal with the girl.'

'Get rid of her. She cannot be here. Not now.'

'She is the best possible cover.'

Sky felt ice trickle through her veins when Karim spoke of her so dismissively, making it clear that she was a means to an end. Well of course she was! She should have listened to Nancy, who had tried to tell her without using hurtful words that men like Karim simply didn't go for women like her unless they had an ulterior motive. She had known it well enough on a visceral level, but that was beside the point.

'Stupid, stupid, stupid!' she muttered, wondering why she was getting so upset. Knowing very well the reason.

She heard footsteps approaching the room and quickly fled to the bathroom, switching on the shower, dropping her robe and stepping into it seconds before Karim opened the door. Steam had already misted up the glass but Sky could still see Karim's outline through it and she was suddenly afraid of him. She wanted to believe in him; to demand an explanation but that wouldn't be possible. He had warned her that his work was dangerous, sensitive and highly confidential. He would never tell her anything. And worse, if he knew she had been eavesdropping, he would likely... well, drop her.

That was a risk she simply wasn't prepared to take.

'Ah, there you are. I wondered what had become of you. I left you sound asleep.'

'I missed you,' she forced herself to say, wondering if he could hear the wobble in her voice. 'So I took a long shower to wake myself up.'

'Good. I have ordered some food. It will be delivered very soon.'

'I can't stay, Karim. I'm sorry.' She glanced at the clock through the open bathroom door. 'It's later than I thought and I haven't prepared for my meeting with the new client tomorrow yet. I want to win the contract so I need to be on top form. I hope you understand. Besides, I have some-thing else I have to do tonight.'

She realised she was babbling when he simply stared at her. She stepped out of the shower and draped herself in the towel that she grabbed from the rail. It was soft and opulent, just like the rest of the place. Ignoring the growing urge to demand an explanation, she busied herself reaching for her clothes, which allowed her the opportunity to turn away from him.

'But, darling, you didn't say.' He frowned, clearly suspicious. 'I thought we would...'

Sky grabbed her phone, pulled up the calendar and showed him an appointment she had for that evening. An appointment with an important client that she had cancelled when Karim phoned, but he didn't need to know that.

'I need this account,' she explained, pulling on her clothes, 'and I cannot afford to let the guy down. I'm sorry.'

'I am sorry too, my love. You work too hard.'

'Nonsense! Everyone my age works hard. It's the only way to get on. It is not as if I am made of money.'

'Not all,' he replied, scowling. 'Many of you English are lazy and live on... what do you call it? Benefits.'

'That is rather stereotyping,' Sky remarked, turning her back to him as she ran a brush through her hair.

'Perhaps, but in my country if you do not work then you do not eat very well. It is as simple as that.'

'Nothing is that simple, Karim.'

He gave her a long look and frowned, causing Sky to realise that her eager-to-please, malleable attitude had been replaced with an urgent desire to distance herself from him. She needed a moment to get her head around what she had overheard and since she was hopeless at putting on an act, he would soon know that his suspicions were on the money and that she had actually listened to his conversation with the mystery man. She had overheard something about orders to kill, which terrified her. What the hell had she gotten herself into? What he might do to silence her if he even suspected that she'd heard their conversation was not something that Sky was in any particular hurry to find out.

'Anyway,' she said, forcing a note of regret into her tone. 'I must go or I will be late.'

'When will I see you again?' he asked, taking her shoulders in a firm grasp.

'Very soon, I'm sure,' she replied, her desire to get away from him making her sound brusque. 'You are the one who disappears at the drop of a hat so I will wait for you to call me. Besides, Nancy is going away and I want to see her before she leaves.'

'Then I shall have to come and keep your company once she has gone,' he said in a persuasive drawl that, she suspected, worked on all women. 'We cannot have you feeling lonely. That would be a cardinal sin.'

A kiss that had seemed so pleasurable upon her arrival had a very different effect upon Sky when it was repeated before she left. She still liked and admired him but the brutal nature of his occupation had been brought home to her during a brief moment's eavesdropping and she no longer knew what to think.

'What have I got myself into?' she muttered, making a dash for the Tube.

Running without looking where she was going she collided with a figure coming in the opposite direction. She glanced up, ready to apologise, but gasped when she recognised the man from the park.

'You!' she cried accusingly.

'We need to talk,' he replied, his expression grim as he took her elbow in a firm grasp and steered her towards a parked car.

6

As the day's events unfolded, Ryan's preoccupation with Sky Kennedy and how best to use her had rapidly been replaced by a blinding anger that was in danger of countering his professionalism where news of an attack upon Steve reached him. The life of a man whom Ryan respected and was privileged to call a friend now hung in the balance. That made the hunt for his attackers personal and the rules, such as they were, had gone out the window.

'How is he?' he asked, his phone clamped to his ear as he headed for Bayswater in an unmarked company car.

'In intensive care,' Bill replied tersely. 'The bullet somehow missed all vital organs. God knows how. He's lost a lot of blood and is still unconscious. They've run a whole load of tests to see if there's permanent damage.' Bill paused and when he spoke again a rare modicum of emotion had crept into his tone. 'They won't know for sure until he wakes up.' Bill paused for a second time and Ryan heard him swallow. '*If* he does.'

'Christ!'

'Yeah, but I don't reckon he had much to do with it.'

'Why has this happened?' Ryan tried to think like the professional he was supposed to be. 'We're invisible. None of the bad guys know we exist.'

Bill guffawed down the phone. 'Don't be so fucking naïve. This is a message, albeit hastily executed: *we know who you are and can get to you at any time.* The question is, why now? The timing has to be significant.'

'Yeah, point taken. Enemies of the state *are* probably aware of our existence but why target one of us and, like you say, why now? They must know that it will unleash a firestorm.'

'Perhaps it's a diversion.'

'Yeah, that thought had occurred to me as well.' Ryan paused to assess that very real possibility. 'Keep me informed.'

'Where are you going?' As Steve was the victim of the gun attack, Bill had assumed command of the unit.

'To get some answers,' Ryan replied, killing the call before Bill could order him back to base.

Ed had told Ryan that Sky had gone out, all dressed up, and turned up in Bayswater, where she had entered the newest and most prestigious hotel in the area. No prizes for guessing who she was visiting, Ryan had thought when the news reached him, frustrated by the convoluted manner in which he was obliged to ferret out the ringleaders of a mysterious group that his sixth sense told him could well be behind the attack on Steve. More frustrated still by his inability to grab Amin by the scruff of the neck and force answers out of him.

He had told Ed to hold fast outside but when news of the attack on Steve had reached Ryan it changed everything. Ryan was tired of skulking in the background, little more than an information-gatherer for the government. The time had come to go on the offensive and on this occasion he would invent a few new rules of his own.

'Any action?' Ryan asked, joining Ed in a shop doorway a discreet distance away from the hotel's smart entrance portico, with its green and gold canopy and a carpet covering the steps up to the glass door.

'This guy arrived about an hour ago,' Ed replied, showing several blurry images of a man wearing a hoodie and jeans.

'He got past the doorman?' Ryan asked, surprised.

'Yeah. They had an exchange but whatever was said got him in.'

And Sky is in there. 'Must be an associate of Amin's.' Ryan made a mental note to check out the funding behind this new hotel. 'He hasn't come out again?'

'Nope.'

'Okay.'

'So what now?' Ed asked.

'Now we wait. We will achieve nothing by storming in there, other than to show our hand and possibly endanger Sky.'

'You think the guy that went in is the one who tried to kill Steve?' Ed lifted a brow. 'A bit of a leap, isn't it?'

'I dunno.' Ryan flapped his hands, feeling helpless, wanting to do something, anything, to get revenge for Steve. But he only had his gut instinct to go on; that and his experience. Now the time had come to appeal to Sky, even if she didn't want to know. Ryan was all out of alternative options.

'Possibly, but he will never admit it.' Ryan felt his frustration growing as he tapped the fingers of one hand restlessly against his opposite forearm. 'You know as well as I do that he will have gotten rid of the gun so unless Beth gets lucky and picks him up on CCTV then we have nothing on him. What we can do is get his prints from Amin's suite once it's empty, then we might stand a chance of finding his identity. That might lead us up the food chain, or at least point us in the right direction.'

Ed grunted, still looking unconvinced. 'They ain't made any basic errors before now. And any one of the dozen cells we know about could be responsible. It doesn't have to be Amin.'

'True, but my instincts tell me the attack on Steve was carried out at short notice. Otherwise, the shooter wouldn't have missed.' Ryan sucked air through his teeth and shrugged. 'It could be the slip-up we've been waiting for.'

'But in the meantime he gets away with it.'

'I don't like it any more than you do, Ed, but we have to be smarter than them if we're to stand any chance of catching the bastards. Hello, action!' Ryan stood a little straighter as he saw Sky emerge from the hotel, her hair dishevelled. Ryan squinted as he attempted to get a better look at her features and concluded that she was close to tears. Amin had clearly upset her. Or something had. Anyway, they were unlikely to get a better opportunity. 'Get behind the wheel,' he said, tossing Ed the keys to the car that he'd parked illegally on a double yellow line.

Ed sprinted off like the professional that he was, asking no questions.

Ryan could see that Sky was preoccupied and so it was easy for him to deliberately engineer a collision with her. She opened her mouth, presumably to apologise, then her eyes widened as recognition dawned.

'You!' she cried accusingly.

'We need to talk.' Ryan grabbed her elbow and steered her towards the car. 'You're coming with me.'

'I'm not going anywhere with you.' Her eyes blazed with a combination of anger and fear as she struggled to get free of Ryan's grip. Her efforts proved futile. She might just as well have saved her strength. 'Let go of me! I'll scream.'

'Scream away, darling,' Ryan replied, opening the car's rear door and pushing her inside, in no frame of mind to adhere to political correctness. He slid in beside her, Ed gunned the engine and the car moved off. The whole episode had taken less than twenty seconds. It was unlikely that anyone would have noticed but even if they had, there had been no time for a Good Samaritan to take the registration number of the car and report an abduction.

'This is kidnap,' Sky declared hotly. 'What do you want with me? I've seen you lurking outside my flat, and on the common. You're a stalker.'

'Hardly. If you mix with terrorists then you must expect the consequences.'

'Terrorists?' She shuddered, no longer able to hide her fear. 'I don't know any terrorists. Who are you?'

'Government contractor,' Ryan replied succinctly. 'And your boyfriend just tried to kill my boss.'

'No, he didn't.' But there was hesitation behind the protest that supported Ryan's as yet unsubstantiated suspicion. 'He can't have. I have been with him for several hours.'

'What makes you think the hit went down that recently?'

'Well I... that is...'

A little of Ryan's anger ebbed away when he realised just how frightened, how confused, she actually was. Without even having questioned her, he had already got a fair way to believing she was an innocent dupe; a distraction. He glanced at her profile, at her smooth, creamy skin and the fear in her wide grey eyes. She was not, he sensed, quite as convinced of Amin's innocence as she was attempting to make out. Whatever had happened to send her scuttling away from his hotel could work in Ryan's favour.

'Where to?' Ed asked.

'To mine,' Ryan surprised himself by saying.

Ed glanced over his shoulder briefly before returning his attention to the road. 'You sure?'

'Yeah.' Ryan spoke with a confidence he didn't feel. He was anything but sure, had allowed emotion to penetrate his professional outer shell and was now running on pure instinct. Taking Sky to his own property would be the height of insanity but he didn't want to put her into a cold interrogation room, designed to intimidate and instead wanted to gain her trust. He couldn't think of any other way to go about it.

Sky had laced her fingers together in her lap but couldn't prevent her hands from shaking. Tears swamped her eyes and Ryan felt increasingly convinced that she was in way out of her depth. What was less clear to him was why Sky had attracted Amin's interest. She definitely wasn't his usual type.

'Discipline,' he muttered as he watched her struggling with her emotions in the periphery of his vision. Until he was convinced other-wise, he would continue to look upon her as being involved in Amin's grubby little game.

'We're here.' Ed cut the engine and Ryan opened the door.

'Come on,' Ryan said, taking Sky's elbow again. 'You'll be perfectly safe, I promise you, just so long as you answer my questions. If you would prefer to do this somewhere more official, that's okay too but it will be a more hostile environment.'

'I don't see why I have to do anything with you,' she protested feebly.

'Oh, I think you do. We need to talk about your boyfriend.' Ryan steered her towards his building and unlocked the street door, leaving Ed to park the car. 'Unless I read you wrong, you already have doubts about him.'

'Doubts?' She opened her eyes very wide and sent Ryan a sassy look. 'I don't know what you're talking about.'

'Sure you don't,' Ryan replied, shaking his head.

'What's this all about?' she asked defiantly. 'Why have you brought me here? I don't know anything about Karim's business activities so abducting me is wasting your time every bit as much as mine.'

'Don't even think about trying to lie to me,' he said, fixing her with a penetrating look.

He indicated the stairs and with a huff, she climbed them ahead of him. Ryan kept his distance, just in case she tried to kick back at him. But she clearly had no idea that in following her up the stairs he had left himself vulnerable – a situation that he wouldn't normally even contemplate.

They reached the landing in edgy silence.

'In here.' Ryan opened his door and ushered her inside. He disabled the alarm and relocked the door from the inside. 'Sit,' he ordered, indicating the chairs in the lounge.

'I am not a dog, in case it's escaped your notice,' she responded with spirit, her earlier tears replaced with blazing anger.

Ryan allowed himself a brief chuckle; something he would have thought himself incapable of since hearing the news about Steve. But there was something about this feisty yet terrified woman's attitude that made him want to smile despite the gravity of the situation.

Ryan said nothing and simply waited until, with a flounce, she sat in the corner of his settee. Ryan selected a wooden chair, turned it backwards and straddled the seat, leaning his forearms on its back and studying her intently. The silence clearly discomforted her and she was the one who broke it, just as Ryan had known that she would.

'Why am I here?' she asked. 'I want to see your identification and talk to someone higher up than you.'

'Not happening,' Ryan replied with the suggestion of a smile. 'You'll have to make do with me. The name's Ryan Callahan and I work in the interests of our government. That's all you need to know.'

'Why am I supposed to believe a word you say when you kidnapped me off the street in broad daylight?'

'If you play with the bad boys, sweetheart, what else can you expect?'

'Karim is not one of the bad guys.' She sent him a scathing look. 'You're really not very good at what you do if that's what you think.'

'What has he told you?'

'That people like you are out to get him,' she shot back.

'And yet you don't seem very afraid of me.'

'Why should I be when you have given me your name and taken me to your own property? If that *is* your name and if this is your flat, obviously.'

She had a point, Ryan privately conceded. Perhaps he had allowed his belief in her innocence to cloud his judgement. Too late now. Besides, Ryan wasn't his real name, she'd got that much right, and he had other places to crash. There was nothing here of a personal nature, even supposing any of her friends could penetrate his alarm and get inside.

'I enjoy having guests,' he quipped.

'Ha!'

Her complexion had regained a little colour and she herself appeared to have developed the will to fight her corner. He liked that about her, even if he questioned her taste in men. The girl had spirit.

'Your behaviour doesn't smack of professionalism but more of desperation. I suppose kidnapping helpless women makes you feel important.'

Ryan couldn't help laughing at that one. He was one of the hardest men in the unit and had never allowed his personal feelings to get in the way of his work. 'What are your friends going to do now that they know where I live?' he asked. 'Shoot me as well?'

She sat a little straighter and fixed him with a challenging look. 'Karim doesn't shoot people. He is a humanitarian. He saves lives. He helps people and is brilliant with computers. He uses his skills for the greater good, which is something you wouldn't know anything about.'

He gave a brief, ironic round of applause. 'You sound as though you are trying to convince yourself,' he said. 'Or as if you're reading from a script. Or could it be that he's brainwashed you into believing every toxic word that spills from his lips?'

'Believe whatever you want to.' She tossed her head and looked away from him. 'You will anyway.'

'Tell me how you met Karim.'

'Why?' she shot back.

'Because I think... no, I know that you are being played by a master and I want to know why he chose you.'

'I'm not pretty enough. Is that what's got your antenna flapping?' She spoke sarcastically but couldn't disguise the hurt in her eyes.

'No, Sky,' Ryan replied softly. 'I think you are too good for him.'

'Oh.' His sincere tone and deep, penetrating look appeared to take her by surprise. 'I see you know my name and also seem to think that a few kind words will cause me to change allegiances. Well, think again, mister. I am loyal to my friends.'

'We have Amin on our radar. Anyone he associates with comes under our scrutiny as a matter of course.'

'Then you'll know Karim's got more reasons than most to hate violence. He's a businessman – he owns the club I met him at, the Alexandria. He's got nothing to hide.' Her voice faltered when she said this.

She knows something, thought Ryan. *Good.*

'Karim's not much of a businessman – inherited a lump sum from Daddy and put most of it in that club, or so it seems. He came to our attention for his hacking skills.'

Her lips curved ironically. 'He's not an incel, if that's what you're implying.'

Ryan stared at her. Was she being deliberately obtuse? 'He's been brought to our attention for a different type of terrorism - Islamist extremism.'

She laughed outright at that. 'Karim's never mentioned religion to me, not once. He drinks, too - I don't think he's a practicing Muslim, even if he was brought up as one.'

'Ya think?'

'Anyway, why would a terrorist draw attention to himself by owning such a high-profile club?' she asked, a modicum of triumph sparkling in her rather distracting eyes.

'You'd be surprised just how deeply certain enemies of Western culture immerse themselves in the culture in question. Anyway, don't let me interrupt. You met at his club and naturally he was drawn to you.'

'Why naturally?'

'Look in the mirror, sweetheart.' When she showed nothing but confusion in response to a highly unprofessional compliment, Ryan forged on, wondering why he felt so out of control in an interview that he had contrived. An interview that he ought to dominate. He had broken far harder women than Sky in his time. *Think of Steve, fighting for his life in intensive care and stop dicking about with the woman who might, conceivably, have helped to put him there.* 'Anyway, how long ago did you meet Amin?'

'Quite recently. A couple of months ago.'

'And he took you to the South of France.'

She gaped at him and then gave her head a soft little shake of disapproval. 'My, my, you have been a busy boy.'

'Why did you come back alone?'

'Karim was called away.'

'To where?'

'I... I don't know.' Uncertainty now showed in her expression, as though she would love to know the answer to that question herself. Unbeknown to her, she soon would. And she would not like it. 'He said it was safer for me not to know.'

'I'm sure he did.'

'What's that supposed to mean?' she asked indignantly. 'I've told you all I know. I would like to leave now please.'

'You met him in the Bayswater Boutique Hotel today.' Ryan pushed his growing interest in a young woman who was, he was now convinced, a totally innocent pawn in a dangerous game to the back of his mind. He was in professional mode once again. Ryan was renowned for his interrogation techniques. Sky would not be leaving his flat until he was convinced that she had told him everything she knew, or even suspected.

He hadn't forgotten how distressed, how distracted, she had been when she left the hotel. Something had happened to severely spook her and set doubts about Amin churning through her brain, even though she was stout in her defence of him. If that wasn't the case she would have kicked up much more of a stink when Ryan had grabbed her off the street.

'Why did you leave in such a tearing hurry?' When she looked at him mutely, Ryan pushed the issue. 'Was it something to do with his uninvited guest?'

She was too inexperienced to disguise her reaction. Her mouth fell open and she gasped at him. 'How did you...'

'It's my job to know these things and let there be no doubts in your mind: I am very good at what I do. If I don't believe what you tell me then I have the power to arrest you and keep you isolated for several days. Give you an opportunity to think things through.'

'You can't do that.' She sat taller and glowered at him. 'There are laws in this country. I have rights.'

Ryan chuckled. 'Keep telling yourself that.'

'It is as Karim warned me to expect. He said something like this might happen. That someone like you would tell me lies about him and bully me into telling you things but I—'

Ryan's raised hand cut off her angry flow. 'You are in love with him?'

'Well, I...' She squared her shoulders and glowered at him. 'That's none of your damned business.'

'And you are gullible enough to believe every word.'

'Karim does not tell lies!'

Ryan allowed a long silence to stretch between them, watching the kaleidoscope of emotions that flitted across her features as she held his gaze. Unexpectedly, sexual tension fizzed between them. He wondered if she felt it too and, if she did, whether she recognised it for what it was. Something had happened to spook her and she was now struggling to give Amin the benefit of the doubt.

Time to up the ante. Sometimes it was necessary to be cruel to be kind.

'He packed you off home early from France because he'd been called away to do something important.'

'If you know that, why are you asking me?'

'Because he lied to you.'

'Well, of course you would say that. You are trying to make me doubt him.' She folded her arms and sent Ryan an assessing look.

'Did you enjoy the hot tub?' Ryan asked into the ensuing silence.

'How the...' Her mouth again fell open. 'You were spying on us?' She recovered quickly. 'Well, if that's the case then you will know he has nothing to hide. It would be easy enough to see the hot tub from the hill behind it. If Karim was up to no good he would hardly display...'

Her words trailed off and it obviously occurred to her that her argument defeated, well... her own argument. What better way for Amin to ally suspicion than to wrap himself round an innocent woman in an easily spied-upon hot tub?

'He didn't go anywhere, Sky. He wanted rid of you, that's all.'

She winced at his harsh words but gamely held his gaze. 'Well, of course, you would say that.'

'Something else he told you to expect?'

'He's only trying to protect me.' She unfolded her arms, seemed unsure what to do with them and crossed them defensively across her torso again. 'Anyway, if he didn't leave Saint-Tropez I expect he had a good reason to remain behind.'

'Oh, he did.'

Ryan took his mobile from his pocket, searched through his picture gallery and handed the phone to her, hardening his heart as he did so because he knew she wouldn't like what she was about to see.

'What's this?' she asked suspiciously, taking a deep breath and hesitating for a protracted moment before her eyes were drawn to the screen. She gasped and immediately handed the phone back to Ryan.

Ryan said nothing but watched her intently, wondering if there might have been a kinder way to break through her defences. He dismissed that possibility. She was smitten with Amin, even if she had doubts about his loyalties. There was no question that her own loyalty ran deep and that invoking her jealousy would be the quickest way to open her eyes.

'It means nothing,' she said dismissively. 'It could have been taken at any time.'

Ryan forced the phone back into her hand and this time she took a longer look at Amin, getting up close and personal in the hot tub with a busty blonde. 'It's date-stamped,' he said quietly. 'This was taken an hour after you left him.'

'Oh.' She looked desolate, clearly struggling to hold back the tears but not immediately dismissing Ryan's statement out of hand. That told him a great deal about her lack of self-confidence but would Amin's double standards make her mad enough to agree to help Ryan? As things stood, he had no way of knowing.

'Clearly you weren't enough for him,' Ryan said, falling back on his training and ruthlessly going in for the kill.

'The... the date could have been faked.' She looked up at him through eyes dulled with pain, still defiant. Still unwilling to believe what she had seen. 'He told me it's the sort of thing you were likely to do.'

'You've been groomed, Sky,' Ryan said softly. 'Accept it and decide what you want to do to retaliate. Skulk away with your tail between your legs or get mad and then help me to get even with him.'

'Why?' She shook her head. 'Why would he groom me? I have nothing to offer him that he doesn't already have in abundance.' She handed his phone back as though it was a poisoned chalice. 'I don't understand.'

'You understand that he cheated on you. Got rid of you under false pretences.'

She appeared to have recovered from the shock with commendable speed and leaned forward, elbows planted on her knees, narrowing the space that separated them. 'Perhaps, but I still don't understand what Karim hopes to gain by grooming me. Grooming me for what?'

'You're a wealthy woman.'

She fixed Ryan with an impatient look, clearly about to ask what that had to do with anything but then thinking better of it. 'Nowhere near in Karim's league,' she replied. 'He goes everywhere first class. His villa in Saint-Tropez is out of this world.'

'It's rented,' Ryan replied dismissively. 'By the week. Sometimes by the day,' he added, ignoring the pain that flashed through her eyes. 'Did you notice anything missing from the picture I just showed you?'

'No, I...' She pondered for a moment. 'The creepy bodyguards weren't there,' she said slowly, recalling the decking devoid of any human presence other than the two people in the tub.

'They're hired by the hour, too, when Amin wants to make an impression. I can give you the name of the agency he gets them from if it will help to convince you. He has them on hand to create an illusion.'

'Hmm.' She nodded, eyes downcast, making it impossible for Ryan to know if she believed him.

'Were they there today?'

Slowly, Sky shook her head. 'And, to think, I was glad about that.'

'He isn't as wealthy as he likes people to believe. He does have an interest in Alexandria but not a controlling interest. Whoever set him up there wants to create the impression of a wealthy playboy.'

'If that's the case, why did he hit on me?' Sky lifted her chin, her wounded pride under control. 'We know from your pictures that he can do much better.'

'I disagree,' Ryan said in an undertone.

'No need to flatter. I've had quite enough of that.' She shot him a defiant look. 'I am aware of my limitations.'

7

A conflicting raft of emotions rippled through Sky as she observed the angry spook, rugged features set in granite, who had abducted her from the street and frogmarched her into his own flat. Well, what could be his own flat. It was so impersonal that it was hard to be sure. These people had what they called safe houses, didn't they? Perhaps this was one of those places.

Scared half out of her wits, even though Karim had warned her to expect an interrogation at any moment if the authorities had picked up on their connection, she still hadn't put up a fight. Up until now she had ignored the tiny voice inside her head that demanded to know why Karim would be of interest to the security forces if he only did good works. Now she was being forced to confront it.

If she'd screamed at the point of abduction the hotel's doorman would have heard her. So would passers-by, she reasoned. Why hadn't she done so? Perhaps because she'd been too shell-shocked. Besides, in London, would anyone actually have been willing to get involved?

She had let the opportunity pass her by, not because she was too scared to react, but because something stronger than her own will had made her think this man, Ryan, had something to say that she would want to hear. Anyway, he had been so angry that he wouldn't have taken no for an answer. She had been afraid of him but he also made her feel safe. How was that even possible, she wondered, baffled by her conflicting reactions.

Having recovered from her humiliation when she saw those pictures of Karim in the hot tub with another woman, a slow burning anger now governed her reactions. She had no doubt that the pictures were genuine, not least because a colourful towel she had left draped over a chair was still in the exact same place. God, but Karim hadn't wasted any time in finding a replacement! Her pathetic attempts to question the validity of the pictures, just to save face, hadn't fooled Ryan and the momentary sympathy that flashed through his stony expression had almost floored her.

But she most emphatically did not want this charismatic man's sympathy.

The champagne she'd drunk with Karim had muddled her thinking initially, made her slow to react to Ryan when he'd snatched her off the street, but she was thinking with crystal clear clarity now. Karim was a womaniser; she had just seen uncontroversial proof of what she'd been trying to deny. Clearly, she wasn't sophisticated enough to satisfy him, which made her wonder why he'd bothered to fly her to Saint-Tropez. She was in no doubt that he would have been spoiled for choice if he'd wanted a more attractive companion.

'Why me?'

'Well, that's the question, isn't it?'

Ryan's response jolted Sky. She'd been lost in a reverie of self-pity and hadn't realised that she'd voiced her angry speculation aloud.

'I dare say you have a theory.' She glanced up at him with a bitterness she struggled to conceal as she fought to keep the antagonism out of her voice. 'I remain to be convinced.'

'No you don't,' he replied softly.

'Don't try to tell me what I do and don't believe!' she cried, exasperated and confused. Part of her wanted to hit him but she thought about the conversation she had overheard and knew that the confidence Ryan displayed was most likely founded on a degree of fact supported by evidence. Even spooks had to gather evidence, didn't they? 'I have known

Karim for a couple of months. If he was a bad guy, I would have picked up on... well, something.'

'Trust me, bad guys have mastered the art of disguising their true agendas.'

'You're not going to let up, are you?' Sky sighed and carried on talking without giving Ryan a chance to respond. 'I feel like such a fool,' she admitted with a wry smile. 'I always thought I was streetwise and wouldn't fall for a slick line. But still, if you're right about Karim having an agenda, then you might just have done me a favour. Saved me from making an almighty fool of myself. Better to know now, before I get in any deeper.'

Aware that she had been babbling, Sky abruptly closed her mouth, not adding that if Ryan was wrong, there was nothing Sky could do to endanger Karim's purpose since she knew nothing about his agenda.

Except that she did, she reminded herself.

She had overheard his conversation with the mystery man and, what's more, she suspected that Ryan knew it. Not much seemed to get past him.

'Right,' he said with a slow nod, eyeing her with open speculation, as if trying to decide if she was being completely transparent.

'Come on, Ryan,' she goaded. 'I don't have you pegged as the reticent type. I've agreed to tell you what I know, if only to prove you wrong, so ask your questions.'

He chuckled, a deep, throaty sound that she reacted to somewhere deep within her core, which infuriated her. It was wrong on so many levels. She was committed to Karim, even if he didn't play by the same rules as her. Although she now had reason to doubt his integrity, she wasn't yet ready to betray him. Or to react to another man, no matter how attractive.

'We have had our eyes on your boyfriend for some time. He's part of a terrorist cell based here in the UK...'

'No!' Sky shook her head emphatically.

Ryan fixed her with a penetrating look that made her feel as though he could see inside her mind. 'Sure about that, are you?'

'I'd never be attracted to someone like that.'

'Leaving aside your poor judgement, try to keep an open mind.'

'Easy for you to say.' But that annoying voice inside Sky's head was making its presence felt again, suggesting that Ryan could be right. It would explain why Karim had homed in on her; she obviously had gullible stencilled across her forehead in capital letters and made good, respectable cover for his nefarious activities. 'It's not like he flaunted our relationship in public, using me as window dressing; quite the reverse.' Sky spread her hands, willing the tears of disillusionment not to tumble down her cheeks. 'So what does he really want from me? I just don't understand any of this,' she finished lamely.

'With your help, we will get some answers.' Ryan's fierce expression softened as his gaze lingered on her features. 'We can find out frustratingly little about the hierarchy of his organisation despite our best efforts, which are sophisticated and up to the minute.'

'How frustrating for you,' she felt obliged to say, clinging on to the belief that there was an explanation. That this man had somehow got it all wrong.

He smiled at her, his first full-on, uncontrived smile and her involuntary reaction to it threatened to weaken her resolve. The gesture lit up his rugged features and robbed his blue eyes of their fierce intensity, albeit fleetingly. Something had happened, she sensed, something serious and it had prompted this... well, impromptu situation.

'You have no idea,' he responded, his smile fading. 'The question we're asking ourselves is why have we been able to collect intel on your boyfriend so easily, whilst the rest of his cell remain shrouded in anonymity.'

'They want you to concentrate on him,' she breathed, getting drawn into Ryan's conspiracy theory in spite of her stubborn refusal to believe without doubt that Karim was capable of anything quite so horrible.

'Now you're getting it. Alexandria is excellent cover, too. It attracts wealthy men of all nationalities and the door is jealously guarded. We can't get in there and even if we could, any meetings are assured of absolute privacy in the upstairs rooms.'

'Presumably you can watch the doors and see who goes in. Don't you people have sophisticated surveillance means?'

Ryan chuckled. 'If only it was that easy. People who don't want to be seen or identified are adept at flying below the radar.'

'They're one step ahead of you,' Sky said tauntingly.

'You may wish that wasn't the case when another attack happens and innocent lives are lost.' His voice was hard again, uncompromising.

Sky nodded as a hundred questions formed inside her head. She wanted to protest, to offer to talk to Karim and resolve the situation. She still felt loyalty towards him, albeit less instinctively than a few hours previously at a time when she hadn't seen that picture of him with the gorgeous blonde – a picture now imprinted on the inside of her eyes. To a time when she hadn't overheard that conversation between Karim and the mystery man, which had caused doubts to form in her mind, even before Ryan had abducted her.

'I don't accept what you say about him, but playing devil's advocate just for a moment, if it's true then he must be the front guy. How did he come to your attention? Am I allowed to ask that?'

Ryan shrugged. 'He hacked his way into the database of a highly sensitive government organisation but wasn't quite as clever as he thought. Our geeks had planted traps and he tripped one of them. That's how we found out about him.'

'But didn't arrest him?'

Ryan grimaced. 'Not yet.'

'So perhaps the ringleaders of his cell, if there is one, know he's been compromised and want you to concentrate on him whilst they protect themselves. They are one step ahead of you,' she mused.

Ryan spread his hands and gave a frustrated sigh. 'It's worrying, I'll grant you. We have tracked and stopped a dozen plots to create terrorist havoc in this country but we've never come across such a secretive cell before and that's very concerning.'

'Perhaps you're worrying about nothing because it doesn't exist and Karim is one of the good guys after all.' She sent him a challenging look. 'You can't be absolutely sure that he's the hacker you just referred to because you haven't bothered to ask him. Has that possibility occurred to you?'

'I'm paid to be suspicious.' Ryan paused. 'What if he's tired of being the poster boy?' he asked.

Sky blinked. 'What do you mean?'

'He knows we suspect him. Perhaps he deliberately tripped that trap. We did think it was a pretty basic error. Now he's taunting us.'

He pointed to his phone, reminding her of the pictures that were so easy for them to capture of Karim in that hot tub. Presumably they had more of her with Karim but pride prevented her from asking.

Sky nodded briskly. 'Yes, I got that, thanks for the reminder.'

'We are experts in surveillance but we can only track Amin when he wants us to. We've lost him on numerous occasions; too often for it to be a coincidence. He doesn't have a private vehicle that we can place a tracking device on, nor can we get near his electronic equipment.' He sighed and spread his hands. 'I hate to make the admission, but he's capable of losing us whenever he feels like it.'

Sky lifted one shoulder. 'Perhaps he gets tired of being followed.'

'If some big Islamist extremist hit goes down in this country, which we have every reason to believe will happen soon, then anyone the slightest bit suspect will be hauled in and left to rot in places where most people don't even know there are places.' Ryan paused and fixed her with a look of steely determination. 'And Amin's name will be near the top of our list. He knows it and won't like being a sacrificial lamb, is my guess. He's got used to the high life and rather enjoys it.'

'You think he wants to disappear?' she asked breathlessly.

'Wouldn't you in his situation?'

'Hard to say without knowing more about his beliefs. But if you're right, why latch on to me?'

'You're wealthy.'

It wasn't a question. Ryan had clearly checked her background and the intrusiveness angered her. 'I suppose you think that's the only reason why a man who looks like him would give someone like me a second glance,' she said, squaring her shoulders in an effort to hide her hurt feelings. 'Go on, you might as well say it.'

'I think any man who didn't give you a second glance would be a few sandwiches short of a picnic,' he said, with so much sincerity behind the words that Sky almost believed him. Almost. She had believed every endearment that Karim had addressed to her. Now she no longer knew who he was, if there was any truth behind the things that he had told her about himself and, crucially, what it was that he wanted from her. 'Has he asked about your money; referred to it in any way?'

'No.' Sky screwed up her eyes in an effort to recollect, too tired and confused to take offence at the suggestion. 'He knows that my parents are dead and that I inherited but he's never asked how much.'

'I found out.' Ryan reached across the space that separated them and gently touched her hand. The sympathetic gesture sent pleasure rippling through her bloodstream but she refused to acknowledge the effect he had on her. Once bitten and all that. 'He could, too, if it's that important to him.'

'Even if he has, I'm hardly going to give him access to my bank account. I might look desperate but I'm not completely stupid.'

'No one said you were. I'm just thinking out loud. Besides, if he wanted access, he wouldn't risk asking you for a handout. He's a first-class hacker.'

'You think he wants to come to my flat so he can get his hands on my laptop?'

'It's a possibility it would be unwise to ignore. You need to put safe-guards in place with your bank, just in case.'

'I think you're overreacting. Most of my money is invested but...'

'But if he spun a convincing enough story, you might feel the need to help him out?'

Sky paused. Would she? Before today, before what she had overheard at the hotel, before meeting Ryan and being semi-convinced by what he'd told her, perhaps she would.

But there were other, far stronger reasons, that made her think otherwise.

She would do what Ryan had suggested and take measures to protect her available cash, which was a substantial amount, held on deposit for a rainy day. Better safe than sorry.

'I remain to be convinced that he has any "cause", other than the desire to avenge himself upon the people who killed his family.'

Ryan leaned forward. 'His parents and sisters?'

Sky's shoulders were fixed in a rigid line as the reminder of Amin's loss reinforced her dwindling belief in him. 'You know about them so why doubt his integrity?'

'What is it?'

Sky's doubtful expression had not been lost on Ryan, she realised. 'It's just that... Well, someone came to Karim's room. I was... asleep.' Sky cursed her inability to hold back her blush but Ryan, if he noticed her embarrassment, refrained from comment. 'I heard some of what was said, including mention of Karim's father.'

'The other man mentioned him?' Ryan leaned forward, frowning and alert.

'Yes. There was talk of hastily executed orders... of killing. The mystery guy was flustered.'

'Shit!'

'What?' she asked.

'Someone tried to kill my boss this afternoon and might very well have succeeded. He's in intensive care.' Ryan ground his jaw, his anger barely contained. That, Sky thought, probably explained why he had snatched her off the street. This was now a personal crusade from his perspective.

'I'm sorry,' she said softly. 'That's awful. I hope your boss pulls through.'

'Yeah, and you can help by telling me what you saw and heard.'

'You don't know that the man had anything to do with...' Ryan's granite expression caused Sky's protest to die on her lips. 'All right, I didn't see the man. Like I say, I was asleep. Something woke me, a noise. Raised voices that were quickly hushed. Karim wasn't in bed and that's when I realised he was talking to someone in the other room. He'd said that he'd order room service and we'd eat alone, so I didn't understand what anyone else was doing in the suite.'

'Go on,' Ryan encouraged when she paused to draw breath, and to wonder if she should temper her words. She decided not to. Ryan would know if she was economical with the truth. Besides, if Karim was innocent then he would have an explanation that would pan out. If he wasn't then Ryan would need her help to reel him in; help that it would suit her desire for revenge to provide.

Slowly at first, and then with increasing confidence, she told him everything she'd heard.

'The man definitely said that the order to kill came from Amin's father and that it was a last-minute decision?' Ryan asked, seizing on that particular aspect of her story.

'Yes.' Sky nodded emphatically. 'Karim wasn't happy about it.'

'That's why you left?'

'Well, of course it is! I don't want to get embroiled with murder. I needed to get away and think.'

'Does Amin know that you overheard?'

'No, I don't think so.' Sky paused to consider her response. 'But he was surprised when I said I had to leave. He asked if he could come to my flat tomorrow, as a matter of fact.'

Ryan frowned. 'Goes against what he said about not wanting to draw you into his world.'

Sky bit her lower lip and nodded. 'The same thought had occurred to me,' she reluctantly admitted. 'I told him that my flat mate's going away for a few days and assumed that's why he'd made the suggestion.'

'It'll save on hotel bills and give him a golden opportunity to breach your banking codes on your computer. Sorry,' he added hastily when Sky winced. 'Like I say, I'm paid to think the worst of everyone.'

'It's okay.' Sky hung her head, wondering what the hell she had got herself involved with. Wondering too why she was so ready to believe Ryan. Perhaps because of that picture, she thought. A woman's pride and all that. 'Do you think his father's still alive?'

'It's a possibility that we hadn't stopped to consider but could explain a great deal. His mother and sisters were killed in that explosion and the remains of a man identified as his father were also found in the wreckage.' Ryan tapped his forefinger against his lips, clearly deep in thought. 'A convenient way to disappear.'

'But if it wasn't his father, whose body could it have been?'

'We shall never know but it's easy to imagine the loss of his nearest and dearest poisoning the man's mind against the West.'

'Was the West responsible for the attack?'

Ryan sighed. 'Warped minds can twist things so that the conse-quences of the perpetrators' actions are always our fault.'

'Yes, I suppose... I don't watch the news much. It's too depressing.'

'When does Amin want to visit you?'

'He mentioned tomorrow evening but I didn't give him an answer. I expect he'll call.' Sky thought how anxiously she had awaited Amin's calls, up until that point. Now, she felt very differently; she was detached and determined. A part of her wanted to turn her back on it all, tell Ryan that she couldn't help him and go back to her organised, predictable, unexciting life. It was safer that way. But she already knew she wouldn't do that. Her determination had nothing to do with national security and everything to do with the thirst for revenge.

If Karim had used her, she wasn't about to let him get away with it.

'What do you want me to do?' she asked, lifting her head and meeting Ryan's gaze as steely resolve pushed aside her despondency.

It was time to fight back.

'I would like to put recording devices in your flat, cameras and sound, and I'd like you to invite him round tomorrow when he calls.' Ryan sent her a supplicating look. 'Can you do that for me?'

'No, but I can do it for me.' Sky stood and paced the length of the room. 'What's less clear to me, though, is what you expect to gain from it. He's hardly likely to admit that his father's death was faked, *if* it was.'

'This is the first opportunity we've had to get anywhere near him,' Ryan replied, standing too and watching her. 'He will be relaxed with you, off his guard, because he doesn't suspect you.'

'You actually think that he wants to get away from his father and needs my money to make it happen?' Sky shook her head. 'It seems far-fetched.'

Ryan lifted one shoulder in a casual shrug. 'That rather depends upon his desperation, and the nature of his relationship with his father, always supposing that he is still alive. It also depends upon what he's been promised in return for putting himself out there and bringing himself to our notice. There's no doubt that he's been well trained, prob-ably for years, but being educated in this country, his beliefs could be different from his father's. He certainly won't relish the possibility of becoming a scapegoat for a cause that he may no longer believe in. He will have no illusions about the treatment he can expect if he's arrested. He doesn't have to be proven guilty of anything in order to be detained indefinitely, especially if he isn't given access to a lawyer shouting to the media about police brutality and suspects' rights.'

'This is all so surreal.' Sky shuddered. 'So cloak-and-dagger.'

'Welcome to my world, darling.'

'It might be better if I tell him I overheard snippets of his conversation with the mystery man and ask him what it all meant,' Sky said pensively.

'No!' Ryan spoke firmly, causing Sky to almost jump out of her skin. Her nerves were shot to pieces and she felt wrecked, disillusioned, frightened and angry. 'That's the last thing you should do. There's no guaranteeing how he'll react.'

'You want my help with a man you've never spoken to, but you won't let me do it my way.' She turned away from him, spoiling for a fight that she would never win, wondering what it was about this glamorous man that made her want to challenge him at every turn. 'Get someone else to do it then.'

'No, you don't understand...' Ryan's phone rang, splintering the tension between them. He was slow to look away from her and glance at the screen. As he did so, his sombre expression turned even darker. 'Excuse me. I have to take this.'

Sky watched his profile as he half turned away from her, comparing him to Karim, the most glamorous person she knew. Ryan, she was forced to accept, could give him a run for his money.

'What?' he asked.

He listened and then nodded. 'When?' He listened some more. 'You sure? Okay, I'll be there.'

He pocketed his phone and Sky sent him an inquisitive look. 'Your boyfriend left the hotel an hour ago by the back entrance with the mystery man in tow. Except that the mystery man is no longer a mystery. His name is Haamid Farook, a small-time crook and general hard man.'

'How do you know this?'

'My man went into the hotel and lifted his prints, which are in the system. He has previous.'

'Of course he does.' Sky shuddered, discomposed by the easy way in which Ryan and the organisation he worked for got things done. 'Do you know where to find him?'

'Yeah, on the banks of the Thames. His body was just fished out the water at Wandsworth Bridge.'

8

Karim paced the length of his father's study, his patience gossamer thin.

'What on God's green earth made you authorise such a ham-fisted attempt on Wingate's life?' he asked.

His anger caused him to forget to temper his words. His father would see them as deeply disrespectful. Despite an extortionately expensive education, Karim was not permitted to have opinions, and was certainly not permitted to express them in front of his father. Karim had lost all respect for the man years since and as his decisions became increasingly bizarre, Karim found it harder to hide his contempt. Ordinarily he was astute enough to keep his feelings to himself but today the old man had gone too far.

He had to be stopped.

'Keep a civil tongue in your head, boy!'

Karim swung on his heel and towered over his father, who had remained calmly seated in his wide leather chair. 'I cannot remain silent when you put us all at risk through your personal vendettas. What did Wingate do to you? He doesn't know of your existence. You have made sure of that.'

'Of course he knows. Don't be so naïve. It is only my generous donations to both leading political parties in this country that ensure my respectability and make me untouchable.' The old man gave a mirthless chuckle. 'Imagine their having to explain taking charity from a man such as me.'

Since his father had given to both ruling and opposition parties, it would be in the interests of both to keep their mouths firmly shut. One such occasion upon which the parties could work together, for the sake of self-preservation rather than the good of the country.

'Making an attempt on the life of the US president will be suicide for the man who has to carry it out,' Karim pointed out, changing tack. 'That will be me, in case you had forgotten.'

'And where will the authorities be looking now that Wingate has been attacked? An attack which he is unlikely to survive.'

'You think that will prevent all the agencies, UK and US, from protecting the president?' Karim shook his head, convinced now that his father had completely lost the plot.

'You are starting to think like them. I have given you too much freedom.'

'You have put me in the direct firing line.'

'Calm down, Karim.' His father waved a placating hand. 'Everything is going exactly the way I planned it. Farook is out of the picture. He cannot talk.'

Karim nodded, not surprised. He knew when he got the call to bring the man here that his hours were numbered. At least this time Karim was not expected to do his father's dirty work. His skills were being reserved for the big one. Karim knew there was a bullet with his name on it in the likely event that he was captured. Such was his father's fanaticism that he would sacrifice his only remaining child in order to survive and continue with his fight.

'There is a woman I want you meet,' his father said, adroitly changing the subject.

Karim rolled his eyes. 'Not again, Father. I don't have the least intention of marrying. I may not have much longer left to live and I will not waste those days on a dried-up old hag of your choosing.'

'She is young and untouched.'

'So I should hope.'

'She is not one of your Western whores, free with her favours.'

Karim suppressed a smile. His father kept a whole string of the whores in question, paying them liberally and then complaining about their loose morals.

'Her father is rich. I need him on our side.'

'Then find another way. I will not marry her.'

'The girl has seen you and set her sights on you. You have a duty to help.'

'Aren't I doing enough?'

'You do not have to set the bomb that will kill the president, if...'

Karim tuned out his father's haranguing. He had never opposed his father quite so robustly before, preferring to toe the parental line in order to ensure a steady flow of funds that enabled him to live his life by his own code. He had always known there would be a heavy price to pay for that freedom and his father was now calling in his marker.

But he was also giving him an out: the carrot-and-stick approach. He had given Karim a few days to mull upon his likely demise or capture. Now he was suggesting that if he agreed to marry then he would be taken out of the direct line of fire. His father must really need the girl's family's support.

What the hell are you playing at?

He threw himself into a chair, pondering his difficulties. He did still want to avenge his mother and sisters; he had never forgotten the devastation he had felt when they had been taken from him, causing his entire life to change direction. His sisters were older than him and had been dedicated to his welfare. He still missed them to this day. The thirst for revenge had never left him but he could no longer agree with his father's means of procuring it. Besides, it would be impossible for him not to be involved with the plot to wipe out the president. He was the computer expert and his skills would be vital.

'Why Wingate?' Karim asked, refusing to be drawn on the issue of the heiress.

'They think they are so clever with all their secret agencies.' Karim's father waved his hand expansively. He held a crystal glass filled with single malt but didn't spill a drop. His hypocrisy wasn't lost on Karim. He decried loose Western ways at every opportunity, but that didn't prevent him from consuming copious amounts of Scotland's finest export, or from keeping a string of mistresses. 'I needed to let them know that we are not as stupid as they appear to think. And to distract them from our true purpose, obviously.'

Karim, aware that it would be a waste of breath to point out that his actions would have had the opposite effect, remained silent. The police would, he knew, be on high alert to the possibility of a terrorist attack, making his difficult assignment now completely impossible. Not that it mattered because Karim didn't have the first intention of carrying it out. He rather enjoyed living, and wasn't about to make a worthless sacrifice. Nor was he going to marry the woman his father had chosen for him.

By his actions today, his father – did he but know it – had just signed his own death warrant. He was already dead as far as the world was concerned, Karim reasoned, and it was impossible for anyone other than James Bond to die twice. Karim also knew that the majority of their supporters shared his own concerns about his father's increasingly bizarre and utilitarian decision-making. There were more obscure ways to make their point without threatening what they had already accumulated in the decadent West.

He thought of sweet, trusting little Sky and frowned when he recalled her abrupt departure that afternoon. Had she overheard his conversation with Farook, despite the fact that they had spoken in whispers? Karim was surprised by the depth of his disappointment when he considered that possibility. If she had then she would have to be permanently silenced; there was nothing else for it. Once his father had been taken out of the equation, Karim had plans – plans that had just been brought forward – and Sky was now a pivotal part of them.

He would definitely be paying a visit to her flat once the flatmate was safely out of the way. The timing seemed providential. He knew that Nancy had warned Sky away from him, suspicious of his motives, or perhaps jealous because she had been overlooked in favour of her less attractive friend. Whatever her reasons, with Nancy out of the way for a while, Karim was confident that no matter what she might have overheard, Sky would still be putty in his hands. She was dynamite between the sheets, where she rapidly shed her inhibitions, and was happy to follow wherever Karim led. She was the best he'd had for as long as he could recall and he wasn't about to give that up.

* * *

Ed brought the car to the door of the block of flats and Ryan ushered Sky into the back seat, joining her there. The windows were tinted and the possibility of her being seen by anyone passing by, or watching, was remote.

'Where to now?' Ed asked.

Ryan gave him Sky's address and the car moved smoothly away from the kerb, joining relatively light traffic. Ryan watched the gambit of emotions that flitted through Sky's expression, aware that she was conducting some sort of inner battle with her loyalties. Hardly surprising; Ryan had given her a lot to think about and refrained from talking to her now so that she was free to consider what she'd learned.

And decide whether she believed it.

Her head accepted that Ryan had told her the truth, he sensed, but part of her heart still belonged to Amin and she was prepared to give him the benefit of the doubt, despite what she had seen and overheard. He felt for her but somehow resisted the urge to take her hand and give it a reassuring squeeze. Steve was in hospital, fighting for his life, he reminded himself, and this girl's boyfriend was indirectly responsible for that situation.

With such sobering thoughts percolating through his brain, he extracted his mobile from his pocket and called Bill for an update. Bill himself had sent several messages when Ryan hadn't answered his calls and Ryan knew that he would be taken to task for being offline.

'Where the hell have you been?' Bill asked, picking up on the first ring.

'How is he?' Ryan asked at the same time.

'No change, which is good, apparently.'

Ryan breathed a fraction more easily as he succinctly outlined his activities, without revealing Sky's identity.

'The lady is willing to help us?' Bill sounded highly sceptical. 'Are you sure you can trust her?'

'She's with me now, she is sure and yeah, I do trust her,' he replied, winking at Sky. 'She needs answers herself. I'll call at her flat tomorrow, once her flatmate has gone off on holiday, and install the devices.'

'Right. Address?'

'Need to know,' Ryan replied, unsure why he was holding out on his temporary boss.

'Damn it, Ryan. It's me you're talking to.'

'Even so, Steve lets me run my operations my way.'

'Keep me informed, then,' Bill grunted, clearly not happy. 'I have some more intel on Farook.'

Ryan listened, unsurprised by what he heard.

'Right. Let me know if there's any change in Steve's condition.'

Ryan cut the connection, glad that Steve had no close family. Few of them in the elite team did. Families equated to weak links that could be exploited by the bad guys. Families equated to a change in priorities. Families meant taking your eye off the ball, which could get you killed. Ryan had learned that much from bitter experience but he had also learned not to allow himself to dwell upon Sarah. Whenever he did so, he tended to lose focus.

Ryan glanced at Sky. There were no tears in her eyes and her expression seemed resolute. She was lost in thought and he sensed that she was barely aware of him. He would have given a great deal to know what was preoccupying her. He could make an educated guess, but no more than that because he simply couldn't get a read on her and felt as though she was holding something back.

'You okay?'

'Am I really doing this?'

It was a rhetorical question but Ryan took the opportunity to reassure her. 'Only if you want to. No pressure. All I ask if you decide against it is that you don't tell Amin of our meeting. It will cost lives if you do.' *And I've taken an almighty chance trusting you with as much as I've already told you.*

'I understand. Can we... No, don't worry.'

'Can we what?'

'I don't want to face Nancy quite yet.' Sky swallowed, looking unsure of herself. 'She will take one look at me and know something isn't right. She half expected me not to come home at all. That was what I'd hoped for.' She sighed. 'Now I don't know what to think.'

'Pull over, Ed,' Ryan said, smiling at Sky.

Ed did so. Ryan opened the car door, slid out of it and held out his hand to help Sky out too. They were in Clapham, where trendy bars abounded. Ryan kept hold of her hand once they were clear of the car and he'd dismissed Ed for the night. Sky didn't object to the arrangement, which pleased Ryan more than it should have. He wasn't being professional but told himself that reassurance was what Sky needed and it was his duty to provide it. After all, he'd got her into something that she would never fully understand. No more did Ryan, but he was paid to take risks.

'Here.'

He pushed open the door to a wine bar he'd chosen at random. The evening was warm and half the clientele were clustered around the tables on the pavement. It was cram-packed inside too with drinkers out for a good time. Ryan managed to procure a small corner table, just as its occupants were leaving. A waitress bore down on them and Sky asked for rosé. Ryan ordered bottled larger and their drinks were delivered fast and efficiently.

'Cheers,' Ryan said, raising his bottle and clinking it against her glass.

'I've already had champagne,' she replied, 'but that seems like another world ago, so this counts as medicinal.'

Ryan smiled. 'It counts as anything you want it to. You've had one hell of a shock and a little Dutch courage can work wonders.'

'Did they really kill that guy, the one from Karim's hotel room?' she asked, after they'd savoured their drinks and watched the noisy, boisterous crowd cramming the space in front of the bar without speaking for several minutes.

Ryan nodded. 'Looks that way. They couldn't trust him not to blab in order to save his own skin. He wouldn't have known who the big guns are but probably knew enough that he needed to be silenced.'

Sky shuddered. 'Brutal!'

Ryan lifted one shoulder. 'That about covers it.'

'He knew Karim and where to find him,' Sky reasoned.

'That hotel is almost certainly a base for Karim's organisation. We have people looking into its funding to see if it leads to other threads. That's often how these plots are exposed: by slow, laborious research done by our geeks. Anyway, a scruffy individual like Farook wouldn't have got past the doorman if the hotel's backers weren't somehow involved.' Ryan leaned in close and kept his voice low, even though the loud buzz of conversation and laughter in the bar made the possibility of their being overheard remote. 'I have to say that we didn't know about the hotel until Karim took you there so you've already helped us out.'

'Let's talk about something else,' Sky said, shuddering.

'Sure.'

'Tell me about you.'

'What do you want to know?'

'Anything you can tell me. If you work for a secret organisation, I suppose that's not much.'

Ryan knew he was being tested. If he told her nothing then she would harbour doubts about him and might renege on their agreement. Besides, he liked talking to her, exchanging confidences. It was a long time since he'd felt a connection to any woman; Sarah's death had seen to that. Sky was on the verge of working for him; she would become Ryan's operative, he reminded himself, and so he needed to keep the relationship professional. Even so, he'd open up to her a bit, just enough to gain her confidence.

'The fight against terror is real and ongoing,' he said after a short pause. 'The more cells we expose, the more spring up to replace them. It's never-ending.'

Sky toyed with the stem of her glass, turning it in circles on the tabletop as Ryan carried on speaking.

'The security services have leeway but still have to play by the rules; the lawyers acting for those they interrogate make sure of that,' Ryan explained. 'But as private contractors we fly beneath the radar, have no official status and can do pretty much as we please.'

'Then I hope you recruit carefully because that's a privilege that could easily be abused.'

'You've got that right. We are all ex-law enforcement or military. All with vital skills that we bring to the party.' He paused and fixed her with penetrating look. 'I'm not married, never have been and don't have any kids. No family either. My parents are both deceased and I don't have any siblings.'

'A bit like me.' She gave a prolonged sigh.

'It has its advantages. I see friends with grown kids who still haven't flown the nest, get into all sorts of scrapes and are dependent upon the bank of mum and dad. And that's just the success stories. Anyway, don't get me started.'

'It sounds as though you don't like kids.'

'I couldn't eat more than one,' he quipped.

'Ryan!' She laughed and gently slapped his thigh.

It was good to hear her laugh, to see her relax in his company.

'Kids?' He went on, sensing that her question had been serious despite her reaction, and that she was disappointed in his answer. She certainly looked wistful when she spoke of them. 'I have to say that I've never much thought about it. Not found the right woman, I guess.' He took a swig of his lager. 'How about you? You sound as though you like the idea of motherhood.'

'I like children, that's for sure, but unlike you, I could cope with more than one. We both know how lonely it can be to grow up as an only child but...'

'But what? Don't stop now.'

She shook her head and he knew the moment had passed; she wouldn't share. 'It doesn't matter,' she said, finality in her tone.

He turned sideways on his chair so that he could properly face her. 'How many do you envisage in your future?' he asked in a teasing tone.

She lifted one hand and waggled it from side to side in a considering gesture. 'Two or three. I dare say they will fight like cat and dog, and hate one another growing up, but into adulthood they are more likely to bond and be there for one another. I like the idea of leaving that sort of legacy but don't suppose I ever shall.'

Ryan thought that a telling statement, making it clear just how lonely she felt, and adjured himself not to get too personally involved.

'You and your flatmate seem close, from what you've said about her.'

'We were at school together so, yeah, there's a strong bond. We're chalk and cheese. She's beautiful, outgoing, confident, all the things that I'm not – but they say opposites attract, don't they?'

'What's her take on Amin?' he asked, not bothering to tell her that her low self-image was totally misplaced. She wouldn't believe him.

Sky canted her head, as though considering a question that probably didn't require much consideration. She and Nancy would have discussed it to death, Ryan was absolutely sure of it.

'We almost came to blows over him,' she admitted with a rueful grin. 'Nancy was suspicious of his motives; I accused her of being jealous because for once I was the one who the guy fancied.' She shook her head. 'I regret that now it seems she was probably right to doubt his motives.'

'You can't tell her what we've discussed,' he warned, briefly squeezing her hand. 'It would put her in danger. But if she's going away for a while, by the time she gets back it should all be resolved.'

She raised a brow. 'You can't know that for sure.'

'True, but women aren't the only ones who work on instinct.'

She laughed at him as she drained her glass. Ryan caught the waitress's attention and ordered another round.

'Actually,' he added, 'I am using intel that's a little more scientific than instinct but it's not stuff I can share with you.'

Their drinks arrived and the conversation turned more general. When she relaxed and stopped worrying about what people thought of her, Sky was very entertaining company. She made him laugh when she told stories about some of her more demanding clients and their propensity for making specific requests and then changing their minds when she adhered to their suggestions.

'Diplomacy and the patience of a saint are basic necessities in my line of work,' she said, finishing her second drink and yawning behind her hand.

'Come on,' he said, standing. 'It's getting late. I'll walk you almost home.'

'You think someone might be watching my flat. Someone other than you, that is?' She spoke lightly but the sparkle had left her eye.

'Unlikely, but I'm paid to be cautious. Besides, your flatmate won't question your arrival at this hour, I assume. Come on.'

He took her arm and shouldered his way through the crowd that parted like the Red Sea to let them through before closing behind them again.

They made the short walk to Sky's street in companionable silence. Ryan stopped on the corner.

'Programme my personal number into your phone under a female name,' he said. 'Just in case Amin gets sight of it and asks questions.'

She sent him a look of mild surprise but pulled her phone from her bag. Ryan reeled off his number and she repeated it back to him.

'Right, Brenda,' she said, grinning up at him. 'I look forward to hearing from you.'

'Text me so I have your number.'

She did as he asked. Ryan's phone pinged and he checked to ensure that her number had come through.

'Thanks for the drinks,' she said, shy now and studying the pavement beneath her feet.

'I should be thanking you for what you've agreed to do,' he replied. 'It takes courage.'

'We never any of us know what we are capable of unless forced into a corner.'

'Very true. But this is a dangerous game, Sky. The stakes couldn't be higher. I'm paid to risk my life.' He fixed her with a hard look, not wanting her to be left in any doubt. 'You are not. Think about that overnight. You don't need to be involved and I'll understand if you reflect and decide that you would prefer not to be.'

'I think it's a little late for that. I am involved, whether I like it or not.'

Ryan placed his index finger beneath her chin, tilted it backwards and briefly, very briefly, covered her lips with his own. *What the hell!*

'I'll call you early tomorrow,' he said, wondering what madness had caused him to act so unprofessionally. 'But call me any time day or night if you have even the mildest concerns for your safety. Are we agreed?'

'Of course.'

The tip of her tongue emerged to moisten the lips he had just kissed, as though she wanted to be sure that the kiss had actually happened. Then she smiled up at him, gave a little wave and walked away. She didn't once turn back. Ryan knew because he stood where he was until she reached her house, fished in her bag for her key, let herself in and disappeared from view.

'What the hell have I got her involved with?' he asked aloud as he turned away, heading for the Tube.

9

When she got home, Sky was surprised to see how late it was. She and Ryan had been in that wine bar for over two hours. The time had flown and it had seemed more like ten minutes. He was so easy – too easy – to talk to. She had revealed more about herself than had been her intention but instinctively knew that her confidences would be safe with him. He wouldn't use them to force her to draw Karim out. He didn't need to since Sky herself wanted answers.

If she was being manipulated for as yet unclear reasons, if she had fallen victim to a few compliments and a handsome face, then she fully intended to find out what it was that Karim wanted from her. Even if his flamboyant display of wealth was all part of the set-up, she could tell that he was accustomed to the best of everything and failed to see how her relatively small nest egg could further his ambitions.

She let herself into her flat, half hoping that Nancy would already be asleep, providing her with a legitimate reason to avoid an inquisition she was unsure she was ready to face. She was a hopeless liar and Nancy would catch her out immediately.

'Damn!' she muttered, when she saw the light shining under her friend's door, aware that there would be no escape. 'I'm back,' she called out, deciding to get it over with.

'Come and tell me how it went,' Nancy called back. 'I thought you might stay over. Anyway, I want all the sordid details.'

Beware what you wish for, Sky thought, as she turned the handle to Nancy's door and found her friend sitting up in bed, phone in hand, clearly in the middle of sending messages.

'You'll see him in the morning,' Sky said, smiling and correctly guessing that Nancy was keeping tabs on Phil - a man who had broken up with her rather than the other way around and then won her back with the offer of a romantic getaway.

'Just making sure he doesn't forget my name, and reminding him I'll chop his balls off with blunt sheers if he even looks at another woman.'

Sky winced as she perched herself on the edge of Nancy's bed and her friend put her phone aside. 'You are a vicious woman,' Sky said.

'Honey, you have absolutely no idea.' Both girls laughed. 'Come on then, give. How was lover boy?'

Sky described the suite, the view, and made up a menu when Nancy asked what they had eaten. She kept checking her phone, though, clearly waiting for a response from Phil. She was thankful that her friend was distracted and didn't appear to notice that Sky was winging it, showing less enthusiasm for Karim than usual.

'Well, I'm glad you're enjoying yourself but be careful. I don't want you getting hurt.'

'Not much danger of that. I'm having some long overdue fun, just like you're always encouraging me to. I don't have any expectations beyond that point.'

'Atagirl!' Nancy yawned.

'I'll leave you to get your beauty sleep,' Sky said, standing. 'Not that you need it, but still...'

'Right. We're off bright and early in the morning. A flight at silly o'clock. I'll try not to wake you.'

'Don't worry.' Sky bent to kiss her friend. 'Have the best time in the world and knock 'em dead in those bikinis.'

'Oh, I fully intend to.'

Sky laughed, her hand on the open door. 'I don't doubt it for a moment.'

Sky undressed quickly in her own room and slid between the sheets, aware that, for her, sleep would be a long time coming, despite being bone weary. Her mind was on overdrive and she needed time to reflect, to work out what she had become involved with.

To decide who to trust.

She had been bubbling with excitement all day at the prospect of seeing Karim but hearing him casually discussing murder had proven to be a passion killer. What was less obvious was her willingness to believe Ryan. Just because Karim had a hidden agenda didn't mean that Ryan was right about him, did it? It seemed so far out there. What reason would he have to invent such an unlikely story, though? She had only briefly been frightened of him when he took her arm so forcefully and pushed her into that car. Then she'd felt drawn to him, persuaded by his candidness to reassess what she knew about Karim.

Her doubts about Karim didn't mean that she'd given up on him though. Allowing the listening devices to be put in her flat would help to prove things one way or the other, she hoped. Ryan had told her that the devices were so sophisticated that they would be able to detect what numbers he called on his mobile. All well and good, but if Karim was up to something untoward and was as cautious as Ryan had implied, Sky rather doubted that he would call anyone on an open line.

She thumped her pillows into a more comfortable nest, turned on her side and curled her legs up, falling asleep not to images of Karim's handsome features, as had been her habit these past days and weeks. Instead, it was Ryan's rugged allure that haunted her dreams. What the hell? Sky condemned herself for her shallowness.

The sound of Nancy moving about woke her when it was only just light. She looked at the clock and groaned. Five fifteen. She couldn't recall the last occasion upon which anyone had persuaded Nancy to get up *that* early. Her version of moving about quietly left a lot to be desired, Sky thought, smiling. She'd put her heels on already and was stomping about on the wooden floor like a demented elephant.

Then the doorbell sounded. Phil had obviously arrived. There was the sound of voices, of deep breathing as presumably they kissed, and then luggage being wheeled. The door opened and closed with a loud bang, leaving blessed silence in its wake, but for Perdita's loud purrs from one of Sky's pillows where she had taken up residence.

Sky knew she wouldn't get back to sleep. With a sigh, she pushed aside the covers and headed for the shower, where she stood beneath the hot jets for a long time, thinking, slowly coming back to full consciousness but no nearer knowing where she stood on the Karim issue.

She had been up for several hours when Ryan phoned a little after eight.

'Just checking in,' he said, his voice a deep gravelly vibration that Sky reacted to somewhere deep within her core. 'Hope I didn't wake you.'

'I've been up for a while. How is your friend?'

'He's unconscious still but stable as opposed to critical. Thanks for asking.'

'Well, that's good, I guess.'

'We'll know more when they wake him up. They're keeping him sedated right now. Something about allowing time for swelling on the brain to go down. He was shot and they seem to think he whacked his head when he crumpled to the ground.'

That didn't sound quite as promising but Sky refrained from pointing out the obvious.

'Has your flatmate left?'

'You mean you don't know? You haven't had someone watching?'

He chuckled. 'You're catching on. I hope you haven't noticed anyone but I won't apologise for wanting to keep you safe if you have. I've dragged you into my world...'

'I'm a big girl, Ryan. I can make my own decisions.'

'I hear you.'

Sky sensed that hadn't been what he'd intended to say but she didn't seek clarification.

'Have you heard from our mutual friend again?' he asked.

'No, but if you're right about him wanting to exploit me then I dare say I will do sometime today.'

'Right. Is it okay if I come over now?'

'Sure.'

'Ten minutes,' he replied before cutting the connection.

Sky wondered where he was and why it would only take him ten minutes to reach her. His flat in Brixton was more than ten minutes away. Perhaps he was the one who'd been watching over her all night. Although she doubted it, the possibility made her feel warm inside as she dashed back to her bedroom, trying to decide what to wear.

She settled for skinny jeans and a casual top that Nancy insisted highlighted her assets. She ran a brush through her hair, dabbed on a spot of mascara and lip gloss and was as ready as she would ever be when the doorbell sounded just eight minutes later. She felt nervous yet resolute as she pressed the buzzer to release the street door.

'First floor,' she told him, aware that he probably already knew that much.

'Hey,' he said, surprising her because he was dressed in jeans with a baseball cap pulled low over his eyes. He leaned forward to kiss her cheek and walked past her into the flat's hallway, taking professional interest in its chequered floor and high ceiling, no doubt trying to decide where to plant his listening devices. For her part, Sky took the opportunity to enjoy the view. In jeans and his tattered leather jacket, with a couple of days' worth of designer stubble decorating his strong jaw, he was every woman's wildest fantasy. Tough, resourceful and oozing machismo, he even smelled good – a combination of citrus soap and pure, unadulterated male.

Sky turned away, still confused by her ability to switch allegiances so swiftly, if that's what she had done. But still, Ryan wasn't offering to step into Karim's shoes in the event that he did turn out to have an alternative agenda and so she decided that she'd best get her thoughts out of the gutter. Once bitten, and all that. Men who looked like Karim and Ryan simply didn't go for the likes of her unless they had ulterior motives, she reminded herself with a bitter little shake of her head.

With that sobering thought percolating through her brain, she felt better able to face Ryan, who had stopped looking at the architecture and had instead focused his attention on her.

'Nice place,' he remarked.

'Coffee?' she asked.

'Mind reader.'

He followed her into the large kitchen that had been sympathetically modernised with cream units and sold oak surfaces. The original iron fireplace was still there, though, and an antique dining table and chairs were arranged in front of it.

'Very nice,' Ryan said, nodding his approval.

Sky didn't respond and instead busied herself with the coffee machine. It felt disconcertingly right to have this man in her kitchen. He made her feel safe and secure in a way that she hadn't known since the death of her father and that worried her. She could no longer trust her own judgement when it came to men and would keep Ryan at arm's length. He could be professional and so could she.

'Milk and sugar?' she asked over her shoulder, conscious of him prowling about the large space, making it feel as though the walls were contracting.

'Just milk.'

He thanked her when she handed the mug to him and perched his backside against the side of the table. 'You're nervous,' he said, stating the obvious.

'I can't think why?' she replied, sarcastically.

'Sorry.' His smile was wide and disarming. 'I guess I'm not used to dealing with people who aren't part of my world. It makes *me* kinda nervous.'

Sky laughed. 'If that's meant to reassure, it's not working.'

She suggested that they move into the lounge and led the way. This time Ryan let out a low whistle of appreciation when he took in the full-length windows, the large fireplace and the intricately carved ceiling.

'It's very homely,' he said.

'Glad you approve.'

Sky sat herself in a wingback chair and Ryan took a place across from her. Better that way, she had decided when selecting her seat. If he sat too close to her it would be... well, distracting. But she needn't have worried. Ryan appeared to be all business and unlike Sky's, his thoughts were probably focused solely on the assignment in hand.

'Will you mind if we track calls to and from your phone?' he asked.

Sky flexed a brow. 'You can do that?'

'Sure. The wonders of modern technology and all that but it might feel intrusive.'

Sky gave a hysterical little laugh. Her lack of sleep was already catching up with her and she felt as if she was living in a parallel universe where none of this was actually happening to her: this attractive man wasn't dominating her sitting room, looking at her with professional concern etched into his features. She would wake up any time soon and be thrown back into the routine of another working day.

'I heard a man talk about attempted murder to my boyfriend. A few hours later that man was fished out the river. You think the boyfriend in question has targeted me for my money and has terrorist activities in mind; you want to install surveillance equipment in my flat and are worried about being intrusive.' She shook her head. 'It's a little late for that.'

'I should have asked if you've changed your mind about helping us, having had time to reflect. You can still pull out,' he assured her, leaning forward to hold her gaze. 'No pressure if you've had second thoughts. Like I say, it's not without its dangers.'

'It's tempting, Ryan, but I need to know for my own sanity whether or not I'm being used by Karim.'

'Okay, if you're absolutely sure.' Ryan looked relieved by her response. 'But once you're in, there's no going back.'

'I'm not a quitter.'

'Good to know.' He paused to draw breath. 'Your phone tap. We won't listen to any calls that don't directly relate to Amin; you have my assurance.'

Sky waved a hand dismissively. 'The content of my calls is likely to send you to sleep. Listen to whatever you like.'

'Good, then we're agreed.' He set his empty mug aside and reached for his phone. 'I'll get my tech guy to come over now and set things up. He and I are the only people who you will have contact with, but mostly it will be me.'

For the next hour Sky watched in a daze as a young guy in jeans and trendy glasses climbed all over the flat like a monkey, hiding miniscule gizmos in the most unlikely places. Even though she was aware that they were there, Sky couldn't see them. The technician and Ryan kept discussing locations in an undertone, never once involving Sky, who felt surplus to requirements. The exclusion was starting to piss her off.

When she heard the technician trying to persuade Ryan that there should be at least a listening device in Sky's bedroom, she'd had enough.

'I am here, you know!' she said, an edge to her voice. 'Ask me, not him,' she told the startled young man, pointing a finger at Ryan for emphasis.

'Sorry,' the man – Josh, she thought his name was – said sheepishly. 'Professional hazard.'

'I'm not comfortable having anyone listening in the bedroom but I guess it's necessary,' she said blushing. 'No cameras, though.'

Ryan didn't look happy but accepted her decision. Josh went straight to work.

'Right, all done,' he said, packing up his bag of tricks. 'I'll leave Ryan to talk it all through with you. Nice meeting you and don't worry, we'll be with you every step of the way.'

'That *is* what worries me,' she said, smiling to take the sting out of her words as she showed him out of the flat. 'Big Brother is alive and watching you.'

Josh grinned. 'Only to keep you safe.'

'Yeah right, keep telling yourself that.'

Sky closed the door behind him and returned to the sitting room, where Ryan awaited her.

'Okay, talk me through this. How does it work and what do I have to do?'

'Basically, we can monitor everything that goes on in here from a van that will be parked close by. We will know everything that happens and if Amin brings anyone else here it could be the vital breakthrough we need to get to the men at the top.'

'Why would he, though?' Sky scowled. 'I assume they have safe meeting places. Why change their habits?'

'Because Amin is acting out of character. I hope he's planning to cut the men above him out, which would explain why he needs funds. Anyway, time will tell. As to the people he might bring here, we can use facial recognition; it's come on leaps and bounds and is one of our best tools to fight back against the bad guys with.'

'I see.' Sky folded her arms beneath her breasts and walked the length of the room, still feeling surreal. 'What do you want me to say to Karim?'

'I'm not going to feed you a script because I want you to act naturally, the way you always would with him.'

'Ha!' She sent him a disbelieving look. 'You tell me he's a terrorist, plotting some atrocity against innocent people, and expect me to act naturally.'

'Put like that it does sound unreasonable,' he conceded, 'but you're not convinced that I'm telling you the truth about him. You want to believe that he is simply a rich playboy. Am I right?'

* * *

Ryan could sense her unease and seriously wondered about the wisdom of the operation that he had put in place. She was right; Amin would see through her in a heartbeat. He would know that something had changed.

Or would he?

He sensed an inner strength, a determination in Sky that he suspected she was unaware she possessed and once again he felt as though she was holding out on him. She had been waiting for an opportunity to prove something to herself, that much he was sure about. She needed to step outside her comfort zone and Ryan would hold her hand, metaphorically speaking, every step of the way. He pushed firmly to the back of his mind his desire to hold her hand in the literal sense too.

Now was not the time.

'Yes,' she said reluctantly, answering Ryan's earlier question. 'I still have doubts about Karim's culpability but I also believe what you have told me, otherwise you wouldn't be here, bugging my private space.' She stopped walking and frowned up at him. 'How is that even possible? Why haven't I run to him and warned him about you?'

Ryan smiled as he placed his hands protectively on her shaking shoulders. 'It's okay to be conflicted,' he said. 'Hopefully things will become clearer over the next few days. Never doubt that I have your back, though. I'll be listening from the moment he steps into this flat and will know if you need to be extricated. Just remember, try not to stare at the places where you know the cameras are hidden. I know it's hard but you could inadvertently give yourself away. If you do that, even though I'll be close by, I might not be able to get to you in time.'

Her shuddering intensified. 'Is that supposed to make me feel better?'

'I just need you to focus, and to understand what we're up against. Remember the guy who tried to kill my boss. Well, he's dead now, which should give you some idea of the ruthless nature of the people involved.'

'Yeah—' Sky started violently when her mobile, on a side table, rang. She glanced at the display. 'It's him,' she said, her voice trembling.

'Answer it,' he said softly. 'Put it on speaker.'

Sky inhaled sharply, her stomach likely tied in knots as she walked across to her phone and pressed the green button. 'Karim,' she said in a commendably natural voice. 'I didn't expect to hear from you so soon.'

Ryan, watching her from across the room, nodded his approval.

'I'm worried about you, Sky. You left so abruptly yesterday. I was afraid that I had done something to offend you.'

'Of course not, but like I said, I had a meeting I couldn't get out of.'

'I hope it went well.'

'It did. I think I have the assignment but I'm waiting to hear.'

Ryan was impressed by the way that she lied so convincingly. No doubt images of Amin in that hot tub with the blonde were still fresh in her mind, giving her impetus. There was a lot to be said for a woman scorned and her desire for revenge.

'That's good. Now tell me how you are.' His voice had dropped, turning gravelly and persuasive. Ryan watched Sky for her reaction but she gave no outward sign of being affected by his seduction technique. 'I hope you have missed me.'

'There has hardly been time.'

'Your friend, has she gone on her holiday?'

'Yes, she left this morning.'

'Then I am going to come and see you. I want to see where you live. I want to know everything about you.'

'Okay. When do you have in mind?'

'What's wrong with this afternoon?'

'Aside from the fact that some of us have to work.'

'Of course. Excuse me. In my anxiety to see you, I had forgotten that.'

'Don't you have to work yourself?'

He chuckled down the line. 'Darling, I make my own hours.'

Sky smiled across at Ryan and rolled her eyes. Ryan wondered if she was starting to enjoy herself, playing the bastard at his own game. That was certainly the impression she gave and Ryan was proud of her. It couldn't be easy; she must be a bundle of nervous uncertainty, but Ryan would never have guessed, and he was watching her closely. He was pretty sure that Amin wouldn't be able to tell either, especially since he couldn't actually see her.

'I will be free at about five,' Sky said. 'Shall I cook for us?'

'No, I will not allow it! We will order something in.'

'All right. I shall see you later. I must go now, though.'

'Goodbye, my love. I shall count the hours.'

Sky cut the connection and looked to Ryan for approbation.

'You were superb,' he said, meaning it. 'A natural at deception.'

'Is that a good thing?'

Ryan chuckled. 'In my line of work, it's an essential skill.'

Ryan's phone chirped. 'Hey, Josh. You got that? Where was he calling from?'

'His club, most likely.'

'Does he have living quarters above his club?' Ryan asked Sky. 'We ought to know but don't, I'm afraid to say.'

'I think so. He mentioned something once but I've never seen them.'

Ryan nodded as he ended the call with Josh. 'I suspect that's where he bases himself when in London. The hotels he uses are for show only,' he told Sky.

'So, what now?' she asked, folding her arms.

'Now we wait.'

'I have work to be getting on with and I am sure you have too,' she said. 'Don't feel that you have to babysit.'

Ryan refrained from pointing out that it was no hardship. He sensed that she needed some alone time to come to terms with the issues she was now faced with. He would give it to her. Josh would let him know if there was even the slightest prospect of her needing him. The only places in the flat not covered by at least sound were her friend's room and the bathrooms.

'Okay,' he said, standing to squeeze her shoulder. 'Call me if you need anything. Anything at all. I won't be far away.'

'I'll be fine.'

She turned her head up to look at him and their lips briefly clashed. Ryan couldn't be sure afterwards who had instigated the 'accidental' contact but wasn't complaining about it. The desire to turn the innocent brush into something a little deeper took all Ryan's self-control. He needed to get out of that flat and get out fast. He'd worked with civilians before, several of them attractive, single women, but none had ever affected him quite so profoundly. Ryan could easily forget his duty in the protection of this feisty young woman and that scared the hell out of him. Without his dedication to his work what else did he have in his life?

He smiled at her, touched her cheek and got the hell out of there.

Once he had done so, his first call was to Bill for an update on Steve.

'I was about to call,' Bill replied, sounding upbeat. 'He's confounded his doctors by waking up and talking semi-coherently.'

Ryan felt as though he'd been holding his breath ever since the hit on Steve and he let it out now in an extravagant whoosh.

'Does he remember anything?' he asked.

'He's not making a lot of sense. He's still pretty drugged up. But he's asking for you.'

'I'll be there in half an hour,' Ryan replied, running to the car that he'd left parked a few streets away, jumping inside and gunning the engine. He heard Bill shouting down the phone, asking for an update, but he ignored the request – the order – and hung up.

* * *

Karim finished his conversation with Sky, feeling reassured. She was still the same trusting little innocent he'd targeted since she'd fallen into his lap. She was simply attempting to play it cool. That was fine by Karim. He liked a challenge.

He lay on a couch in his offices above Alexandria, having insisted that he was not to be disturbed. He wasn't likely to be, he knew, since his office and all that it implied was a sham. He didn't run the club, he left that to some of the little people better equipped for the drudgery. This was his personal bolthole – the office and suite of rooms beyond it. It was sacrosanct and he seldom invited anyone into his private domain.

Meetings were sometimes held in the other rooms on this floor – meetings of all types. The girls employed to act as hostesses in the club were all beautiful and highly professional. There wasn't any service they wouldn't supply for Karim's special clients – men who needed to be kept happy – for a price. But the rooms were all wired for sound and vision. Karim suspected that included his own; his father didn't completely trust him and that knowledge rankled. He was loyal enough to be trusted with the assassination of a US president but not left to his own devices to play with the big boys.

That was why he planned to conduct meetings at Sky's flat. His father didn't know anything about her. It was perfect. Karim intended to wipe out his father and inherit his legitimate businesses, which would see him set up for life. Most of his father's generals were disillusioned and the only men still loyal were the half-dozen who guarded the old man's private domain. Well, all of them bar one.

And Karim had plans to neutralise them.

Karim would make it clear to them that he was retiring from that aspect of the family firm but knew that his father's associates all had reasons of their own for wanting to create financial turmoil within the global markets. Self-interest was alive and kicking and they would all be aware that killing the US president would have a disastrous effect upon the stock markets worldwide, wiping millions off their assets – a situation that they would go to almost any length to prevent.

The easier course of action would be to leak details of the plot to one of the security forces but the danger level to Karim would be unacceptable. It meant that the plot would have to go ahead and the perpetrators would have to be caught red-handed. Which meant Karim would be apprehended. If he was subsequently released then his father would know who had ratted him out and Karim's life wouldn't be worth diddly squat.

Karim stirred from his prone position on the couch, stretched his arms above his head and smiled. He had a good feeling; the sort of feeling that came with shaking off restraining shackles that had started to chafe. He considered sending for one of the girls to service him but decided against it. He wanted to be bursting at the seams when he met with Sky later so that he could fully satisfy her. The prospect made him harden in anticipation. Some assignments weren't too arduous.

And once he'd softened her up, he'd spin her a line that would give him access to her deposit account. Failing that, he'd simply drug her and hack into her computer while she was sleeping it off.

10

At the hospital, Ryan flashed his credentials to the armed policeman standing guard duty outside Steve's room. The man studied them carefully, then nodded Ryan through. Steve was lying in bed, attached to what seemed like a jumble of tubes and beeping machines, his eyes closed.

'Fucking hell!' Ryan breathed.

'My thoughts exactly,' Steve croaked, lifting the oxygen mask away from his face in a gesture that appeared to exhaust him.

'I can see we didn't need to worry about you,' Ryan said, feeling a sweep of relief surge through him as the nurse told him not to tire her patient. 'You're being your usual curmudgeonly self.'

Steve closed his eyes and Ryan wondered if he'd gone back into a coma. His eyes opened again though when another nurse bustled into the room.

'Giving you a hard time, is he?' the nurse asked, checking Steve's vital signs.

'Normal service resumed,' Ryan quipped.

'Hmm.' The nurse checked some monitors and seemed satisfied with what they told her. 'I guess if he can complain, then he'll do okay without it for a while,' she said, nodding towards the oxygen mark. 'If he starts gasping for breath, ring the bell. Don't tire him out,' she reiterated. 'You can have five minutes.'

Steve flexed his jaw repeatedly, his face drained, exhausted. Ryan knew that the visit might not even last the five minutes he'd been given and so he needed to get straight down to business. He could find out more about Steve's prognosis later. Right now he had other priorities.

'What do you remember about the attack?' Ryan asked.

'Fuck all,' Steve replied, his voice still slurred but easier to understand. Ryan guessed he must be drugged up to the eyeballs. He shared the nurse's disbelief at his powers of recovery. 'Just felt a thump in the back, a searing pain, a crashing fall and bang on the head and then the lights went out.'

'Right.' Ryan was disappointed but not surprised. 'The guy who we think was the shooter is dead, if that makes you feel better. He's just been fished out the river.'

Steve closed his eyes and blinked. 'Tell me.'

Ryan succinctly explained.

'You were right about Amin then,' Steve said, eyes still closed, when Ryan ran out of words. 'Should have let you follow your instincts.' Steve's voice rasped. Ryan moved to the side of the bed, picked up a sippy cup and held the straw to Steve's mouth. He drank slowly, then released the straw. 'Thanks,' he gasped, appearing to be near the end of his strength. 'You sure this girl won't run to Amin and tip him the wink?'

'As sure as I can be. It's the best lead we've had so I have to run with it.'

'Keep Bill up to speed. The whole team will have your back.'

Ryan nodded, not ready to disagree with Steve in his current dilapidated state, but still convinced that someone connected to the team was leaking, or more to the point suppressing intel. It was the only explanation that made any sense. They had ears to the ground, informants in the most unlikely places, but rumours about a high-profile imminent attack were suspiciously thin on the ground.

Too thin.

'Will do,' he said.

'Okay. Get out of here and let me get some sleep.' Steve lifted a hand with tubes running from it a few inches above the bed covers but it fell straight back down again with a soft thud, as though the effort had sapped the remnants of his strength. It very likely had and Ryan knew that Steve would hate being seen in such a weakened condition. All his colleagues in Steve's elite unit prided themselves on their physical fitness.

'Hang in there, buddy, and don't be giving those nurses any grief.'

'You're mistaking me for you.'

Ryan laughed and left the room, optimistic that Steve would, against all the odds, recover. He was too tough and stubborn to do anything else.

Outside the hospital, Ryan extracted his phone and called Bill.

'How is he?' Bill asked, picking up on the first ring.

'Weak but he'll make it. We need to meet. I have intel.'

'Come to the office.'

'No, somewhere else.'

'Who put you in charge?' Ryan and Bill hadn't always seen eye to eye, mainly because Bill was a little too fond of pulling rank, which irked Ryan. Theirs wasn't the sort of organisation that worried about stature. Working off the books and spending time mixing with the dangerous dregs of society tended to be a leveller; it was a code that everyone with the notable exception of Bill lived by.

'This isn't a pissing contest, Bill. Just do as I ask. I have my reasons.'

'Pachino's in half an hour,' Bill said curtly, referring to a back street café close to the office.

Ryan made his way to the meeting, aware that he couldn't allow his personal feelings to influence his judgement. He and Bill didn't get along but Steve had worked with Bill for over a decade and trusted him implicitly – a situation that Ryan accepted since Steve's judgement was almost always on the money.

Ryan arrived on Bill's heels, ordered a coffee and the two men took a table at the back of the café that gave them a good view of the door. The place was half empty and no one spared them a passing glance.

'Steve doesn't remember anything about the attack,' Bill said, getting straight down to business. 'So why was he so keen to see you?'

'We have a lead on Amin.'

'How the hell did he know about that? I didn't have a chance to say anything. Not that you told me fuck all.' Bill scratched his ear, clearly agitated. Ryan refrained from pointing out that Steve couldn't have known but even half-conscious he had shown that his instincts were still spot on. 'Why are you so unwilling to share the details of this civilian woman you're running?' Bill asked, his voice briefly rising.

'There's nothing for you to know yet. I told Steve about her before his accident but he didn't think it had legs at the time.'

'Okay, but why meet to discuss it here?' Bill glanced over his shoulder, even though there wasn't anyone close enough to overhear their conversation.

'Because the girl is taking one hell of a risk. She's a member of the public with no training in our line of work and I'm not prepared to take chances over her safety.'

'We'll get a small team together to monitor the surveillance.'

'No need. Josh is on it.' Ryan paused for emphasis. 'So am I.'

Bill leaned forward, his face puce with rage. 'I don't know who you think you—'

'Cut it out!' Ryan held up a hand and stemmed the angry flow of Bill's words. 'I recruited the girl so I get to say how we run her.'

'I know you think there's a leak in the team but you're wrong. I'd personally stake my reputation on the integrity of the whole lot of them.'

'Then you're a damned fool!' Ryan took his turn to lean forward. 'But we can resolve the situation easily enough by putting out duff intel and seeing if it gets acted on. We should have done that months ago.'

'I advised Steve against it. It will only create division within the team.'

How the fuck did this guy rise through the ranks, Ryan wondered, refraining from rolling his eyes. And yet he had... risen, that is. Despite being more or less deskbound nowadays, Bill had once been a tough marine entrusted with delicate and dangerous missions, decorated with some of the highest honours. He had proved his loyalty time without number, saved lives with his quick thinking, and yet there was something about him that Ryan still didn't trust.

'If we have a bad apple, best root it out before it infects us all. You know as well as I do that some of the official agencies resent our existence and the fact that we can do more or less as we like, with no accountability. If we have a wrong 'un, that could be enough to see our funding cut.'

Bill's head jerked up. He loved numbers. A stickler for pristine expense accounts and balancing the books, he now focused his full attention on Ryan.

'What do you have in mind?' he asked.

'I'll file an encrypted report to say that the man fished from the river has been traced to the Bayswater Boutique Hotel,' Ryan said. 'It will only go to you, Steve and three others who need to know.'

Bill knew who the three were and gave a reluctant nod. 'Let's hope you're wrong,' he said. 'I'll arrange outside surveillance of the hotel and we'll see what pops.'

'Good.' Ryan drained his coffee cup and stood up. 'I'll be in touch.'

* * *

Sky wondered why she didn't feel more nervous as she awaited Karim's arrival. Surely she should be suffering from acute anxiety by now, yet she hadn't even agonised over what to wear, settling for cut offs and a skimpy top. If Karim was innocent, and part of her remained convinced that he must be, why didn't her willingness to put him to the test trouble her conscience? Images of Karim and that blonde in the hot tub flooded her mind, answering her question. If he was guilty and even suspected that she was on to him, then her life would be in danger.

And yet she felt perfectly calm. Ready to face him.

The doorbell rang before she was expecting him but she knew it wouldn't be anyone else. She squared her shoulders, took her time traversing the length of the hall and peered through the screen that showed him standing on the outside step, smiling for the camera. Sky's heart lurched.

'First floor,' she said, pressing the door release.

She waited for him at the door to her flat, watching him run up the stairs and plastered a welcoming smile on her face. His good looks momentarily robbed her of the ability to think straight and finally she did feel a fluttering of nerves. She squelched them down, took a deep breath and ushered him inside.

'You're early,' she said.

'I hope not too early. I don't want to disturb you.' He entered the hall, closed the door behind him and handed her a bouquet of two dozen red roses.

'Goodness, thank you,' she said, putting the flowers to her nose and partially hiding her face behind them as she breathed in their heady scent. 'They're beautiful.'

'Not as beautiful as you.' He took the flowers from her again, put them on a side table and pulled her into his arms. 'I could not wait to see you again.'

'I've finished my work for the day, so you aren't disturbing me.' She tried to sound breathlessly excited, as the old Sky would have been when the recipient of such extravagant compliments. In actual fact, she barely believed a word.

She never had, not really.

His kiss was deep, probing, and despite her doubts about him, Sky felt herself responding to it. She was aware that they were standing directly below the camera in the hallway and that Ryan, or whoever was monitoring the situation, would be able to see everything. She told herself that she was acting, playing a part, and needed to be convincing. She told herself that Karim still deserved the benefit of the doubt.

'Your flat is wonderful,' he said, releasing her and glancing down the hallway like a prospective purchaser. 'I love the feeling of space.'

'The living room is this way.'

She picked up the flowers. He took her other hand and she led the way.

'Magnificent!' he said, releasing her in order to stand in front of the full-length windows and admire the view of the common in the distance, visible above the intervening rooftops. 'How do you get any work done?'

'It's nothing compared to the hotel suites that you take for granted,' she replied, laying the flowers down again, turning to the drinks cabinet and pouring him a measure of the malt whisky she knew he preferred. Whisky that she had bought with him in mind the moment she returned from France, having learned of his penchant for the spirit whilst they had been there. Now she almost resented the cost.

'Thank you, my darling.' He noticed the bottle and raised a brow in evident surprise. 'You are very thoughtful. But what are you going to drink? Let me wait on you.'

'I have a bottle of wine open in the fridge.'

She turned away from him, picked up the flowers again and went to fetch it before he could provide her with that service. Already, she felt the strain of pretence playing on her nerves and was having second thoughts about what she'd signed up for. Every innocent word that Karim spoke made her look for hidden meanings. After just five minutes in his company she wasn't sure how much longer she could keep this up. She was already a wreck and there was every possibility that he would want to spend the night with her.

She really hadn't thought this through properly, she realised. A situation that twenty-four hours ago – having Karim in her flat, loving and attentive – would have filled her with joy now made her feel nauseous.

Karim prowled behind her as she entered the kitchen. She was conscious of him taking everything in, his eyes darting into every corner, as if he knew the bugs were there. *Keep it together.* Sky reminded herself that there was no way he could possibly know. Even so, her hand shook as she poured wine into her glass. For something to do, she sought out a large vase and took her time snipping the stems of the roses and arranging them in it.

'Nervous, darling?'

Damn it, Karim had noticed the tremor. 'I don't want you to dislike my home,' she said, aware that it was still partly true. Her standards were not nearly as grandiose as his own and she only had Ryan's word for the fact that Karim's opulence was all an illusion, created to give the impression of immense wealth.

'My darling, your taste is exquisite.' He clinked his glass against her own. 'We ought to be drinking the best vintage champagne.'

Sky couldn't think what to say in response and so led the way back into the sitting room, wondering what they would talk about. Ryan had warned her to let Karim take the lead. If he had a specific reason for being there, the death of the man from the hotel would have made the expedition of his plans necessary and Karim would not waste too much time softening her up. In other words, he felt confident about his ability to manipulate her.

Keep telling yourself that.

Unable to stand the silence, Sky flipped through her Spotify playlists and the sound of mellow jazz soon filled the room, but not so loud that it would make Ryan's job of listening in too hard.

The conversation remained general for half an hour. Karim made her laugh several times. He was a natural raconteur, a man of the world, and as she started to relax into her role her doubts about his objectives re-emerged.

After they'd finished their second drinks, Karim insisted upon ordering food in. Korean was agreed upon – more to the point, it was suggested by Karim and Sky didn't want to look unsophisticated by mentioning that she'd never tried it. Karim ordered for her and their delivery arrived within a very short space of time.

They ate in the kitchen. Karim seemed to realise she had no idea what she was putting in her mouth and explained the contents of each dish without sounding patronising. How could this man be something other than what he appeared to be, she wondered, briefly glancing up at the camera above her head, but looking away again before the direction of her gaze became obvious.

'That was lovely,' Sky said, pushing aside her plate. The food she had forced past the lump in her throat lay heavy in her belly.

Karim stood to help her stack the dishwasher. She wondered if he had ever done anything quite so domesticated before but refrained from asking. She made coffee for them both and they returned to the sitting room. Now, she sensed, would be the defining moment. She would get her answers. She darted a glance at the camera hidden in a light fitting as she curled her feet beneath her on the corner of the couch. He sat beside her, placed his coffee on the end table and slipped an arm around her shoulders.

'You make me feel so contented, Sky,' he said on a long sigh. 'I had forgotten how pleasurable simple... well, pleasures can be when you're with the right person.'

'You have known the right person before?' she asked, because the question sprang spontaneously to mind and seemed like the right thing to ask.

He chuckled. 'You must not be jealous.' His lips brushed the shell of her ear, sending shivers down her spine. 'There has been no one else in this world for me since meeting you.'

Had it not been for the pictures she had seen of him in the hot tub, she would have believed him. She would have believed him because he was so very convincing and because a part of her still desperately wanted to think that she hadn't been played for an idiot.

'I suppose in your line of work it's dangerous to form lasting attachments.' She looked up at him with confusion. 'Which makes me wonder what you are doing here with me.'

'I am thinking of retiring.'

'Retiring?' Sky jerked forward, dislodging the arm that was still draped around her shoulders. 'Is that even possible? All the films I have seen imply that if one is involved in covert work then one signs up for life.'

'That is all Hollywood but yes, to a degree it is true. Even so, you have made me think the unthinkable. Made me yearn for what I have lost.'

'A family,' Sky breathed, not having to act. Whatever she had expected from him, it most certainly hadn't been anything quite so dramatic. 'Goodness.'

'However, you are right. It is not so easy to put behind me what I have been attempting to achieve all these years. I know too much.'

'Surely you have proved your loyalty?'

Karim chuckled. 'I would like to think so.'

'Well then...'

'It is not as though one can simply resign, that much is true. There are those within the organisation who would suspect my motives. We have jealousies and rivalries just like everyone else.'

Sky fixed her gaze on the floor. 'I don't understand any of this,' she said, shaking her head.

'And I would give my life to protect you from it but if we are to have a future together then I have no choice but to ask for your help.'

Sky glanced instinctively up at the light fitting, despite her best efforts not to and her stomach lurched. 'Help?' Sky spread her hands. 'You know I will help you if I can, but what can I possibly do?'

'There is wide dissatisfaction amongst my colleagues. I am not the only one who hankers after change. Some of us are not happy with the direction we are being led in but, as I say, individually there is nothing we can do about it.'

'I still don't see what's so dangerous about helping displaced people.' She paused to fix him with a probing look. 'That is what you do, isn't it?'

'It is, but it's not as simple as you make it sound. There are dangers, expenses, risks, laws to be circumvented. New identities to be created.'

Sky gasped. She was absolutely sure that Karim must be involved in people smuggling – a possibility that she hadn't previously considered – and felt repulsed. Everything she had heard about it implied that the men responsible charged displaced people a fortune, with no guarantees of getting them to where they needed to be.

'But there is safety in numbers. Some of us can right a lot of wrongs being perpetrated by our current leader.'

Is he talking about his father?

Sky nodded, wondering how much of this was true and how much of a line she was being fed. There seemed to be an element of fact behind his words but Sky didn't trust her own judgement.

'You are a humanitarian.'

'Precisely so, my darling.' He caressed her back with sweeps of one large hand. 'I desperately want to ensure the future of our operation. There are so many people who need our help and so I need somewhere safe to meet with them. Your flatmate is away so would it be asking too much to...'

'You want to meet your friends here?' Sky flexed a brow and pretended to think about it, wondering how Ryan could possibly have predicted that exact requirement. 'Will it be dangerous?'

'No, darling. I would not ask if there was the slightest element of risk to you. It is just that we are often watched in our usual haunts but no one is aware of this place. Nor do they know about you.'

'If you are watched you could have been followed here and it would be easy enough to check ownership of this flat online.' Sky feigned terror. 'The place could already have been compromised.'

'No, my darling. I was not followed.' He smiled and shook his head, extremely confident. 'Even so, I have asked too much of you, I can quite see that. I should not have made the suggestion. Pretend that I did not. It is only my desire to live openly with you that made me voice it.'

'I want to help you, Karim.' He rested a hand on her thigh and she gave it a squeeze. 'You know that I do, but this,' – she waved her arm in an arc – 'this business you are involved with.'

'Helping victims of terrorist attacks, displaced people who have lost their homes in wars, to put their lives back together.'

'Yes, I have no idea how you do that.'

'Which is for the best. Suffice it to say that we help the persecuted who can no longer stay in their home countries to start again elsewhere. That sometimes requires us to bend the rules.'

'You encourage people to come to Britain illegally?'

'That is harsh and simplistic way to categorise our activities but accurate enough. These people cannot officially seek asylum. They know too much and would be silenced, sometimes only for revenge.'

'I see.'

Sky paused, as though considering a situation that required no real consideration. The fact that it had followed almost the exact course that Ryan had told her to expect quelled any lingering hope that Karim was being completely honest with her. Well of course he was not! Men like him targeted women like her for one reason and one reason only. She had known it but had been slow to accept the fact, until now. But if Ryan was right and Karim's ultimate target was her money, at least she was one step ahead of him.

'Of course you can use the flat Karim,' she said, sliding her arms around his neck. 'If it will help. I will arrange not to be here so that you are assured of secrecy but it will have to be this week. Nancy is only away for six days.'

'My darling, if you are absolutely sure.' He pulled her into his arms. 'You have absolutely no idea what this will do for me. For us.'

He kissed her and his hands roamed over her body. Acutely conscious of the fact that they were being watched, Sky pulled out of his arms.

'Will you stay tonight?' she asked, hoping he would decline, aware that it would look odd if she didn't ask.

'Alas, I cannot. I have to be at the club.'

'That's a shame,' she said. 'Talking of which, why can you not have your meetings there? Didn't you once mention that you have your own suite of rooms?'

'Too many ears, my love. What I intend to suggest is far too sensitive to take the risk.'

The fact that he was playing her for a fool had begun to seriously rankle and Sky absolutely did not want him in her bed. He couldn't stay the night but would almost certainly want sex. How to get rid of him without arousing his suspicions?

The problem was resolved when her phone rang. The timing was so providential that she knew before checking her screen and seeing Brenda's name flash up that it could only be Ryan.

'Hello, Brenda,' she said. 'How did the new hairstyle turn out? Are you pleased with the highlights?'

Ryan chuckled. 'They have exceeded my expectations. You have played your part but now look as though you require rescuing.'

'I'm glad it worked out well. Perhaps I will follow your suggestion.'

'Can I send you those urgent suggestions for our picky client?'

'Hell, well I suppose if you must. Send them through now.'

'What is it?' Karim asked when she hung up. 'Don't change your hair, it's perfect.' He chuckled. 'Why do women find the subject so endlessly gripping?'

'Because we are expected to look our best for you men. But I'm sorry, Karim. Brenda is my assistant. She has been working on proposals for the client I met last night and I have to approve them before our next meeting tomorrow. She's sending them over now, so I will be tied up for the next few hours.'

'Ah, that's a shame.' He gripped her shoulders and lowered his head, but not so quickly that she didn't see the suggestion of a smile forming on his lips. He had dodged a bullet insofar as she had given him an out. Not being required to take her to bed clearly wasn't causing him too much heartbreak. 'But I understand.' He glanced at his watch. 'I too must be going but I will be in touch and let you know when I want to take up your kind offer. It will be soon, though. Perhaps as soon as tomorrow. The quicker these things are arranged, the less chance there is of being betrayed.'

They both stood, he kissed her long and deep and she then led him into the hall, anxious to be rid of him.

Once he had gone, she went back into the sitting room and looked up at the light fitting. 'What now?' she asked it.

A few minutes later the doorbell sounded and this time her heart did lift because she knew before looking at the screen that it would be Ryan.

11

Ryan and Josh had both listened in as Sky entertained Amin. For the majority of that time, Ryan's jaw had been set in a rigid line and his fists remained clenched so tight that his nails had worn grooves in his palms. He felt helpless to protect Sky from the guy's smooth technique. Never had professionalism felt more like voyeurism. Never had he felt more invested in a situation, more anxious for the safety of a civilian.

And yet despite the fact that she must be nervous and conflicted, still wanting to believe that the bastard was sincere because no one liked to be played, she had handled the situation, for the most part, superbly. Josh had worried about the number of times she'd glanced up at the cameras but Amin hadn't picked up on it. He was so arrogant, so supremely confident in his ability to talk Sky round, that he'd probably put her nervousness down to a desire to please him.

'The presumptuous wanker,' he muttered, as he rang the doorbell, tapping his foot impatiently.

'Ryan,' she said, standing at her open doorway as he ran up the stairs.

'Hi,' he replied, smiling. 'You okay? You did just great.'

He stepped into the hall and closed the door behind himself. It took every last vestige of his training not to pull her into his arms and offer her reassurance in the exact same spot that Amin had. Only the thought of Josh still monitoring the cameras held him back, even though he was supposed to be standing down until needed.

'Thanks.' She shuddered. 'It didn't feel that way. I was sure he'd realise something was different about me. I kept expecting him to ask if I'd overheard him and that guy in his room yesterday and I wasn't sure if I'd have been able to respond convincingly enough to reassure him.' An uncertain smile broke through her reserve. 'I'm a terrible liar, in case you hadn't noticed.'

'Hush, it's okay. The guy's dead. Amin will know it. He might even have carried out the deed, so any danger to him died right along with Farook.'

'I guess.' She glanced at her feet and didn't look convinced, leaving Ryan with the impression that she was still struggling with her conflicted feelings for Amin.

'You believe me now?' he asked as he followed her into the kitchen and nodded when she pointed to her coffee machine.

'Yeah. I knew you'd got it right the moment he asked to use this place to meet his buddies.' She busied herself making coffee. Her hair fell over her face, making it impossible for Ryan to read her expression. 'I feel humiliated. And used.' She turned to hand him his coffee and her hair swung back over her shoulders, revealing eyes blazing with anger. 'And furious,' she added unnecessarily.

Ryan perched his backside against her kitchen table as she bustled about, finding things to do with her hands as she worked through her anger. 'Is it any consolation that I think he was mixing business with pleasure?'

'Not much, no.'

'Sorry. Stupid thing to have said.'

'No, I'm the one who's sorry.' She let out a long breath and finally took a chair at the table, looking him directly in the eye. 'I thought I'd learned that when something was too good to be true... which just goes to show.' She let out a long, resigned breath. 'Anyway, what do you need me to do?'

'Absolutely nothing. You've more than played your part. The moment he rings to tell you he needs access to this place you just need to let him in and make yourself scarce.'

'It's not quite that easy, though, is it?' She leaned her elbow on the table and rested the side of her face against her clenched fist. 'What if he is trying to scam me?'

'He won't. Your money is safe.' He ran the knuckles of his left hand gently down the side of her face, his professional need to reassure his asset warring with a personal desire to protect her at all costs. Hell, he needed to get a grip! ',We won't let him get near your funds. Trust me on that. But we do want him to lead us to the big guns and, thanks to you, that might finally happen.'

'I'm glad to have helped and wish I could do more.'

'You've done more than enough.' Ryan turned serious. 'It's dangerous. You've seen how ruthless they are. They used Farook to make a point, then bumped him off. The loyalty amongst thieves mantra is a myth and I'd prefer to keep you well away from the coal face.'

He turned his back so that the view from the camera would be partially obscured and took her hand, running his fingers down the length of hers. She looked taken aback by the gesture, almost as taken aback as Ryan himself felt at having instigated it. He thought at first that she might snatch her hand away and half hoped that she would. One of them needed to maintain a level of professionalism and right now he knew that wouldn't be him. Instead, she sighed and briefly curled her own fingers around his. Then she stared at their joined hands, looked a little astounded and broke the contact.

'It's a little late for that,' she replied, 'especially if my money has always been the attraction.'

'If that's the case then the man's an idiot.'

Sky gave a sad little smile and shook her head. 'You don't need to be kind. I am aware of my limitations.' Her expression turned pensive and Ryan knew it would be a waste of breath trying to convince her that she underestimated her attractiveness. Living with a beautiful woman who was full of confidence had undoubtedly contributed to Sky's low self-esteem since she would have become used to being overlooked. 'What concerns me is that if Karim's goal is my money then he's playing a long game.' She frowned. 'How did he even know about it beforehand? It's not something I advertise. I've been caught out before and learned to be cautious.'

Ryan gave a nod of approval. Her quick wit had gone straight to the heart of the problem. 'As I said, we think he's considering breaking away from the group.' Ryan scratched his ear. 'That implies he's either desperate or has a death wish. You can't resign from a terrorist cell and expect to live a full and active life, so if he wants to disappear and let the dust settle before reinventing himself, it takes money.'

'Why do you suppose he wants to quit?'

Ryan shrugged. 'Could be any number of reasons but if I had to hazard a guess, I'd say that he's become a little too fond of the Western way of life, and resents having to follow orders.'

Sky nodded as she stretched her arms above her head. 'Well, he went to a lot of trouble with me. That trip to France was over and above. He already had me hooked so it wasn't even necessary.'

'It hasn't occurred to you that he took you because he enjoys your company?'

Sky gave a harsh little laugh. 'Not even momentarily. Well, not since I found out what really makes him tick but even before that I couldn't figure out why he'd chosen me.' She paused. 'Anyway, you still haven't told me how you think he found out about my money.'

'Easy enough nowadays.'

'Yes, but he had to know that I had dosh first. He would have needed to know my name and where I live.'

'Ah, now I see.' And Ryan did. Amin had hit on her in favour of Nancy even before he knew she was loaded. Or there again, as she'd just suggested, he did know. 'Perhaps he liked what he saw.'

Sky flapped a hand. 'Well, it doesn't matter.' She swallowed as she leaned towards him. 'I've helped you out; now it's payback time.'

'Whatever you need,' he replied without hesitation.

'When Amin and his cronies are here, plotting to blow up the world, I want to be in your van, listening to what they have to say for themselves.'

She held up a hand when Ryan opened his mouth to protest. 'That's non-negotiable, Ryan. I've put my neck on the line, been manipulated at the hand of a master, and now I need to know why me.'

'I'll tell you as much as I can.'

'No need. I will hear it for myself.' She folded her arms and set her chin in a stubborn line. 'Either that or I'll tell Karim I've changed my mind when he calls.'

Ryan shook his head. 'I am trying to be noble and keep you safe, Sky! This isn't a game.'

'Nor is it the Middle Ages,' she shot back at him. 'I don't need your well-meant protection. What I need is answers.'

Ryan knew when he was beaten. Besides, he could kind of see her point of view. If she was now disillusioned with Amin, that was a good thing but he absolutely didn't want her going off-piste in a wild attempt to exact revenge. Better to keep her where he could control her, or so he chose to tell himself.

'Okay,' he said, holding up a hand to ward off further justification on her part. 'I'll get approval for you to be part of the surveillance.' Not that he needed it. This was his operation. Bill was a stickler for doing things by the book, which was one of the reasons why he didn't fit in with the field operatives, who took all the risks. Every team needed an office manager, someone to keep the bean-counters happy, but the book didn't have much of a part to play in their line of work, where life and death decisions were made on the fly.

'Thank you,' she said so primly that it broke the tension and they both burst out laughing.

'You should laugh more,' he said, hoping that Josh had gone offline, as promised, but not especially caring if he was being unprofessional and listening in. 'You're beautiful when you react spontaneously. When you're being yourself and not what others expect you to be.'

Her smile faded. 'I've learned to be cautious, or thought I had. I've had one or two disappointments since my dad died...'

'Men after your money?' Ryan shook his head. 'Idiots.'

'Nancy is always telling me I'm too trusting, but I let my heart rule my head. I can't seem to help myself.'

'Not surprising, given the loss of your parents' Ryan leaned back in his chair and crossed one denim-clad leg across his opposite thigh. 'You found yourself alone, swimming with the sharks and needed a safe haven.'

'Something like that. Guys found out that I own this flat and... well, suddenly I was Miss Popularity. Anyway, like I say, I wised up. Until I met Karim.' She closed her eyes for an expressive moment and let out a deep sigh. 'He literally swept me off my feet and it felt wonderful to be treated like I was made of porcelain.'

'Your friend didn't warn you?'

'She did, or tried to, but I wasn't willing to listen. Something that felt so right couldn't possibly be wrong, even though a part of me wondered "why me?" right from the word go.' She frowned. 'Does that make any sense?'

'It makes total sense.' Ryan resisted the urge to reach forward and touch her hand. To offer her the reassurance that he sensed she urgently needed. He knew the gesture might be misconstrued, though. The last thing he wanted was for her to think that he was chancing his arm too. He might well make a move, when the time was right. But now wasn't that time; it might never come.

'You want to be appreciated for yourself,' he said, 'not for your money. Trust me, there are dozens of men out there who would value the opportunity to make you see just how much you have to offer that has nothing to do with your bank balance.'

'That's what Nancy says. She reckons I should be more like her. Have my fun and not take it seriously. Not believe all the promises and move on when I get bored.' She shook her head. 'But that's just not my style.'

'No, I reckon it's not. We can't all be like the Nancys of this world.'

'I don't suppose you have too many issues when it comes to self-esteem,' she said with the suggestion of a smile.

'Don't judge a book by its cover, darling. We all have our issues.'

'Tell me something about yourself... something personal,' she remarked, pushing a plate of biscuits across the table towards him. He took one and bit into it.

'Not much to tell.' He spread his hands.

'That's not fair!' she protested. 'You've probably found out more about me than I know about myself through spooky, Big-Brotherly means. Now you're falling back on all that need-to-know codswallop because you can't be bothered to tell me about your nearest and dearest.' She sent him a look of mild rebuke. 'That is so not fair.'

Ryan laughed, feeling relaxed and enjoying himself in a way that he hadn't since he couldn't remember when. Relaxing when he was supposed to be working but then, if this was work, bring it on! 'Okay, what do you want to know?'

'You said you were an only child. Are your parents still alive?'

'Not sure about my mother. She left us when I was a kid.' Ryan spoke in a bland tone, surprised at just how much that recollection still hurt. 'My father was a colonel in an elite regiment. Overseas a lot on top-secret missions. We were almost always left behind. I guess my mother got lonely. It happens a lot in the military. Anyway, when I was ten she started an affair with an enlisted man and finished up running off with him when he quit the regiment.'

'And left you behind?' Her face was a study in sympathy, which had not been his intention but was the normal reaction whenever he told the story – which was infrequently. 'Have you seen or heard from her since?'

'She tried to get in touch a while back. Seems she married the guy and became a baby factory. I now have four half-siblings. None of whom I have met, or have any desire to meet.'

'What about your father?'

'He was killed by an incendiary device in Kabul.'

'I'm sorry. Your life growing up must have been lonely.'

'Nah.' He waved the suggestion aside with a casual flap of one hand. 'The army was my family and made my career choice a no-brainer. Turns out I was a natural. Went through some tough training and became a member of an elite squad which... well, kinda led on to what I do now.'

'What about personal relationships? I'm sure there must be a Mrs Callahan wannabe waiting in the wings.'

Ryan laughed. 'In my line of work, personal relationships are discouraged.'

'Blimey.' She elevated both brows. 'You live for your work, no attachments permitted.'

'I'm no saint. I do date but my work tends to preclude permanent attachments. Women, I've found, become less understanding the more dates that are broken at short notice. Especially when I can't explain what's more important than they are. They all think I work in a government advisory capacity, which implies regular hours, whereas nothing could be further from the truth.'

'Ah well, that would take some explaining,' she replied, smiling.

'There again.' Ryan fixed her with a probing look. 'Perhaps I haven't met the right woman yet.'

Sky blushed, got up from her chair and started clearing the cups away. 'What happens now?' she asked.

'Now, it's a waiting game, as it so often is in my line of work. We wait for Karim to contact you again.' He grinned at her. 'Welcome to the glamorous world of espionage, darling.'

She shuddered. 'Waiting makes me nervous,' she said, as she leaned over to stash cups in the dishwasher.

'I'll stay and keep you company if you like.'

She turned to face him, arms folded defensively across her chest. 'I'm a big girl. I don't need babysitting.'

'I'm not suggesting that you do.' He leaned his backside against a kitchen surface, watching her bustling about unnecessarily. 'Okay, tell me something about yourself that I won't have found out through spooky, Big-Brotherly means.'

'Is there anything?'

'Well, I shan't know that unless you tell me.'

She smiled, more relaxed again. 'Okay. Did you know that I had a favourite uncle who took me under his wing?'

'Can't say that came up in my enquiries. An actual uncle?'

'Yeah, my mother's brother. He was part of the furniture; he always seemed to be at ours and I adored him. He was ten years younger than Mum and only twelve older than me. He was Uncle Brian who played with me, made me giggle, bought me treats and special presents on birthdays and at Christmas.'

'What happened to him?'

'After Dad died he seemed to think that he could move in and take over control of my affairs. And me.'

'If he was a favourite uncle, why didn't you let him?'

'Because I heard him and Dad arguing not long before Dad drove his car off the road.' She paused. 'They were arguing about money. Uncle Brian was after a handout and I got the impression that it wasn't the first time he'd asked. Accusations flew, voices were raised and a month later Dad was dead.'

'You think his death wasn't an accident?' Ryan frowned. None of this had shown up in his research but then, he hadn't delved that deeply into her personal circumstances. Besides, if no questions had been raised about the supposed accident, there would have been nothing for Ryan to have found.

'Well... no, not at the time anyway. Dad was in a terrible state after Mum went.' She stared out the window without, Ryan suspected, actually seeing the view. Instead, she was lost in the past, reliving a difficult time in her life that she'd probably buried because it was too painful to confront. 'If he had died soon after I might have understood his need to be with her, but it had been three years. We were moving on with our lives, Dad and me. We had each other and he would never have left me of his own volition.' She shook her head. 'As an adult I can see all the flaws in my wonderful uncle that weren't apparent to me as a child, but I don't think he'd resort to murder, which is what you appear to be suggesting.' She sent him a direct look. 'Then again, I guess you're paid to see the dark side of every situation.'

'Sky, I'm sorry. I didn't mean to...'

'It's okay. I suppose a small part of me did have questions that I was too grief-stricken at the time to confront. Then I smothered the possibilities, even when Uncle Brian went to Dad's solicitors, insisting that he'd been appointed to look after my affairs. When he discovered the error of his ways, he tried confronting me, accusing me of all sorts of things when the soft touch didn't work.' She shuddered. 'The last I heard he was living in Thailand.'

'Let me have his full name. I'll check to see if he's back in this country.'

'Brian Greaves. But if he's back or not, I don't see what that has to do with anything. He hasn't contacted me, nor is he likely to.'

'Even so, it pays to be thorough.'

12

Thorough about what, Sky wondered. She knew there was something significant about Ryan's remark, something fundamental that ought to have been immediately obvious to her. Always alert and on duty, he seldom made throwaway comments. She wondered if he saw her as a duty and concluded that he very likely did. That was okay. She could do professional; it was safer that way. She had definitely learned her lesson since being faced with the truth about Karim and would not be swayed by another handsome face, even if the face in question happened to be on the good guys' side.

Despite this latest stark reminder about her lousy judgement when it came to men she still had trouble concentrating when Ryan looked at her in such a deep, intense way. She felt privileged because he'd opened up to her about his own fractured childhood and sensed that he didn't often share that aspect of his past. Even so, she wasn't about to be lured in by another smooth-talker. In his way, she reminded herself, he was as keen to manipulate her as Karim appeared to be. Neither of them gave a toss about her as a person and both were using her as a means to an end.

Then again, she thought, men didn't have the monopoly on manipulation.

Or on the desire for revenge either.

She could tell that she'd surprised Ryan when she'd stood her ground and insisted upon listening in when Karim and his cohorts met at her flat. She felt proud to have gotten her way. It was probably against all sorts of protocols but hell, she was the one who'd been played so she deserved to know what was going down and further her own plans, the details of which she wasn't about to share with Ryan.

'You okay?' asked Ryan. 'You look as though you're away with the fairies.' Sky blinked. She hadn't realised that she'd drifted off into a reverie.

'Sorry. I was thinking about what I overheard. About Karim's father, I mean,' she said, turning to face Ryan and frowning, still struggling to make sense of a senseless situation. 'Do you think that man, Farook, was actually talking about him? He definitely said *your father*.' Her frown intensified. 'Why would Karim tell me his father's dead if he isn't?'

'He is, as far as we're aware so I'm in the dark too,' Ryan admitted. 'What he told you about the incendiary device that killed his parents and siblings is a matter of record.'

Sky tapped the fingers of one hand against her opposite forearm. 'Unless the man whose body they found wasn't his father.'

Ryan nodded, his expression grim. 'Quite,' he said softly. 'That's a possibility we hadn't considered.'

'A good way to carry out terrorist atrocities and fly beneath the radar. No one suspects a dead man.'

Ryan conceded the point with another brief nod. 'My thoughts exactly.'

She sent him a challenging look. 'A man with all those high-tech resources at your fingertips.' She glanced up at a hidden camera to emphasise her point. 'Surely you can find out, otherwise what's the point?'

He smiled in that gentle way of his that melted Sky's heart, or would if she'd permitted the gesture to affect her. 'Unlikely, much as it pains me to make the admission. If Amin senior faked his own death, then he will have covered his tracks so well that we'll never get to the truth. Worse, if we start delving, word will get back to him, putting him on his guard and he'll go even deeper under cover.'

'That might give him second thoughts about carrying out an atrocity in this country,' Sky pointed out.

'It might delay the inevitable; nothing more. Fanatics always move on to the next target.'

Sky nodded, suspecting that much was true. Aware that they were ruthless people who, presumably, had an agenda. 'What you said about my uncle,' she remarked, blinking when a possibility that had previously eluded her popped randomly into her brain. 'You think he might have told Karim about my circumstances?'

'Don't you think it's a possibility that needs investigating?'

Sky plopped herself down on a stool and leaned her elbows on the table, propping her chin in her cupped hands. 'I suppose they *could* have met somewhere along the way.' She shook her head, far from convinced, but it *did* make sense on so many levels. 'But I still find it impossible to imagine that my uncle would even have thought to raise my name in front of a stranger. What would he hope to have gained by it?'

'You said you separated on bad terms.'

'True, but that was a few years ago.'

'Has he been in touch since then?'

'A few times but not for over a year. He offered an olive branch, said he regretted that we'd separated on bad terms, that he'd only been trying to protect my interests, blah, blah. But, bottom line, it was just a fancy way of trying to invoke my guilt so that he could ask for handouts.'

'Did you oblige?'

Sky shook her head. 'The blinkers had come off and I saw straight through him. Harsh things had been said at a time when I was feeling very vulnerable and those things couldn't be unsaid.'

'You make it sound as though your uncle leeched off your parents.'

'Looking back, I think that he probably did. Like I say, he was ten years younger than Mum and could do no wrong in her eyes. But once she was gone Dad decided enough was enough.'

'Men like that, in my experience, manage to convince themselves that whatever they're given is theirs by right, that they've earned it, and they feel aggrieved when funds are curtailed. That, in turn, leads to a burning desire for revenge.'

'Well, if that's the case then my uncle has played a patient waiting game. Last I heard he'd hitched up with a wealthy widow in Thailand so he wouldn't need to fall back on what little he hoped to extract from me.'

'Unless she saw through him and gave him the boot.'

'In which case, he would have come crawling back to me.'

'Not if you'd made it clear that your cheque book was closed.'

Sky shrugged. 'He can be fairly devious, I suppose, but even so...' She paused, wondering why she was trying to think up excuses for a man who had totally disillusioned her and who possessed the morals of a slug. 'Would he really involve himself with terrorists? He was never one to take unnecessary risks.'

'Amin would hardly introduce himself as a terrorist for hire,' Ryan said with a smile. 'You mentioned that your uncle was a womaniser, so too is Amin. Sorry,' he hastily added when Sky winced. Pointing out her stupidity was most definitely unnecessary. Sky had gotten the message, loud and clear. 'Kindred spirits who prey upon the vulnerable.'

'I'm sure...' Sky started violently when her mobile, on the table between them, buzzed with an incoming call. 'It's him!' Sky could hear the tremor in her voice when she glanced at the display.

'Okay, sweetheart. Take a moment to compose yourself before you answer. He'll wait. In fact, it'll be better if you make him sweat for a bit.'

Sky swallowed and nodded. Her palms were clammy when she picked up her phone. Perhaps she wasn't cut out for all this cloak-and-dagger stuff, she thought, but she was damned if she'd express her doubts. Ryan would pounce on her momentary weakness and insist upon cutting her out when things got interesting.

Not happening!

'Here goes nothing,' she muttered aloud as she pressed the green button to take the call. 'Karim,' she said, infusing warmth she didn't feel into her tone. 'I didn't expect to hear from you again so soon.' She put the call on speaker and placed her phone back on the table before it slipped through her clammy hand. 'Is something wrong?'

'Does anything need to be wrong for me to want to talk to you? I have missed you for every second that we've been apart.'

Sky rolled her eyes and Ryan grinned. She could see that he was back in full work mode and she attempted to school her expression accordingly. What they said about women scorned was right on the money, she could now attest, and she was enjoying playing Karim at his own game.

'I wonder if I can take you up on your kind offer, *chérie*, and use your lovely flat for a few hours tomorrow afternoon?'

She glanced at Ryan, who responded with a terse nod. 'Tomorrow? Goodness, that's short notice. I'm in the middle of preparing a major pitch and I'm not sure if I can arrange to—'

'I know, but you must be aware how anxious I am to resolve my affairs so that we can be together. I will not allow a moment's unnecessary delay. Besides, it just so happens that all the people I need to talk to are in town. It would be a shame to miss such a golden opportunity.'

Words that would once have caused Sky to burst with joy, now sounded empty and hollow. Had she really been so shallow that she'd fallen for his spiel? Very likely and the desire for revenge had never been stronger.

'What time would you like to come over?' she asked. Ryan waved a hand in warning and she realised she had been too brusque. 'I can't wait to see you,' she added, but her voice sounded lame, unconvincing.

'At two tomorrow, my love. I would like to spend a few minutes with you before my guests arrive. Will you be able to arrange something to do for two hours?'

'That long?'

'There is much to discuss. I cannot talk about it on the telephone.'

Ryan nodded his encouragement, indicating that would be plenty of time to make his own arrangements. 'All right, then. I will phone a client who is overdue for a visit. He's normally available at any time.'

'Thank you, my darling. I will see you very soon.'

Sky let out a loud breath as she cut the connection. 'Sorry,' she said. 'I didn't handle that well. Do you think he suspected anything?'

'You did just fine.'

'How is it possible for me to despise a man who once made me want him so badly?' she asked.

'No one likes to be played for a fool. Are you okay?' Ryan asked, placing his hands on her shoulders and staring into her eyes. 'If you've changed your mind...'

'Not a chance!'

'Okay, just so long as you're sure. Now then, about tomorrow. Wait for him to arrive. Then, when you leave, take the first right, as though you're heading for the Tube. I'll know when you're there and I'll come and get you.'

'Fine.'

She tried to turn away but Ryan kept his hands on her shoulders, effectively pinning her in place. 'Proud of you,' he said softly, dropping a light kiss on the top of her head and then letting her go. 'But now...' He glanced at his watch.

'I know, you have arrangements to make. Go!' She made shooing motions with her hands. 'I shall be fine here alone.'

'Call if you need me. Or if you just want to talk.'

She promised that she would and he headed for the front door. He paused with his hand on the knob, turned to wink at her and then disappeared through it.

Left alone and ordinarily comfortable with her own company, the flat now felt too large. And too empty. That wasn't good. Sky had plans of her own to finalise, arrangements to put in place, and she had to do those things alone. No more depending on men to fight her battles for her.

She got through the evening alone without resorting to wine for Dutch courage and turned in early, convinced that she would never sleep. To her surprise, she slept well and woke feeling refreshed and determined.

She didn't hear from Ryan that morning but put him from her mind and concentrated on the work that she'd neglected for too long. As the hours ticked by and she could no longer put off thinking about Karim's arrival, Sky decided against changing for his benefit and remained in her casual workday clothes. She ran a brush through her hair, slapped on a little lip gloss and left it at that. The image that stared back at her was barely recognisable – a combination of defiance, determination and controlled fury.

Sky realised that she had grown up, was tired of being exploited and was ready to fight back.

Don't get mad, get even. How often had her father offered her that advice? She considered now what she hadn't allowed herself to dwell upon previously. Uncle Brian had always had another scheme to make money that couldn't possibly fail but always did. Once Mum was no longer there to fight her brother's corner, had Dad grown tired of financing his madcap schemes and banished him from the house, much as she'd just suggested to Ryan?

More to the point, could that had been why her dad had died?

It had always been at the back of Sky's mind that something untoward had caused his accident, even though the coroner had ruled it as a suicide. Dad was devasted when he'd lost Mum, but he had known it was coming, was devoted to Sky and wouldn't have been selfish enough to leave her alone, grieving for them both.

That was what she'd told Ryan and was a matter of fact.

'What did you do, Uncle Brian?' she asked in an undertone, aware that the listening devices would be back in play.

She almost jumped out of her skin when the doorbell sounded. She glanced at her watch. Karim was early. Sky resisted the urge to give her appearance a final check, glanced up at the camera in the kitchen's light fitting, pressed the buzzer to release the street door and made her way to her own door.

'Goodness, Karim,' she said, summoning up a smile as he appeared at the top of the stairs. 'You are very punctual.'

He walked into the hall, pulled her into his arms and kissed her. Sky did her level best to participate and not draw attention to the stark change in her feelings towards the man.

'I cannot believe how lucky I am to have met you,' he said when he broke the kiss.

* * *

Ryan joined Josh in the communications van early the next afternoon, having kept himself busy all morning while resisting the urge to contact

Sky to ensure that she was still on board. He knew that she would be and also knew that it would be a mistake to let his personal interest in the lady intrude upon such a sensitive operation.

He had slipped away from Sky's flat the previous evening, phone glued to ear.

'Run me a background check on Brian Greaves,' he told Beth when she picked up. He gave her as much information as he had on the man. It wasn't much but didn't need to be. He knew that Beth would find him in the system in double-quick time if he was there to be found.

'On it,' she replied, cutting the connection.

Ryan considered returning to the office but decided against it. He didn't need Bill poking his nose into his delicate operation. Instead he returned to his flat, tidied up a few loose ends online regarding other cases and turned in early.

'Hey,' Josh said, when Ryan rapped at the door and Josh opened it to let him in.

'Everything okay?'

Josh looked offended by the question. 'Of course,' he said, staring at a screen that showed a clear picture of Sky's living room.

'Sky will be joining us once Amin arrives at hers.'

Josh swivelled his head to look at Ryan, finally giving him his complete attention. 'Is that wise?' he asked.

Ryan lifted a shoulder. 'Better to keep her where I know I can find her,' he replied. 'She's determined to involve herself and I don't want her doing anything rash.'

'Well, I guess you know what you're doing.'

Ryan wished he shared his colleague's confidence.

'Hey up, show time,' Josh said, pointing to a screen that showed the outside of the door to Sky's flat. Amin smiled as he mounted the stairs, looking at one point straight at the hidden camera on the landing.

Ryan leaned forward, watching the kitchen camera as Sky took a deep breath, looked directly up at Ryan and then went to answer the door. He was obliged to clench his hands when he watched them embrace, attempting to remain professional and detached. They came apart again fairly quickly and made their way into the lounge.

'Is he early in the hope of a quick leg-over?' Josh wondered aloud.

Ryan didn't respond. Instead he continued to watch the scene unfold.

'Will two hours be enough for you?' he heard Sky ask.

'More than enough, my darling. Thank you.'

'Then I'll leave you to it,' she said.

'Idiot!' Ryan muttered. 'He'll wonder why she's so keen to get away.'

The two men watched, the ultimate voyeurs, as Sky bustled about, collecting up her bag and laptop. She had, Ryan noticed, left her desktop logged on, just as Ryan had asked her to. The pair embraced again and Sky left the flat.

'Watch him,' Ryan said as he slipped from the van. 'Let me know if he goes anywhere near her computer.'

Ryan was waiting when Sky rounded the corner as though her tail was on fire.

'Whoa!' He placed his hands on her shoulders, much as he'd done once before, to stop her headlong flight. 'Did he frighten you that much?'

'No.' Her cheeks were flushed and she was breathless but surprisingly resolute. 'I just felt repulsed when he touched me.'

'It's okay.' Ryan allowed himself the luxury of a brief hug but released her again almost immediately, before instinct overcame common sense. 'Come on.' He took her laptop bag from her. 'We don't want to miss the show.'

They reached the van and Josh let them in the moment Ryan hammered on the door.

'Hey, Sky,' he said, not taking his eyes from the various screens in front of him. 'Welcome to daytime television.'

His careless attitude helped to ease the tension that Ryan could sense in Sky. She grinned and took the seat next to Josh in the cramped van, leaving Ryan to hover behind them.

She scowled when Amin sat at her computer and started pressing keys. 'What's he doing?'

'What I thought he'd do,' Ryan replied. 'Checking your bank balance.'

Sky scowled. 'The nerve! Are you sure he can't get at the cash?'

'Absolutely.' It was Josh who answered her. 'He can't move large sums without the bank sending a code to your phone. But he's a computer expert so he can find a way round that.'

'Clone my phone number?'

'Yep.' Josh actually took his eyes away from the screens for a brief moment and turned to smile his reassurance at Sky. 'Don't worry, we have it covered. As far as he is concerned, he will have to move the lot in one hit if he wants to get away with it. He knows you'll notice any unauthorised withdrawals, so he will do it now or not at all. To him, the transaction will look as though it's gone through, but it won't go anywhere.'

Sky nodded. 'Clever. Just so long as you don't lose my money then I'm good with that. Not that he'll find as much as he hoped to. The majority of what I have is stashed away in offshore investments, safe from his grasping hands.'

'Here we go.' Ryan pointed to the camera outside the street door. Three men stood there, their heads turned away from the camera. 'Party time,' he said.

13

Karim chuckled to himself. Obliging little Sky had left her desktop logged on, saving Karim the trouble of guessing her password. She was *sooo* trusting that she was almost no challenge. Karim's smile quickly faded when he reminded himself that this was no game and that it was a sense of self-preservation that drove him. Perhaps he'd allowed himself to become distracted by his problems because, much as his pride balked at the possibility, he was obliged to concede that Sky didn't seem quite as dedicated as she had once been, hanging on his every word, almost salivating every time he turned on the charm. That could be because her flatmate had stuck her oar in, warning her off Karim because she was jealous.

Yeah, that would be it, he decided.

Not that it mattered if Sky had revised her opinion of him, he reminded himself. He had access to her flat. And to her computer. Her feelings, or lack thereof, were inconsequential. In fact it would be better if she'd had a change of heart. That way the heart in question wouldn't be broken when he bailed on her, so he'd be doing her a favour. He had one chance and one chance only of escaping the downward spiral that his father's fanaticism had dragged him into, and that required money.

Large sums of it.

Sky's money, of which he had been assured there was a copious amount just waiting for him to help himself to.

He found Sky's banking codewords in a locked drawer which he opened in seconds. He swore when he saw the totals, threw back his head and howled with frustration. He had been misled. There wasn't nearly enough for his needs *and* the bulk of it was in a ninety-day notice account. Where the fuck were the rest of her funds? He rummaged through her filing drawer and cursed some more when he found evidence of offshore investments that were untouchable, at least in the timescales available to him.

'Damn it!'

He thumped his fist so hard against the desk that a pen holder wobbled and fell to the floor. Its contents rolled under a settee. Karim barely noticed and certainly didn't give thought to retrieving the spillage. He had made a point of not talking to Sky about her finances, worried that she would suspect his motives. Besides, he hadn't needed to. He was aware of her full net worth. Her late father's assets had been a matter of public record following probate. Well, public record if one knew where to look without leaving a trail.

He would have to take what she had in her no-notice accounts and disappear. That had always been his intention. Time was not on his side. He ignored the niggle of guilt he felt at scamming her, to say nothing of the pang of regret that ripped through him because he'd never see her again. She'd gotten to him, he admitted, and the irony wasn't lost on him. He thought of all the high-maintenance women with traffic-stopping figures who had tried and failed to become permanent fixtures in his life. None had come close to succeeding. And yet Sky, with her insecurities and negative body issues, had somehow wormed her way beneath his guard.

He shook his head, wondering if her blind adoration had stroked his ego. Not that it mattered. Women were ten a penny. He'd find a replacement soon enough and forget all about her.

The sound of the street doorbell roused Karim from his pity party. He closed down Sky's browser, checked the video camera in the hallway and saw his guests waiting outside. He pressed the buzzer to release the street door, then opened the flat door and stood at the top of the communal stairs, watching as three hard men climbed them, at which point doubts assailed Karim. If he had got it wrong, if even one of them still had total faith in his father's leadership, then he was royally screwed. There was no mercy for dissenters in his father's world, especially if his only son proved to be disloyal.

'Gentlemen,' he said, pushing his doubts aside and ushering them inside. It was too late now to have second thoughts, he knew, as he glanced in both directions to ensure they hadn't been seen by an inquisitive neighbour before closing the door to the flat. 'Come through to the kitchen. We can talk freely in there.'

His guests appeared both uncompromising and uncomfortable and shared several speculative looks as they preceded Karim down the corridor.

'Please, be seated,' Karim said, gesturing to the table with a wide sweep of one arm. 'What can I get you?' he asked, because it would be the height of bad manners not to make the offer. Fortunately, they all declined.

'We are not here to socialise,' Arham Khan said, pulling out the chair at the head of the table and seating himself.

Karim wasn't surprised that he had taken the lead. Arham had served Karim's father longer than anyone else in the room and was one of his most trusted lieutenants. He was the man whom Karim would have to convince. If he managed to do so then the others would follow his lead. Unless, of course, one of them saw an opportunity to climb up a few places in his father's organisation by ratting out both Karim and Arham. They would have to have a death wish to attempt it because Arham was highly influential but people had been known to do crazier things.

'Who owns this place?' Mehmood Shah asked, glancing around the spacious kitchen through eyes narrowed in suspicion.

'A friend who will not disturb us and who no one in the organisation knows anything about. We're safe here.'

Arham grunted. 'If that's what you think then you're a fool. Someone always knows something. Besides, you have yet to explain why we need to meet in secrecy. What is wrong with Alexandria?'

'If you believed that your movements were under scrutiny then you would not have come here today,' Karim replied affably. 'Trust me, I know how to keep a low profile. I should do. I've had enough practise at it.'

'What's this all about?' Chamali Hassan asked, an impatient edge to his voice.

'Chamali...' Karim stopped and took a deep breath. The time had come to lay his cards on the table and his doubts intensified. He glanced at Arham, who watched him from the opposite end of the table with the suggestion of amusement underlying his expression. *He knows and will force me to spell it out.*

'Gentleman, I think we all agree that our leader has gone too far.' Karim allowed a significant pause. No one broke the silence and he breathed more easily at the lack of protest. 'His ambitions exceed the reasonable and we are the ones who will be sacrificed when the mission fails.'

'We all knew there were risks when we became involved,' Arham remarked, sitting sideways on his chair, leaning one arm along its back and crossing his legs. Karim knew the casual pose was just that; the man's intelligent eyes were laser sharp and he was definitely interested in what Karim had to say.

'We were willing to die for a cause that we believed in.' *Or were brainwashed and intimidated into believing in.* 'Speaking personally, I have never looked upon myself as being the martyrdom type.'

'A little too fond of the playboy image?' Arham asked in a provocative tone.

Karim smiled, refusing to be riled into defending himself. 'I am loyal to the cause but not to committing suicide,' he said calmly.

'How can you be sure that we will not go straight to the top and report your disloyalty?' Arham asked.

'I cannot be,' Karim replied. 'But I do need you to know that I don't have the slightest intention of attempting to assassinate the president of the United States, and if I do not then one of you will be expected to take my place in the direct line of fire.'

* * *

'Holy fuck!' Ryan's mouth fell open as he stared at Sky and Josh in dumb stupefaction. Whatever he'd been expecting, it sure as hell hadn't been anything quite so recklessly untenable.

'Well, at least we now know the target,' Josh said, looking equally shocked.

'The president is coming to this country, to a summit,' Sky added, nodding in a dazed fashion. 'I read about it. But surely, he will be too well protected for anyone to get close enough to kill him.'

'A sniper could take him out,' Ryan said. 'There's always an element of risk of that nature whenever he appears somewhere publicly. Even so, I get the feeling that a sniper won't be used. It will likely be something more devastating. Probably a bomb activated by a computer.'

'And our friend Amin is a computer whizz,' Josh added, returning his attention to his screens.

The three of them fell silent as they continued to listen to Amin's tone growing in confidence as he answered the questions raised by his visitors.

'Karim wasn't sure if his guests would agree, which is why he's so nervous,' Sky said, impressing Ryan with her ability to go straight to the heart of the matter. 'He must be desperate to have called them together.'

'The prospect of near-certain death would do that to a man,' Ryan agreed. 'I suspect from what we've heard that the attack will take place at Chequers. It's the only stop on the president's agenda that will provide an opportunity. The security services will jam internet access for the duration, and Amin will know that. So that means Amin would have to be pretty close, operating his computer from a separate server which…'

'Which is why he fears dying in an abortive attempt to kill such a well-protected man,' Sky finished for him.

Ryan gave a grim nod. 'Precisely.'

Josh had run a face-recognition programme but only one of the visitors, Arham Khan, was known to the agency.

'What do we know about him?' Ryan asked, peering over Josh's shoulder.

'Not a great deal. He came to this country as a teenager to live with an uncle. He was known to associate with subversives as a young man but not connected to anything specific. He was questioned a couple of times but let go without charge. That was years ago. He's now a supposedly legitimate businessman who—'

'Imports and exports.' Ryan tapped his fingers as he continued to read from the screen. 'The name of his company. Can you run it through the system? There's something about it niggling at the back of my mind.'

'On it.'

Ryan watched as Josh's fingers ran over the keyboard at lightning speed and scrolls of information flashed up on his screen.

'Here we go.'

Ryan leaned in closer and gave a little cry of triumph. 'Khan's company, Algeria International Exports, is owned by a shell company.' He tapped a finger on the screen. 'Sound familiar?' he asked.

'Jesus!' Josh ran the fingers of one hand through his hair, flattening it. It sprang straight back up again at odd angles. 'Fisher and Company, Logistics.' He looked up at Ryan, his expression set in stone. 'That's the lorry those illegals were recently found in. We have our link.'

'We have confirmation but we are still no nearer to nabbing the leader.'

'Surely we ought to take this lot in, or at least inform our American cousins that we have uncovered a plot to kill the president,' Josh said.

'We will, but not just yet. Let's give them something more concrete to go on. Come on,' Ryan cajoled the screen. 'Give us a name for the head honcho.'

'Our lives will be worth nothing if we disobey direct orders,' Chamali said, throwing up his hands. 'I do not like the idea of taking on such a risky assignment any more than you do, Karim. The chances of success are minimal but if we succeed every accolade will be heaped upon us. We will become legends and live out our days in the lap of luxury.'

'If the president of the United States is killed on English soil, then every exit point will be closed down,' Amin pointed out. 'They have contingency plans for such situations and will be on high alert. No stone will be left unturned and someone will let our names slip to the authorities, just to let up the heat on their own activities. Every suspected enemy of the British will be pulled in and grilled without the benefit of legal representation, then left to rot until someone eventually breaks. Even if we miraculously escape the scene and avoid arrest, there will be no safe hiding place.' He paused. 'Perhaps even our leader himself will, as they say in this country, grass us up in order to save his own hide.'

'Your father would do no such thing!' Khan cried, no real conviction in his tone.

Ryan shared a worried look with Sky.

'I am not the only one who enjoys the Western style of life. Besides, Father has a lot of high-ranking politicians and policemen in his pocket. He can call in favours and will be listened to because those people will be thinking of self-preservation. It will do nothing for their careers if it can be proven that they've been associating with terrorists for years *and* no doubt accepting favours and gifts from the old man.' Amin gave a mirthless chuckle. 'You have to hand it to the old devil. He's feathered his own nest well.'

Ryan noticed that none of Amin's visitors disputed the statement.

'Perhaps,' Khan said, 'but I have yet to hear a viable alternative that will keep us alive if we fail to follow orders.'

'I hope you are not thinking of squealing to the authorities and demanding new identities,' Chamali said. 'We all know that is not an option. Someone will find us eventually and until they do we will spend the rest of our limited days on this earth looking over our shoulders, wondering who will come for us and when. Suspecting every stranger we meet. Endlessly worrying.'

'Why not simply send an anonymous tip-off to the authorities? If they know that the president is the target and that the plan is to take him out at Chequers they can change his schedule at the last minute,' Khan said calmly. 'That way we cannot be blamed for the mission's failure.'

'We will still have to go through with the preparations and be there, which means we will almost certainly be captured. Chamali and I have reconnoitred the lie of the land and there are only two possible locations in which to lay the explosives and have a hope of detonating them using our own network successfully. If we found the sites using Google maps and binoculars you can be sure that the security forces will be one step ahead of us.'

Ryan shared a look with Josh.

'Shall I report up the chain now?' Josh asked.

'Not yet.' Ryan held up a staying hand. He could see that Josh was confused by the order. They had discovered something vital that they couldn't keep to themselves. That shouldn't be kept secret at all. But Ryan was more concerned about the leaks emanating from their team, increasingly convinced that Bill was the guilty party. They were *so* close to getting a lead on the head man, but every tip off they'd had so far had turned out to be a blind alley.

And yet Josh was right. This discovery couldn't be kept from Bill for long, not now that he was acting team leader.

'You are right.' Mehmood kicked at a leg of Sky's table.

'Oi!' she cried indignantly.

Ryan smiled at her and briefly touched her arm.

'Right about what?' Khan asked. 'Other than fearing for his own skin.'

'It will be suicide and also likely to do more harm than good to our cause,' Mehmood insisted.

'Even if that is correct, we have already ruled out alerting the security forces, do not have a hope of disappearing and living to enjoy our old age and also have little or no hope of succeeding with the mission,' Khan said, counting off the points on his fingers. 'So what is it precisely that you are suggesting?'

'Nothing could be simpler,' Amin replied. 'We carry through with the plan but the explosives fail to detonate.'

'Failure will not be tolerated,' Khan retorted.

'Do you have a better suggestion?' Amin asked in a challenging tone.

'Cut off the head and allow more reasonable men to take charge,' Khan replied matter-of-factly.

'Kill my father?' Amin's mouth fell open.

'The conniving bastard,' Ryan muttered. 'He's pretending to be shocked but he's forced Khan to make the suggestion he's been rooting for all along.'

'How can you be so sure?' Sky asked, glancing over her shoulder at Ryan, who was still standing close behind her in the cramped van. Close enough to be able to inhale the fragrance of her shampoo, to sense her combination of shock and anxiety.

'Experience,' he replied, placing a reassuring hand on her shoulder. 'Years of interviewing suspects and learning from what they don't say.'

They both returned their attention to the screens when Chamali spoke in a considering tone.

'It is not such a bad idea,' he said, nodding pensively. 'His ambitions, his hatred of those who killed your family, Karim, although understandable, has overcome caution and he believes himself to be invincible. Too well protected by the forces mentioned earlier for any accusations to stick. But then, it is easy to be ruthless when one is not in the direct firing line because one is already dead.'

'Our leader is so well integrated into society that no one suspects his real motives,' Mahmood added. 'As we all know, he gives generously to charities and to both leading political parties.'

'What name does he use?' Ryan muttered, tapping his foot impatiently. 'Where does he live? Give us a clue.'

'Only the half-dozen men who guard his Islington base are loyal, I suppose,' Amin said pensively. Ryan gave a little hoot of triumph. 'The rest of us have grave doubts, or are unswervingly loyal to you gentlemen first and foremost, so it is only they whom we would have to overcome.'

'You would have to overcome them, Karim,' Khan said conversationally.

'What?' Amin's eyes bulged. 'You expect me to commit patricide?'

'If you want to continue breathing and living the life,' Khan replied. 'Only you can get close enough to do the deed. Your father does not even totally trust me.' Khan's expression remained set in stone. 'With some justification, it would appear.'

'Possibly.' Amin gave a reluctant nod, reinforcing Ryan's opinion that the discussion was going in precisely the direction he wanted it to take and that his reluctance was all part of the act. Clearly, the man had serious issues with his father's authority. 'I can see him in private but how do I get past the guards if I finish him off? And more to the point, what about Malek?' he asked.

'Who's Malek?' Sky asked.

Ryan shook his head, as much in the dark as she was. 'Head bodyguard, by the sounds of things.'

'I will take responsibility for Malek.' Khan's expression hardened, making Ryan think that he had a personal score to settle with the man.

'Very well.'

Ryan listened with rapt attention as they talked round the issue, deciding that two of the others would call for an audience as they put it directly after Amin was admitted. It seemed that Khan and Mehmood would not be turned away.

'All well and good,' Khan said suavely, 'but if we cut off the head, who steps into his place?' He fixed Amin with a steely look. 'I hope you are not planning to take over. You really aren't ruthless enough.'

Amin offered a thin smile. 'And you are?'

'Without a doubt. And I have the respect of the men. Your father and I have been allies since before you were born and they know it. It was I who helped your father to reinvent himself after the death of your mother and sisters.'

Amin bowed his head. 'I was not aware of that.'

'Arham would make a wise leader,' Chamali said. 'I would swear allegiance.'

'As would I,' Mehmood agreed.

'Then so be it.' Amin spoke as though admitting defeat but when he turned away from his colleagues a small, satisfied smile played about his lips.

'They have done what he wants,' Sky said, shaking her head. 'You read it exactly right.'

'Looks that way. Presumably, if Amin's father is as wealthy as implied then Amin will inherit and be absolved from his responsibilities to a cause that he no longer believes in,' Ryan replied. 'Very clever of him.'

'But what does it all mean?' Sky looked confused. 'If he has a wealthy father to inherit from, why does he need my money?'

'A contingency fund,' Ryan replied. 'If this plan fails he will have to scarper until the dust settles.'

'The meeting's breaking up,' Josh said, bringing their attention back to the screens.

'Okay. Let's try and narrow the search down for the father. It would be too much to assume that he's still using his given name, although we know that Amin is.'

'Well, the father can't. Not if he's supposed to be dead,' Sky pointed out.

'Islington's a big place,' Josh said. 'Where do we start looking? It's not as though any of those guys will have the address written down and about their person if we pull them in. Not that it's my problem but I'm curious.'

'Let me worry about that,' Ryan replied, fixing Josh with a considering look. Could he be the leak? Why else would he take an interest in a part of the operation that wasn't his domain? He always had the latest technical gizmos to hand and wasn't afraid to use them but Ryan didn't know much about his personal life.

Not yet.

Since he hadn't authorised the release of the intel they'd just collected, Josh and Sky were the only ones who knew what was being planned. It was golden intel that would bring Josh a hefty payday, always assuming that his loyalty was suspect. If that was the case, if he was doing this for financial gain, then he wouldn't be able to resist tipping Amin's father the wink.

'It will be somewhere big yet not ostentatious,' Ryan added when he realised he'd fallen silent and the other two were watching him expectantly. 'Somewhere that guards won't look out of place.'

'Which covers half of Islington,' Sky said, rolling her eyes. 'The area is awash with posh houses and people who overestimate their importance. I know because I have a client there whom I visit regularly.'

'Hey up!' Josh's curt exclamation had them all turning their attention back to the screens. Someone else had just rung the street bell. Amin again checked the video screen and pressed the door release.

'Holy fuck!' Sky breathed when the man entered her flat, lowered his hood and unwittingly looked straight up at a camera. 'That's my uncle.'

14

Karim could have done with a little longer to gloat over the ease with which he'd manipulated some of his father's oldest allies and toughest men. But gloating would have to wait. His next visitor was right on time and Karim knew better than to leave him loitering on the street. There was CCTV everywhere and experience had taught him the inadvisability of having anyone recognisable to the authorities behaving suspiciously in a public place. That would give whichever agency spotted him an excuse to haul him in for a grilling and he didn't trust Brian Greaves, who didn't know the meaning of loyalty, not to give Karim up in order to save his own skin.

There was no earthly reason for Sky's flat to be under scrutiny but even so...

God, but he was tired of all this! He wanted to disappear, forget about fanatics, about a cause he no longer believed in and probably never had and simply live a life of sophisticated pleasure. And there was only one way he could think of to achieve that ambition, a method that the men who had just left had obligingly agreed to facilitate. Even so, Karim needed to plan carefully. If the plot to assassinate the father he despised went pear-shaped, as it so easily could – he hadn't survived for this long without having eyes and ears everywhere – there could be no loose ends floating about that would come back and bite him on the arse.

'Fucking hell!' Greaves said, looking about the hallway and letting out a low whistle. 'My bitch of a niece did well for herself and hasn't spared me the crumbs from her table, even though I made all this possible by getting rid of her old man.'

'Not exactly the sort of information you could share with her.' Karim had led the way into the sitting room and nodded towards a picture, in pride of place on the mantelpiece, of Sky with her father, both of them smiling. Sky's hair was blown across her face and she looked happy – beautiful. There could be no doubting the pride and adoration in her father's expression as he looked at his daughter rather than the camera.

She had told Karim that the picture had been taken a year before her mother's death and that she hadn't known such total peace since then. She had told him as well that she'd loved and respected her father above anyone else on earth and missed him every single second of every day. But he didn't bother to tell Greaves that she'd likely lynch him with her bare hands if she knew the truth. Let the man live with his grievances; he was of more use to Karim that way.

'I did her a favour. The man was a tight-fisted control freak.'

'What you didn't tell me was that almost all her dosh is tied up in investments or long-notice accounts,' Karim said, holding on to his temper by the sheer force of his will.

'How the fuck was I supposed to know that? I told you about her and as much as I knew about her circumstances.' Greaves frowned and then gave a guarded chuckle. 'Did you really think she'd have it all stashed under the mattress and would give it to you if you asked her nicely?'

'That's hardly the point.'

'Look, mate, we have an agreement and I'm ready to collect. Half a mil is small change to her, and it's less than I'm owed. I'm betting she's got the hots for you and will be putty in your hands, you lucky bastard! Marry her, make her promises of undying love and all that crap. You don't need me to tell you that women love all the bullshit. They're still the weaker sex, and you know how to play her.' Greaves paused and his expression turned dark. Karim had once seen him lose his temper and pummel a guy to within an inch of his life with his bare hands. 'I have obligations and no time to wait.'

'Yeah, I hear you.'

'Get me my cash or else dear little Sky goes the same way as Daddy dearest.' He ran a finger across his own neck in a cutting motion. 'Then, as her only living relation, I'll cop the lot.' He pointed the same finger at his chest for emphasis. 'I happen to know that she ain't got no current will so there's no one to challenge my right.'

The thought of Sky being brutally murdered sent a chill through Karim's entire body. 'No need for that,' he said calmly, hoping like hell that the plot to kill his own abusive father would go off without a hitch. He would certainly have no qualms about putting the knife in, quite literally. But he did need to think about getting away without having to confront his father's annoyingly loyal guards. The same guards who were required to give Karim access to his own father's house, made their contempt for him obvious in lots of subtle ways, and who never left him alone, apart from when he was with his father or in his private rooms.

He had a score to settle with those guys and knew they would be held to account if they allowed their charge to be stabbed in his own library. Karim knew that his father he was highly regarded by a lot of dangerous and powerful men, which was why he would have to settle his estate from a distance and keep a low profile, at least until the guards had paid the ultimate price for their laxity. And until Arham Khan had calmed the storm created by such a high-profile assassination.

He knew he was taking an almighty risk but Karim was running out of options fast. Not only had Sky's bank balance, or lack thereof, been disappointing but he also had a feeling Greaves had known that would be the case all along and had put Karim on to her for that reason. He had recognised the desperation in Karim to escape from beneath his father's iron fist and had exploited it quite ruthlessly.

Karim almost admired his manipulative qualities.

Almost.

'Got to you, has she?' Greaves chuckled maliciously. 'Well, that doesn't surprise me. She always was a spritely little thing, right from the time that she turned from girl to young woman, unaware of her own attractiveness. There's so few of them around nowadays that they have a novelty value.' Greaves ran the side of his hand across his lips. 'I seriously thought of having her myself. Could have done, but didn't want to kill the golden goose. Her ma, my sister, was a pushover but never would have forgiven that.'

Karim sent him a scathing look, which bounced harmlessly off Greaves' thick outer shell. How had he been reduced to dealing with men of his ilk? Karim wondered. Where was the deference, the respect, the loyalty that was Karim's by right? More to the point, why boast about lusting after his niece? Had he done more than just window shop, despite his denials? The very possibility caused Karim to seethe.

'Give me three days and you will have your money,' Karim said, a plan to literally kill two birds with one stone springing to mind. 'And more besides, if you will provide me with a small service.'

Greaves grunted. 'How much more?'

Karim wasn't surprised that was the first question he came back with. 'As much again.'

'I'm listening.'

'Can you make sure you're on duty the night after next?'

Greaves sniffed. 'Possibly? Why do you need to... No!' He held up a hand to halt his own flow of words. 'On second thoughts, I don't want to know. I can be on duty. It's just the three of us at night, as you know. The old man likes to have the house to himself so he can entertain his floozies whilst pretending to be holier than though.'

'Very well.' Karim suppressed a smile, aware that Arham would deal with Greaves before either of the others. He would make an excellent fall-guy but was too thick to realise it. 'Stand by and you will have your instructions.'

'And you'll have my cute little niece in the meantime, I suppose.' Greaves sniffed. 'Lucky bastard!' he said as he left the flat.

Karim closed the door behind him and simultaneously closed his eyes. 'Game on!' he muttered.

* * *

Sky collapsed into Ryan's arms the moment her uncle left her flat, consumed by a combination of disillusionment and fear. Ryan held her, soothing her back with calming sweeps of his large, capable hands until the worst of the storm abated. She barely heard him curtly order Josh to keep up the surveillance.

'Come on,' he said, holding out a hand. 'Let's get you out of here.'

'I'm not... not going back there,' Sky replied, pointing to the screens showing various rooms in her flat. 'I don't want to be anywhere near him.'

'Nor will you be. Don't worry.'

Sky noticed Josh in the periphery of her vision open his mouth to speak. He then studied Sky closely and closed it again with no sound emerging, immersing himself with his technical stuff instead.

'You can pack up here once Amin leaves the building,' Ryan told him. Josh nodded to confirm he'd heard Ryan's instructions but didn't look up from the adjustments he was making.

'Where are we going?' Sky asked, blinking when they emerged into the sunshine. 'And anyway, Karim won't leave. He'll wait for me to get back and he'll be suspicious if I don't appear.'

Ryan shook his head. 'You'll call him in a minute and tell him you've been caught up with your client.'

'He might insist on waiting. I can't stay away indefinitely.'

'Sky, you just heard your uncle casually suggest that Amin should kill you. And if he bottles it, you can be sure that the uncle won't. Anyway, you're in no fit state to face Amin. He'll be able to tell in a heartbeat that something's changed.'

'The consequence of hearing your nearest and dearest plotting to kill you.' She swallowed. 'And hearing them casually admitting to killing your father,' she added, anger driving away her fear. 'Take it from one who knows.'

'Let's take a moment to process what we've learned,' he insisted.

'Okay, where are we going to do that?'

'Back at mine. We can talk there without anyone hearing us.'

He took her elbow and steered her in the direction of his car, which he'd parked in the next street. He unlocked the vehicle with his remote, opened the passenger door for her and waited until she'd settled herself before closing it again. He then trotted round to the driver's side, slid behind the wheel and fired up the engine. But he didn't pull away from the kerb. Instead, he punched in a number on his mobile and gave whoever answered it instructions, not to stake out possible locations in Islington as Sky had imagined would be his intention but to follow Josh when he left the van.

'Josh?' Sky blinked at Ryan in bewilderment. 'Surely he's on our side.'

'I sure as hell hope so,' Ryan replied, setting his jaw in a rigid line. 'But someone is leaking highly classified information. It's hard enough to get any intel on the various cells and soul-destroying when it leads to nothing because someone has been either coerced or paid to rat us out.' He pulled the car away from the kerb. 'Phone Amin, and let him know you won't be back for a while.'

Sky shuddered. She didn't want to talk to him and hated knowing that he was in her flat alone, no doubt rummaging through her possessions. Preparing to steal from her. Or worse. But the shock was already wearing off. Ryan had warned her and she was glad that she'd believed him, proving that her judgement wasn't entirely skewed since she was already prepared to fight back.

She called his number and he picked up on the first ring. 'Perfect timing, my darling.' His voiced oozed down the line, causing Sky to shudder. 'My meeting is finished and I cannot wait to see you.'

'You will have to wait a little longer, I'm afraid. Some problems have arisen with my client's account and I will have to resolve them before I leave. It could take a couple of hours.' *Which will give you ample time to empty my bank account and scarper.* 'Sorry.'

'Don't be. We all have to work but alas, I cannot wait that long. I have somewhere else that I have to be.'

'That's a pity.'

'Perhaps we can do something tomorrow.'

In your dreams. 'I'd like that.'

Sky listened to him ramble on for a bit and then cut the connection. 'Bastard!' she muttered.

'I'm sorry that he's hurt you,' Ryan said, touching her shoulder.

'What he's done is make me as mad as hell.' Sky sighed, anger fuelling her emotions. 'I suppose I always knew deep down that it wouldn't last. When something seems too good to be true it almost always is.'

'You are the one who's too good for him. Don't let a pretty face and a fake sophisticated air influence you, sweetheart. You're worth ten of that bastard.'

Sky smiled at Ryan, aware that it was within his best interests to keep her focused on the job in hand and that his compliments weren't genuine.

She fell to contemplating and they drove the rest of the way to Brixton in comparative silence. She was grateful that he left her to work through what she'd just seen and heard without feeling the need to fill the silences with meaningless reassurances. His phone rang a couple of times but he glanced at the names on the in-car display and dismissed the calls.

'Here we are,' he said, pulling into his parking space at the back of his building. 'Let's get you a drink. I reckon you could do with it.'

Sky didn't bother to pretend otherwise, even though it was only the middle of the afternoon. He opened the street door and led the way into his flat. It was as minimalistic and tidy as on her previous visit but when he opened the door to the fridge and produced a bottle of chilled Chablis, she wondered who he'd had in mind when he'd purchased it. He didn't strike her as the white wine type, proving her assumption right when he also pulled out a bottle of beer for himself.

He opened the wine with the same smooth efficiency that appeared to govern everything he did, poured her a glass and handed it to her.

'Cheers,' he said, clinking his bottle against her glass. 'You okay?'

'Sure.' She took a long slug of wine and gave a casual shrug but was furious when the act was ruined by the tears that trickled from the corners of her eyes. 'Sorry,' she said, brushing them impatiently aside. 'I'm fighting mad and yet feel as though I'm grieving for my dad all over again.'

'That's natural.' He led the way from the kitchen into his small sitting room, indicated the couch and took the space beside her once she'd settled herself. 'You just heard a man you once liked and respected boasting about killing your father. Just about anyone else would have fallen into hysterics.'

'I'm actually glad that I know the truth. Dad's supposed suicide was bugging me.'

She turned sideways to face Ryan as she attempted to articulate her feelings, conscious of his close proximity and of the pressure of his thigh against hers as the small couch forced them together. She wondered if the contact was accidental and then mentally berated herself for the direction her thoughts had taken. What the hell was wrong with her? She had just learned that her father had been murdered by her own uncle and yet her mind seemed determined to take a sensual detour. A subconscious displacement activity perhaps? Her brain helping her to process the shock, even though she wasn't nearly as shocked as Ryan seemed to think she ought to be?

'How my uncle could be so ruthless is another question. A more immediate one, though, is how, if he tampered with Dad's car, the sabotage wasn't picked up on when the crash was investigated?'

'Was there a suicide note?' Ryan asked gently.

'Well yes, but it was typed and addressed to me. Dad apologised and said he couldn't go on without Mum but I never really bought that. Yes, he was devastated when we lost her but that had been three years before. Anyway, we knew the end was coming, we were prepared for it and he told me he was relieved that her suffering was over. We both were. Anyway, I told the police that Dad never typed anything. He barely knew how to switch a computer on and if he was writing to me, he would definitely have put pen to paper and not used such an impersonal method of communication. Uncle Brian took over dealing with the police, though, and probably told them something completely different. I was too devasted to force the issue but, like I say, I've always had niggling little doubts.'

'The note probably explains why they didn't examine the car more closely. Funds are tight and if there was no suggestion of murder and no motive for it then they wouldn't have spent much time on the investigation.' Ryan took her hand and squeezed her fingers. 'But we know the truth now and your uncle *will* pay for his crimes; trust me on this.'

'Won't the evidence from the cameras be inadmissible?' Sky asked. 'He didn't know he was confessing to an audience. Clever barristers always seem to successfully argue that point on TV dramas.'

Ryan smiled and shook his head. He still had hold of her hand and Sky didn't see any pressing need to claim it back. The feel of his fingers absently stroking hers was comforting. 'It's your flat and you gave permission for the surveillance equipment to be placed in it.' He smiled at her. 'Don't worry. He won't wiggle out of this one but we won't bring him in quite yet. He needs to serve his purpose first.'

'You'll have to find him, then. I have no idea where he lives.'

'I had people watching your flat and gave instructions for Greaves to be followed when he left.'

'Ah, that was the cryptic message you sent when I was falling apart. You didn't want Josh to know what you were doing.' She frowned. 'He seems like a good guy. I really hope he's on the right side.'

'So do I, but in my line of work it pays to be suspicious of everything and everyone. Less likelihood of being surprised that way.'

'Yep, I get that.' She paused. 'You think my uncle is acting as a bodyguard of some sort for the man at the top of the tree? For Karim's father?'

'Sounds that way. And anyway, I get the impression that your uncle will be up for anything that pays well.'

'Including bumping me off,' Sky said, shuddering.

Ryan released her hand and slipped an arm round her shoulders. She gratefully rested the side of her face against his broad shoulder.

'He won't get anywhere near you, darling.'

'Nonsense!' She jerked upright and sent Ryan a disapproving look. 'I won't make myself a target but I won't hide myself away either. If my uncle is serious then he could catch me unawares in the street at any time and I refuse to turn into a hermit, afraid of every unfamiliar sound. Afraid of my own shadow.'

'Which is why I'll draw him into a trap just as soon as he's led us to Amin's father. That will happen over the next day or so; I can't keep to myself what I know about the plot to kill the president for longer than that. I shouldn't withhold it anyway, could lose my job for keeping my mouth shut, but sometimes it's necessary to follow one's instincts.

Besides, if the Americans knew then they'd be all over Chequers and that would give your boyfriend a legitimate reason to abort.'

'Isn't that what we want?'

'Nope. We need to keep Amin on track.' He looked down and sent her a smile that she reacted to all the way to her toes. And back up again. 'You only have to lie low for a couple of days, and not return to your flat.'

She shook her head emphatically. 'Not happening,' she said firmly. 'We have the upper hand and I intend to exploit that situation. I do have an email address for my uncle and—'

Ryan's body jerked upright. 'You should have said,' he replied in a tone of mild rebuke. 'Josh could monitor it.'

'I only just remembered. Anyway, if I ask him to meet me, we both know he'll be unable to resist seeing what it is that I want.'

'You'll make yourself an easy target.' It was Ryan's turn to shake his head.

'You don't get to decide,' she replied hotly, sitting bolt upright and glaring at him. 'This is my life and my father I intend to avenge.'

'And we will!' Ryan placed his hands on her shoulders and forced her to meet his gaze. 'We have all the evidence we need. It will serve absolutely no purpose if you go off without a plan of action after a resentful and dangerous man.'

Sky could see that Ryan was getting annoyed with her, probably assuming that her reaction was immature. He could well be right but Sky had never felt a more pressing need to take control of her own destiny.

'I have always been a follower, never a leader,' she said, attempting to explain a position that she barely understood herself. 'With friends like Nancy who always shine in any social situation, I suppose that's hardly surprising and it's never bothered me before. I just kind of accepted that she wasn't the sort of person I'm supposed to be and I was happy with that. I don't like being the centre of attention. Then Karim came along and for a brief moment I understood what Nancy gets out of being admired. Even now, after I realise that he targeted me because my uncle had told him about my money, I still get a buzz out of the way I felt being on Karim's arm, ridiculous as that sounds.' She looked up into his handsome face, wanting him to understand the changes in her psyche brought about by recent events and the desire that drove her. 'I guess we all have our dreams, but that's all mine were.' Her expression turned deliberately self-deprecating. 'Pride before a spectacular fall, and all that.'

'The man is a snake, a charlatan. You've had a narrow escape and, for what it's worth, I meant every word when I said earlier that it was he who was lucky to have you in his life.'

She smiled at him, still unwilling to believe him. 'Well anyway, my eyes are well and truly open now. I just heard my uncle admit to killing my father, hoping to extract from trusting little me the money that Dad wouldn't give him.' She paused. 'It was obviously well orchestrated, our initial accidental meeting at that club, I mean. Nancy received complimentary tickets for the night we went. I didn't think anything of it. She's on all the main club's mailing lists and women who look like her often get freebies.'

'I see. Your uncle assumed that you'd turn to him, your only remaining relation, after your father died. When he overplayed his hand and scared you off, he had to think of a different way to reel you in.'

'It might have worked if I'd been a bit younger.' Sky canted her head and took a moment to consider. 'But even before he started trying to take control of my affairs, I suppose, I saw something dark and resentful in him that I didn't like, even though I didn't realise it at the time.' She gave a careless little laugh. 'You're not the only one who falls back on instinct, it seems.'

'You're a good judge of character.'

Sky thought how easily she'd fallen for Karim's line and sadly shook her head. 'When I declined my uncle's repeated requests, things turned ugly. I'm surprised he didn't let his temper get the better of him and bump me off then and there. He clearly has anger issues and an unjustified sense of self-entitlement.'

'But he's not stupid. If you were killed so soon after your father and he inherited the lot then there would have been a thorough investigation.'

'Yeah, I guess, so he waited a couple of years, saw an opportunity and pointed Karim in my direction instead.' Sky folded her arms and turned away from Ryan. 'I suppose I ought to be grateful that he only wanted him to defraud me, not kill me, although that situation has obviously changed.' She huffed. 'Honestly, did he really imagine that I'd keep all that dosh in a no-notice account?'

'Probably not but he wanted to get Amin invested so that he'd do the dirty work. Your uncle will have to be miles away, with a ton of people, if Amin makes a serious attempt on your life. He'd also have to make sure that there's no connection between him and Amin in the event of Amin being caught. And there isn't, since we don't know where Amin's father is precisely, or what name he's using and Amin's father is the only link between them. You can be sure that Greaves won't tell the truth about his employment history, drawing the forces of law and order to Amin senior's door. That would be suicidal.'

'Well, I don't care what you say, I fully intend to have a private conversation with uncle dearest,' Sky said stubbornly.

'Oh, for the love of God!' She turned in time to see Ryan pace the length of the small room, muttering beneath his breath and clearly running out of patience with her. The tension was palpable but Sky ignored its interfering presence. Her mind was made up and she had absolutely no intention of backing down. This was her fight just as much as it was his. Aware that the plot to kill the president wouldn't be allowed to grow legs now that they knew about it, she felt justified in conducting a very different campaign of her own.

'Use the sense you were born with, Sky. What can you possibly hope to achieve by poking the bear?'

'You didn't seem to be getting very far in catching the men controlling Karim before I came along,' she responded sweetly, her mild tone in direct variance with his anger. 'If I were to meet with my uncle in a public place and tell him that we listened to his entire conversation with Karim, knowing what a cowardly bastard bent on self-preservation he actually is, don't you imagine that he'd point us in the direction of the boss in return for us letting him scarper?'

15

Karim hung up, concerned about Sky's unexpected non-availability. It wasn't like her to miss an opportunity to spend time with him, which reinforced Karim's belief that she'd gone off the boil. How could that have happened? Far more sophisticated women than her had been known to cling to him like limpets, even when he made it clear that he wasn't in it for the long haul. God forbid that she suspected the truth! He couldn't see how that would be possible; he had been so careful and she was so trusting, so willing to believe all the garbage that spilled from his mouth.

What had changed in the interim?

He slumped in a chair, his eye constantly drawn to the blinking light on Sky's desktop. He didn't consider himself to be an emotional man. Ha! Little chance of that, given the hostile atmosphere in which he'd been raised by a father who left his care in the hands of a series of house-keepers and then the strict regime of a top boarding school, where he'd rubbed shoulders with the sons of elite British society. The only attention his father had given his one remaining child was in grooming him to believe in the cause. Pleading lack of interest was not an option for Karim – the punishments would be harsh and cruel if his father even suspected his lack of enthusiasm.

Karim, at first keen to impress in order to gain his father's longed-for approval, soon learned that he would never achieve that ambition. Why he had been sent to an establishment that routinely turned out English gentlemen when he was destined for another future entirely had often perplexed Karim. He had seen what doors were opened to his peers, simply because of their educational credentials, and had yearned early on to be accepted by society's elite. His father, on the other hand, appeared to see that acceptance as cover for his own ideals.

'Fuck the cause!' he shouted to the rafters.

The sound reverberated around the large room but didn't bring him any closer to resolving his problem. Taking what Sky had in her current account would be pointless. With his luxurious standards it wouldn't last him five minutes. But he also had to pay Greaves off, he knew. They'd struck a bargain and Karim wouldn't be permitted to renege on that. Even so, the thought of Sky being murdered filled him with abhorrence. Perhaps he had grown a conscience, despite everything. He chuckled at his lousy sense of timing. The only way to prevent her uncle from doing away with her would be to marry her.

Or to let her be and concentrate on taking his father out, trusting to luck that he didn't fail.

Walk away from her; that would be the sensible thing to do, but for reasons Karim failed to comprehend, he didn't want to wipe Sky out of his life. Marriage it would have to be, he decided. He felt rather pleased with his altruistic stance. For once he wasn't putting his own interests first. He was, however, getting ahead of himself. He had to have an escape plan in the event that the hit upon his father failed and he managed to evade his avenging guards. That required money.

Copious amounts of it.

He could 'borrow' from the coffers at Alexandria, and would have done but for the fact that there was very little actual cash floating about nowadays. Everyone paid by card and if he transferred the amount he needed into his private account it would be noticed and questioned within hours. His father ran a very tight ship and was kept abreast of any anomalies in his legitimate enterprises.

Karim was unsure whom he feared more – his father or Greaves. Both were ruthless individuals when crossed. What the hell had he been thinking, allowing Greaves to talk him into targeting Sky and believing Greaves when he assured him that a pot of gold would be his for the taking? Life was never that simple but greed and a healthy sense of self-preservation in the light of his father's increasingly untenable ambitions had made him desperate.

'Face it, you're fucked whichever way you go,' he said aloud, thumping the arm of his chair in frustration, determined to be there when Sky got home. He needed to be sure that she still adored him, for the sake of his ego as much as anything else.

And he needed to protect her from her uncle. The recollection of his gloating expression as he blithely described how badly he'd wanted to force himself on his own niece had Karim clenching his fists again. How he hadn't smashed one of those fists into Greaves's face he couldn't have said. Self-preservation, he supposed. Karim fought reluctantly and, because he had no choice in the matter, with his brains, not his fists. Greaves, on the other hand, was a hard man who punched first and asked questions afterwards. Karim had the good sense to know that he would literally be on a hiding to nothing if he challenged him physically.

His reflections were interrupted by his phone ringing. His hopes that it was Sky calling to let him know she was on her way were dashed when his father's private number flashed up on the screen. It took all of Karim's self-discipline to answer the call, aware that there would be consequences if he did not. There was never a satisfactory reason for ignoring the great man, Karim had come to learn the hard way.

'Yes,' he said curtly.

'I need to see you. Get over here at once.'

The line went dead, his father simply assuming that his orders would be obeyed without question.

'Arrogant prick!' Karim muttered, sighing as he gathered up his jacket and prepared to respond to the royal command. 'What the hell's so important?' he wondered aloud, as he closed the door behind him and ran down the communal stairs.

His father seldom summoned him without good reason and Karim knew better than to assume that filial affection had suddenly become the root cause. His father felt no affection for anyone other than himself.

Karim went cold all over as he commenced the laborious business of getting to Islington without being followed. His father lived openly in his palatial house, the epitome of the successful businessman who gave generously to charitable causes, accepted because he had bought his way into society. Nevertheless, resented by many. Racism was still alive and kicking in British society.

No one even suspected him of extremist connections and the man was determined to keep it that way. If the ridiculous plot to wipe out the president did go ahead and by some miracle succeeded, nothing would lead back to the old man.

He had made very sure of that.

The need to take double the time for what should have been a forty-five-minute journey was another necessity that had grown old. Karim thought wistfully about simply jumping on the Tube and heading straight for his destination, leading the service to his father's door. Now wouldn't that just put the cat amongst the pigeons, he thought, managing a mirthless chuckle as he fantasised. His father had carefully constructed layers of protection but remained paranoid about having his true identity discovered. Karim had avoided being the cause of his ultimate unveiling but only because his own involvement in nefarious activities would inevitably come to light as well. Activities that had resulted in the mass loss of innocent lives couldn't be ignored and would see him rot in a jail cell for the rest of his days. Until such time as another inmate, intent upon becoming a hero, stuck a shiv in his ribs.

Unfortunately, that situation still prevailed.

His heart stuttered when he considered the possibility that he'd been ratted out by one of the men he'd just conspired with. Was that the reason for the parental summons? He breathed more easily once he'd reasoned the possibility through. If his loyalty was suspect, he wouldn't have been summoned. Instead he'd have been grabbed by his father's goons and thrown in the back of a Transit van, familial connections notwithstanding.

It had been agreed that Arham Khan would take over at the top and the other two were loyal to him, secure in the knowledge that their respective stars would also be in the ascendency if there was a change of leadership. Even so, his father had eyes and ears in the most unlikely of places and Karim needed to go prepared. If necessary, he would wipe his father out then and there, secure in the knowledge that their upcoming interview would take place in private. That would very much be a last resort, though, since the guards would almost certainly fall back on their training before he could reason with them and he would finish up dead too.

After taking a different convoluted route by way of a change, Karim arrived at his father's residence and suffered the humiliation of being conducted through the house by a silent, muscle-bound goon. He refrained from exchanging a word with the Neanderthal, preferring to remain aloof and to preserve his dignity as much as the mortifying circumstances permitted.

'What's so urgent?' he asked his father, the moment he had been admitted to his inner sanctum and the door had been closed behind him.

His father looked up sharply from the newspaper he had been reading, unaccustomed to being addressed so curtly, even by Karim. Especially by him. 'Keep a civil tongue in your head, boy!'

Boy? Karim perched on the edge of a chair and waited his father out in silence. He would get to the reason for the summons in his own time but if he was waiting for Karim to apologise before he did so then he would die of old age first. It felt good to meet the old man's evil eye and not back down. He should have done it a long time ago. He could see that his father was perplexed by the changes in Karim, unsure what to read into them.

'You failed to update me on progress,' he eventually said.

'That's because there is nothing to update you on. You know as well as I do that we communicate only when necessary. You are the one who doesn't want me hanging around the place, making it look untidy. Those, I believe, were your exact words the last time I remarked upon my lack of welcome at your abode.'

His father looked down his long beak of a nose and sniffed. 'I want you to include Malek in all aspects of the plan.'

Karim knew it wasn't a suggestion when his father pressed a button, the door opened immediately and the most senior of his in-house guards filled the aperture with his bulk. Karim's father trusted Malek more than anyone else on the planet, treating him as a confidante and friend. He had been pivotal in reinventing his father's identity after his 'death' and was looked upon more as a son and heir than Karim himself was. Malek certainly didn't have to knock and wait to be granted entrance to the house. Unlike the other guards, he lived in permanently and occupied a suite of rooms as luxurious as those occasionally used by Karim. One of Malek's duties was to procure escorts for his father. Karim happened to know that the hypocrite also enjoyed their favours himself.

Up until now, the favouritism hadn't unduly concerned Karim. It took the spotlight away from him, which was just the way Karim liked it. Malek had never bothered to hide his contempt for Karim and had probably suggested the US presidential assassination plot to his father in the hope that it would wipe Karim out. Well, it *would* wipe him out if he went ahead with it, leaving Malek as the only viable heir presumptive, which was undoubtedly Malek's intention.

Karim had little trouble believing that Malek had persuaded his father to involve him more directly. With Malek breathing down his neck Karim would have to give the appearance of going through with the assassination. That he could do; he had grown adept over the years at hiding his real agenda, but how the hell was he supposed to further his plans with Arham and the others if he was under such close scrutiny? They had burner phones but their use was still dangerous and so kept to a minimum. The various agencies had an annoying habit of tracking down their phones and monitoring their conversations. It hadn't happened to Karim yet, at least not so far as he knew, but that was because he remained so vigilant.

Karim knew that he would have to risk making phone contact and that Arham would have to step out of the shadows, perhaps eliminate Malek prior to Karim taking out his father. Malek's presence would severely hamper their plans otherwise. The man could sniff out disloyalty at twenty paces with the wind in the wrong direction.

This development was concerning. Did his father suspect that Karim had no intention of going through with the mission? Had he got wind of a plot to usurp him? That was a possibility that Karim couldn't afford to ignore and would account for the manner in which his father constantly sent him assessing looks. Malek treated him to a knowing little half-smile – more of a warning grimace – and remained stationed inside the door, bulky arms folded across his impressive torso.

'Get Malek fully up to speed with the plan,' his father said in the commanding tone of a general addressing his minions, secure in the knowledge that his orders would be followed to the letter.

'What do you know about computer technology?' Karim asked, returning Malek's forbidding look with a challenging expression of his own, well aware that Malek barely knew how to switch a computer on, making his inclusion in the planning all that much harder to fathom. What the hell was his father up to? What did he think he knew?

Karim's palms had turned sweaty and his heart was beating at an irregular rate. *Calm down!* He took a deep breath, aware that he could tell Malek anything and the idiot wouldn't know any better. Nonetheless, he laid out the details he'd worked out for appearance's sake more or less as they were, conscious of the fact that the two men assigned to help Karim with the planning would be able to confirm them, and that Malek would definitely apply to them for that confirmation. When lying, stick as close to the truth as possible, was the mantra that life had taught Karim to live by. The logistics, the placement of the explosives, would be easy enough for Malek to check out. But the remote detonation of said explosives was way beyond Malek's comprehension.

And also beyond the comprehension of the men assigned to help him.

That was Karim's ace in the hole. If all else failed and he was required to implement the suicidal mission then the explosives would fail to... well, explode.

And Karim would leg it somewhere safe, rat out his father and wait for the dust to settle.

His father followed the discussion with laser-like concentration, frowning constantly but not interrupting. *He really thinks this crazy scheme will work.* If Karim had harboured doubts about committing patricide, which he had not, not seriously, then that moment would have convinced him. He was dealing with a madman. But, then, he had known that since childhood, since the day his father had calmly taken him out of school and sent him away to England. That had happened an hour before the car containing his mother, her forbidden lover and his two sisters had been blown to smithereens. The girls, it seemed, had not been spared because, being older than Karim and more often at home, they had been aware of their mother's affair and of her intention to leave her husband.

That could not be permitted and the girls had signed their own death warrants by choosing their mother's side. Karim had only been spared because he was ignorant about the affair he had subsequently discovered when his father discussed the matter with him on one occasion only, after he'd left school. For that reason and because his father hoped to raise a son in his own image. But Karim knew that as an adult he was a grave disappointment to the father in question and wondered if his father knew that the feeling was mutual.

'Now then, Karim,' his father said, once he'd explained the plot to Malek with sufficient technical detail to, he hoped, make the man's thick head ache. 'Perhaps you can explain to me how the authorities latched on to our association with the Bayswater Boutique Hotel.'

* * *

Ryan turned to face Sky, frowning as he attempted to figure out precisely what her intentions were. He could understand her desire for revenge and admired the speed with which she'd recovered from the shock of hearing her uncle casually admit to committing murder, not to mention his plan to repeat the crime with her as the intended victim. But being aware that Greaves was such a ruthless individual surely ought to have made her want Ryan's protection rather than setting her off on some sort of crazy quest for self-imposed justice.

'Just give it a few days,' he said, knowing he was probably wasting his breath. 'Once I've figured out a way to stop the American president from being assassinated on British soil, you can be sure that we'll present the evidence we have to the police and Greaves will be arrested and charged. You don't need to take any silly risks.'

'Has it not occurred to you that I want to talk to my uncle? To find out what motivated him.'

'Greed. Self-entitlement. Resentment. Laziness.' Ryan counted the points off on his fingers. 'All of the above.' He threw up his hands when she shook her head, clearly not ready to listen to the voice of reason. 'Who the hell knows what goes through the mind of a sociopath?'

'You're thinking with the brain of a professional with tunnel vision and I do understand you need to protect us all, including visiting dignitaries. You, in return, must try to see things from my perspective. My family has been torn apart by a man I once trusted. I need to understand why and I'll never get the chance to ask him that question once he's been arrested.'

'I assume, despite your uncle's words, you have a current will,' Ryan said, forcing himself to remain professional, detached, when all he really wanted to do was take her in his arms and kiss some sense into her. There was more than one way to influence hearts and minds. *Get a grip, Callahan.*

'What on earth has that got to do with—?'

'You haven't, have you?' Ryan shook his head, deliberately goading her. 'Better do something about that before you go off confronting psychopathic murderers.'

She seemed undaunted by his taunts and stubbornly determined to do things her way. A way that would likely see her killed. 'Absolutely. I'll take care of it today. Thanks for reminding me. I've been meaning to get round to it.' She sent him a scathing look from beneath partially lowered lashes. 'You called my uncle a sociopath a moment ago. Now he's psychopathic. Which is it?'

'Alright!' Ryan let out a long sigh, aware that he'd met his match, not bothering to answer her question. 'If you're determined to confront him, I'll help you, if you'll agree to wait until after we've tracked Amin's father down.' He spread his hands. 'I can't sit on the intel that I have and it has to be my priority, you must see that.'

Her expression softened. 'Of course I can see that a president's life takes priority over my murdering and grasping uncle,' she said.

'International relations would never recover if the president died in this country.'

'Thank you.' Some of the tension drained out of him. He crossed the room, stood in front of her and held her gaze. 'You'll stay here for the next couple of days?'

'Okay, I guess,' she replied after a long considering pause. She glanced towards the door, a reminder to Ryan that there was just one bedroom.

'I'll take the couch,' he said.

She looked down at the two-seater. 'It's a bit small for you.'

He shrugged, aware of sexual tension fuelling the atmosphere between them, wondering if she sensed it too. She pushed an escaped strand of hair behind her ear. Her cheeks were flushed and she absently moistened her lips with the tip of her tongue.

'I've slept in worse places.'

She looked away from him, seconds before he gave into temptation and kissed her. 'I have no doubt.' She let out a long breath. 'I will need to go back to the flat and collect a few things. And bring my cat back here.'

'I'll come with you. Damn!' he added when his phone rang, he extracted it from his pocket and took the call. 'Yes,' he said curtly, aware that he couldn't ignore a third call in succession from Bill.

'There's a lot of activity in at the Bayswater Boutique Hotel,' Bill replied.

'What sort of activity?'

'Change of shift patterns, increased telephone activity. I hate to admit it, but it seems you were right about the leak.'

'They're cleaning house?'

'Looks that way.'

'Who did you leak the connection to?'

Bill paused. 'Only Beth.'

'Shit!' Ryan threw back his head and closed his eyes. 'I didn't want it to be her. Okay, do nothing for now. I'll come in shortly. I need to talk to you alone about something much bigger. I have an important lead I need to chase down.'

'Don't tell me what to do or not do!' Bill shouted. 'I'm in charge, in case it had escaped your notice.'

'I can always depend upon you to remind me of that. Later,' Ryan said curtly, cutting the call.

'What's wrong?' Sky touched his arm.

'I've just found out that the man who's taken temporary charge of our agency is disloyal,' he said, grinding his jaw, his mind racing. 'And very likely orchestrated the attempt on Steve's life.'

'I'm so sorry,' she said breathlessly. 'How can you be so sure?'

'Because he told me that Beth is the mole but I know for a fact that she's as loyal as I am.'

'She's obviously your friend and you don't want her to be the guilty party but how can you be so sure that she isn't?'

'Because she was engaged to another guy in the unit who was killed by extremists. She was in another branch of the service at the time.' Ryan walked away from Sky, rubbing his chin as he contemplated the simple way in which Bill had fallen into a trap. 'Beth has independent means, no living close relations who can be manipulated into making her cooperate with enemies of the state, and a burning hatred for the scum who took out the love of her life. I knew it wasn't her but did suspect the other two names I fed to Bill.' He glowered at the uninspiring view from his window without actually seeing it. 'You realise what this means?'

'You can't tell Bill that we know about the plot to kill the president.'

'Precisely. The rats will run to ground and all will be lost.'

'It would save the president's life.'

'But wouldn't stop your boyfriend's father from plotting something even bigger. He clearly wants to go down in the annals of terrorist history as the greatest of all time,' Ryan said scathingly.

'Presumably your new boss knows that you suspect Karim,' Sky remarked, not taking issue with his reference to Karim as her boyfriend, which had been cruel and unnecessary given what she now knew about him but Bill's disloyalty had sent Ryan temporarily crazy.

'Sure, but not what we've discovered, unless he grills Josh. I will have to warn him and I can only do that in person. But you...'

'I'm a big girl. I can stay here on my own and collect my stuff later. No one knows where I am.' She touched his arm. 'Go. Do what you have to. I promise not to run off and leave you with anything else to worry about.'

She stood on her toes and briefly placed a kiss on his lips. It wasn't nearly enough for Ryan, despite the fact that he had more pressing issues to deal with. Like preventing the leader of arguably the most powerful nation on earth from being killed on British soil. Grunting, he pulled her into his arms and kissed her long and deep. She wound her arms around his neck and responded to Ryan without hesitation. He felt heat going straight to his loins, with the predictable reaction. He cursed his lousy timing. Now was most definitely not the right moment.

Perhaps there would never be one.

Releasing Sky and holding her at arm's length, he smiled. 'We'll pick up where we left off later,' he assured her. 'This is definitely not over.'

She looked dazed and nodded, running the tip of her tongue over her lips as though looking for proof that she hadn't imagined the entire episode.

'Is there any food in the flat?' she asked. 'I'll cook something.'

'Good idea,' he replied, gathering up what possessions he would need in order to confront Josh and then Bill. Anything to keep her occupied worked for him. 'Not much in, I'm afraid, but there's a convenience store just around the corner.' She would be safe enough going there, he decided, since no one knew where she was. 'We'll collect the cat later.'

'Okay. Stay safe,' she said.

'That's my line,' he replied, grabbing his jacket. 'There's a spare set of keys in that drawer.' He pointed to the appropriate place. 'Lock yourself in once I leave and don't let anyone other than me back in again.'

'Got it,' she replied.

'Call me if you have any concerns. Any concerns at all.'

'I'll be fine. Just go!'

'Later,' he said, turning to take one last look at her before letting himself out of the flat and forcing himself to concentrate on the business in hand.

16

Ryan slammed the door as he left. The sound reverberated through the now eerily silent flat, playing havoc with Sky's skittish nerves. She fiddled with her phone as she checked her messages, then wandered into the bedroom, not having ventured over its threshold before, curious to see what it would reveal about the man who occupied it.

The bed was made with military-style precision but there was nothing of a personal nature in the room to give her more of an insight into Ryan's character. No family pictures, no discarded clothes, no books, nothing. She opened the wardrobe to reveal a few pairs of jeans and sweatshirts; nothing formal. Nothing to identify their owner's idiosyncrasies, making Sky wonder what had happened in his past to make him so devoid of emotional attachments. There had to be something. Not that he'd seemed emotionally barren when he'd kissed her earlier but she suspected that had been a rare and brief lapse in his iron self-control.

The room was impersonal and yet Sky felt Ryan's almost overpowering presence in every square inch of it. How was that even possible, she wondered, and why did it give her flailing confidence such a massive boost? She didn't need Ryan, or any other man to fight her battles for her. She was a capable, independent woman who fully intended to exact her own form of justice for the wrongs that had been done to her, regardless of the fact that the stakes had risen to a level of international importance.

It would be easy to use matters of national security as an excuse to delay what had to be done, Sky conceded, since she did care about the security of her country. Should that be enough to make her sit back with her knitting and let Ryan get the justice on her behalf that he'd promised to exact once he'd saved the world?

Not a chance!

She hadn't come this far only to let someone else have all the fun. This was personal. The justice system would never punish her uncle in the manner that he deserved to be punished; not even Ryan's form of justice, which didn't appear to recognise suspects' rights.

She glanced out the window which overlooked the parking area, watching Ryan as he strode towards his car, his long legs eating up the ground. He glanced up, saw her at the window and paused to raise a hand. He then climbed into his car, fired up the engine and drove off at speed. How had he known she would be at his bedroom window, she wondered. Had he sensed her presence or was she allowing her imagination to get the better of her?

'Stay safe,' she muttered, reiterating her earlier words to him, aware that what she was about to do, what she *had* to do, would aggravate him and put an end to their fledgling friendship. Unfortunately, that was insufficient to make her revise her plans.

She wanted to think about that kiss; about the intensity behind his words when he'd said that they had unfinished business. Unfinished business that she now knew they wouldn't get around to finishing. Her actions would kill that possibility stone dead. She felt a deep pang of regret, aware that she had made him a promise, albeit with her fingers crossed behind her back. When she broke that promise the trust would be gone and that would be that. She hesitated for a protracted moment, wondering if she should stick to their agreement but dismissed the possibility before it could take root.

'Sorry, Ryan,' she said, gathering up her bag. 'I've got too much invested in this business to back down now.'

She took a last look around, then left the flat, not bothering to take the spare keys with her. Whatever happened over the next few hours, she would not be returning here.

An icy sense of calm came over Sky as she caught the Tube to Canning Town. She recalled little about the journey afterwards, or about her fellow passengers, all of whom either stared at phones, or at the Tube maps on the walls of the carriage, a spaghetti of different colours tunnelling their way beneath the capital. Sky spent the time mentally fine-tuning her strategy, attempting to anticipate her uncle's reaction to her proactive stance. Suppressing the fear that recollections of her childhood and the man's influence over it brought to the surface. Memories that she had buried in a shallow grave, ready to be re-examined when the time was right.

Sometimes she had thought – hoped – that the right time would never come and that she would find a way to slam the door on the past and move on. But the time had inevitably arrived, she was no longer a vulnerable child and as ready as she would ever be to face it.

She left the Tube station amidst a small gaggle of other passengers and made her way to an address she'd committed to memory. An address she had visited once before, a year previously, just so that she knew where it was. She had never been inside.

For the second time in her life she stood outside the shabby terraced house – even shabbier than she recollected as sunlight glinted off grimy windows and peeling paint – that was converted into equally shabby bedsits. The pedestrians who pushed past her were young and already looked disillusioned with life. One or two sent her speculative glances but something about her demeanour appeared to stop them from approaching her.

Her uncle, she had made it her business to discover, occupied one of the attic rooms in this salubrious abode. She had deliberately withheld that knowledge from Ryan and the reminder caused her conscience to twang.

She had no intention of pressing a bell that probably didn't work and giving Brian Greaves advance warning of her arrival. She had surprise and a few other tactics on her side and wanted to keep it that way. The problem of getting past the street door proved to be no problem at all since it wasn't locked. A hefty push was all it took to make the hinges protest as the door scraped open over stained flagstones, giving way to the pressure and crashing against the inner wall.

Presumably no one had bothered to fix the lock since even the most desperate of thieves would look for richer pickings, Sky decided, wrinkling her nose as she ascended three flights of increasingly dirty stairs. The soles of her shoes stuck to the treads and she preferred not to dwell on the nature of the substances now adhering to her trainers. The smell of urine – either human or canine – prevailed. Someone had thrown up and not bothered to clear up their vomit. There was drug paraphernalia in plain sight.

How desperate must people be to live like this?

Her moment of sympathy gave way to fresh resolve. She knew that her uncle didn't need to rough it, or he hadn't before his latest sojourn as a guest at Her Majesty's pleasure, presumably after the rich widow in Thailand gave him the push. A spell inside that probably accounted for his association with radical elements. Prisons were known as recruiting grounds, Ryan had said. Presumably her uncle had an alternative agenda, had seen an opportunity to enhance his own situation. That was a fact that Sky had been banking on in coming here. Money had always been the only god he ever worshipped and she very much doubted if anything had changed in the interim.

A dog barked behind a closed door as she reached the first landing and a rough voice yelled at it to shut up. A baby cried in another part of the house and Sky felt depression grip her as she continued with her ascent. This was no environment in which to raise a child. The poor scrap didn't stand a chance.

A youth ran down from the top floor, barging into her and almost knocking her from her feet without appearing to notice. He didn't pause to apologise – of course he didn't – but at least he didn't try to mug her. Sky breathed a little more easily when he didn't even look back at her.

'What am I doing here?' she asked aloud, aware of the answer to her own question. Her patience had been rewarded. She had the proof she needed, fully intended to confront the guilty party *and* just possibly help Ryan out too.

She reached the top floor and stood outside her uncle's door for a moment to recover her breath and solidify her resolve. Jittery nerves caused her to do something she'd vowed not to do. She extracted her phone from the pocket of her jeans and typed a brief WhatsApp to Ryan, telling him where she was. But she didn't send it. It was a failsafe. A last resort if things went pear-shaped.

Feeling a little calmer now that she had a backup plan of sorts, she raised a hand and knocked loudly.

'Fuck!' she muttered when no sounds emerged from within. God forbid that she had come all this way and he wasn't even at home. Sky doubted if she'd be able to raise the courage to repeat the journey. 'He must be here,' she muttered, tapping her foot. 'He has to be.'

She raised a fist and knocked again, louder and for longer. This time she was rewarded by the sound of someone swearing from within. It was unquestionably her uncle's voice and it made her shiver with apprehension. Her finger hovered over the button that would send the message to Ryan and hopefully bring reinforcements barrelling in, but she resisted the urge to ask for his help. Just knowing that he would be able to get to her in record time and feeling almost sure that she would be able to prevent her uncle from attacking her, at least for a short period of time, prevented her from turning tail and scrambling back down the grungy stairs. If she did she knew that she would never be able to lay her demons to rest and get on with the rest of her life.

The door was wrenched open and her uncle stood there, bleary-eyed, wearing only a pair of boxer shorts.

'Where the hell's the fire... Fuck me!' His eyes widened when his gaze fell on Sky. 'Well, well.' He rubbed his hands together gleefully. 'Must be my lucky day. Come in, darling. Come in. Excuse the mess. It's the maid's day off.'

Sky had prepared herself for a pigsty and wasn't disappointed. A rumpled bed with sheets that had probably once been white occupied half the room. There was a tiny kitchenette at one end with dirty plates and empty bottles occupying every surface. What she assumed must be a shower room stood at the opposite end, the door half open, the sound of a constantly dripping tap coming from within. There was a large TV sitting on an upturned crate and a couple of easy chairs.

None of that came as any great surprise but the collage of pictures stuck to one wall, all of them of Sky in different public locations, all of them recent, completely took the wind out of her sails.

'Admiring my artwork, I see,' Brian said, leering at her.

* * *

Ryan rang Josh from his in-car phone. The tech guy picked up on the first ring.

'Yo,' he said.

Yo? Gotta love the rich diversity of the English language embraced by the young, Ryan thought with a cynical elevation of one brow. 'Where are you?' Ryan asked with equal verbal economy.

'Still packing up equipment. Why?'

'Hold fast. I'll be there in ten. Don't talk to anyone in the meantime. Especially not Bill.'

'Er, okay. I guess.'

A combination of surprisingly light traffic and Ryan's fast driving brought him back to the van in less time than anticipated. Josh's geeky teenager look hid a vast intellect, Ryan knew, and he would read between the lines in seconds if Ryan attempted to bullshit him. So he cut straight to the chase.

'We have a leak in the organisation,' he said without preamble, the moment he'd entered the van and shut the door behind him.

'Don't look at me, man.' Josh leaned back in his chair, gangly legs splayed in front of him, and lazily pushed his palms towards Ryan. 'I just do as I'm told. So long as I get to play with my toys then I'm golden.' He glanced lovingly at his equipment. Far from packing it up, Ryan recognised a popular game on one of the screens. Josh had clearly been involved in a battle to the death on some inter-galactic planet.

'Yeah, I know.' Ryan scratched his ear. 'The thing is, I think I've narrowed it down to Bill.'

'Holy fuck!' Ryan had finally said something to jolt Josh out of his complacency. 'You sure, man? I mean, like, he's our temporary boss.'

'I'm sure. He's trying to pin it on Beth.'

'Beth's solid,' Josh said, nodding his head so firmly that his ponytail cascaded over his shoulder.

'I know that.'

'What you gonna do about it?' Josh leaned back even further in his chair, all boneless limbs that he spread in impossible seeming directions. 'More to the point, why involve me? This is above my paygrade.'

'I'm ducking his calls right now, so the chances are he'll be on to you, wanting to know how this operation went.' Ryan paused. 'I need you to feed him dud information.'

'Okay.' Josh sat forward again. 'I can probably manage that. What do you need me to say?'

'That Amin turned up with some other guys that aren't on the system. They talked about the assassination of the US president and fine-tuned their plans. Didn't go to *Alexandria* to have such a sensitive talk because Amin thinks the security there's been compromised.'

'The truth, in other words.' Josh paused. 'Bill will have to pass on the intel about the president to our American friends,' he said, scratching the back of his neck.

'He will if he thinks the intel is genuine but if he insists that the evidence is inconclusive then we will have definitive proof that his loyalties are skewed.'

'Won't he ask to see the footage we took?'

'Yeah, about that.' Ryan grinned. 'I was hoping you'd be able to splice something convincing together that leaves out all the stuff about wiping out their leader.'

'Christ, you don't want much!' But Josh's eyes gleamed and Ryan knew he'd rise to the challenge.

'Of course, if that's above your paygrade too...'

'I didn't say that but miracles take a little longer.'

'I need the bits where they all expressed their doubts about being able to pull it off. That will give Bill a reason not to pass it on, if he can convince himself and others that it's too speculative and there was no real intent.'

'But if the Yanks find out that he knew of a plan, no matter how speculative, and didn't tell them...'

'He won't care. He'll be long gone, if I'm right about him and he knows he's living on borrowed time because I made a point of telling him that I suspect a mole in our organisation. He also knows I won't stop digging until I root out the guilty party.'

'Unless someone roots you out first, man.'

'Occupational hazard,' Ryan replied crisply. 'Anyway, Bill's being well paid for his disloyalty.' He scowled at Josh's screens as though he bore them a grudge. He hated disloyalty above just about every other human frailty. His thoughts briefly dwelt upon Sarah, but he pushed her firmly to the back of his mind. Now wasn't the time to open that particular can of worms. He needed to remain focused on the job in hand and didn't need distractions of a personal or emotional nature. 'This is the big one. Regardless of whether or not the attack succeeds, Bill knows that the investigation will be far-reaching, that his involvement will be uncovered and there will be no place for him to hide. He will have an escape plan drawn up, ready to implement.'

'Right.' Josh looked a little shell-shocked.

'How soon can I have the edited copy?'

'Give me an hour and I'll send something to your phone.'

'Good man!' Ryan slapped the geek's bony shoulder.

'Yeah, that's me. A prince amongst men. Bill? Blimey!' He scratched his head. 'Not many of us good guys left, it seems. Can't trust anyone nowadays.'

'Amen to that.'

Josh turned back to his screens and immersed himself. Ryan thanked him and left him to it.

'Let me know if you hear from Bill,' he said from the open door.

Josh lifted a hand to indicate he'd registered the request but, fingers flying over his keyboard, he continued to mutter to himself about disloyalty and didn't look up.

* * *

Sky stared at her uncle, her jaw flapping open in disbelief. 'You've been stalking me. You really are one sick bastard,' she said, shaking her head as she recovered the power of speech, recognising how important it was to go on the offensive.

'Hardly stalking. Just looking out for you. It's not against the law to keep a watchful eye on my only living relation, or it wasn't last time I checked.' His bloodshot gaze was fixed on her, his whisky-fuelled breath hot on her face, but Sky resisted the urge to step away from him. Now wasn't the time to show weakness, or fear. 'Someone has to keep you safe.'

'Safe from what?' she asked, struggling to keep the repulsion out of her tone.

He managed to imbue his responding chuckle with a wealth of resentment. 'You're rich and vulnerable, Sky, and not nearly as streetwise as you like to think. You'll become a target for every chancer this side of Watford Gap.'

The mingled aroma of an unwashed body, alcohol and fried food was almost unbearable. Sky itched to open a window but doubted whether the warped frame would withstand the attempt. The renewed wails of the baby on the floor below drifted through the floorboards, momentarily distracting.

'Oh, I'm streetwise, Uncle. I ought to be. I had a rude awakening in that respect.'

'Ah, so you've come to your senses and are here to thank me for helping you to wise up.' He smacked his lips together. They were cracked, Sky noticed, and his once handsome face looked haggard. 'How did you find me, as a matter of interest?'

'It wasn't difficult,' she lied. She had employed a private investigator to do the legwork when her doubts about her father's death had surfaced and refused to be quelled. He'd followed Uncle Brian from his favourite watering hole shortly after his release from prison to this house often enough for there to be no doubt that it was his only place of residence. But hearing from Ryan that her uncle was employed by terrorists had come as a complete shock. She assumed that employment must have come about in the last year, after she'd dispensed with her PI's services, since there had been nothing in the reports she'd received about him frequenting large houses in Islington.

'So, how do you want to repay me for services rendered?' he asked, scratching his scrotum through his grungy boxers and taking a step towards her.

'I've come to give you the opportunity to turn yourself in for murdering my father,' she replied calmly, lifting her chin and meeting his repulsive gaze. She felt a modicum of euphoria when a combination of surprise and fear briefly flitted through his expression.

'You don't wanna go bandying unsubstantiated accusations like that about,' he said, recovering quickly but actually taking a step backwards. His expression had turned dark, forbidding, and he clenched his fists tightly at his sides. 'Bad things happen to little girls who don't know what they're talking about.'

'You really think I'm stupid enough to come here accusing you without proof?' She raised a brow imperiously.

'I think you're stark raving bonkers to come here at all, if all you want to do is provoke me.' He spoke with increasing confidence but she could see that she'd rattled him. 'All this is pillow talk, I'm guessing, but that's hardly proof. Fucking Amin,' he added in an undertone. 'He's always had it in for me.'

'Really?' Sky withdrew her phone from her pocket, pressed a button and the sound of her uncle's own voice, boasting about killing Sky's father, filled the room.

It was Uncle Brian's mouth that fell open in shock this time. 'You fucking wired the place!' He gave a slow handclap as he recovered a modicum of control and an equally slow, terrifying smile spread across his face. 'Well, well. So the kitten has finally developed claws.'

'You overreached yourself when you pointed Karim in my direction,' Sky replied, ignoring the fear that had welled up inside of her by reminding herself that she held all the aces. 'I smelt a rat at once shortly after I met him. He took an urgent phone call and I heard him mention your name. It all fell into place then. Men who look like him go for women like me for one reason and one reason only. But I let him think he'd convinced me, even pretended to fall for his hype, hoping that I'd get the proof I needed about the murder I suspected you of committing. Of course, I had no idea about Karim and his father and their true loyalties.'

'What do you know about that?' Genuine fear swept across her uncle's features.

'More than either of you could possibly imagine.' She imbued a wealth of confidence into her expression, almost enjoying herself. 'Being underestimated, overlooked, has its advantages.'

A volley of barks from the floor below stopped abruptly when the dog yelped.

'Leave it, Sky! For your own good.'

'I'll take advice from a man I have on record threatening to kill me?' She shook her head slowly. 'I don't think so.'

'If you're so sure that what you have is enough to hang me with, what are you doing here?'

'I wanted to see your face when you realised I'd finally got the upper hand,' Sky replied mildly. 'It's taken a while but I have to say, the longer it takes, revenge is definitely all it's cracked up to be.'

'Revenge? What are you talking about, girlie?' Greaves subjected her body to an insolent sweep of his eyes. 'You were up for it. You wanted it as much as I did. Came on to me. Offered it to me on a plate with your micro miniskirts and provocative looks.'

Sky couldn't believe what she was hearing but also wondered why she was so surprised to... well, be hearing it. Her uncle hadn't changed and was attempting to blame her for his debauchery. She inhaled sharply as she sent him a look of deep loathing.

'I was fourteen and you were the uncle I admired. The man I went to with my problems. The man who I thought had my best interests at heart.' She gave a scathing little laugh. 'When all you were actually doing was grooming me; I can see that now. And you know what, I never told a soul. I was ashamed. Thought it was my fault, but then that's what men like you depend upon, isn't it? They want their victims to feel guilty, and dirty, too afraid to speak out.'

'Victims?' Greaves shook his head. 'You were no victim, darling, but tell yourself that if it makes you feel better.'

'Looking back, I think Dad knew, or suspected. He asked me why I didn't hang out with you any more. I made an excuse that he probably didn't believe, but the moment Mum died, Dad cut you off. He didn't do so before only because he knew it would upset Mum. And once your meal ticket came to an end, you retaliated by killing him, thinking you could get your grubby hands on his wealth through me.' Sky was actually enjoying venting her spleen and the fact that her uncle didn't attempt to interrupt, or to defend himself, confirmed that she'd got it right. 'You actually thought that after what you'd done to me, I'd still be the naïve, trusting little Sky, ready to believe every word that fell from your vile lips.'

'It's all water under the bridge now and anyway, it looks to me like the actions you brought upon yourself helped you to wise up. You should be thanking me instead of bearing unhealthy grudges.' He sniffed and then wiped his nose on the back of his hand. Repulsed, Sky looked away. He had fallen lower than she'd realised. The uncle she remembered had been suave, well-mannered and always impeccably dressed. 'Anyway,' he added, folding his arms defensively across his still well-defined chest, 'what do you intend to do with this supposed evidence of yours? If you wanted me prosecuted you'd have taken it straight to the police, not come here whining about ancient history.'

'Oh, I fully intend to see you prosecuted for murder,' Sky replied, 'but the length of your sentence depends upon how willing you are to cooperate.'

He sent her a lascivious smile and glanced at the wall filled with her pictures. 'Oh, I cooperate with you every night when I go to bed, darling. You have no idea.'

'Give me the name and address of Karim's father and it will go a long way towards mitigation,' Sky said, ignoring his vile suggestion.

'Ha! Not a chance. Cross those ruthless bastards and I'm a dead man. Thanks, but no thanks. I'll take my chances. Besides,' he added, pacing towards her with a menacing smile, 'I'm guessing no one knows you're here, so...'

He reached for her phone. Sky had been ready for him and brought up a knee, straight into his scrotum. He howled and hopped on one foot and Sky followed up with a roundhouse kick to his head, which narrowly missed its target. Greaves recovered quickly and made a renewed grab for the phone. Sky backed up but there was nowhere for her to go. She frantically called up her WhatsApp and pressed send, hoping the message that she'd prepared for Ryan, telling him where she was, had gone.

She had no way of knowing because Greaves snatched the phone and threw it across the room. It hit the wall and shattered. And then he was on her, pressing her body against the wall, his fetid breath hot against the side of her face.

17

Ryan returned to his car and sat behind the wheel, taking a moment to consider his next move. He found it hard to concentrate, mainly because his mind kept veering towards Sky, alone in his flat where she would be perfectly safe. And yet his instincts kept telling him otherwise. She knew what ruthless people they were dealing with and wouldn't do anything stupid.

Would she?

She'd promised to wait a few days to get the revenge she so badly craved on an uncle she'd just heard admit to killing her father. But she didn't know where to find Greaves so she couldn't run off half-cocked, he repeatedly told himself.

He was almost grateful when his phone rang and the display showed it was Bill calling.

'Give me a straightforward traitor to deal with any day,' he muttered. 'Much easier to understand than the workings of a woman's mind.' He pressed the green button. 'Yeah. What's up?' he asked.

'That's what I ought to be asking you.' Bill's high-pitched, whiny voice echoed down the line, severely irritating Ryan. 'I've been waiting for your report on Amin's meeting. When were you planning to share?'

Never. 'Just about to come in for a debrief. How's Steve? Any change?'

'None as far as I'm aware.'

In other words, Bill hadn't bothered to check, Ryan thought, his mouth turning down in disapproval. 'That's good, I guess. Has Beth done anything to arouse suspicion?'

'Hardly but I shall have to suspend her pending an investigation.'

'I would advise against it right now. We'll just keep what we know from her. If our American cousins get wind of an internal investigation, and we both know that they will, they'll be all over us like a rash.'

'They have no jurisdiction—'

Ryan gave a cynical little laugh. 'Right, keep telling yourself that. We both know they have eyes and ears everywhere.' *And you won't want them digging up any dirt on you, scumbag.* 'Anyway, I'm on my way.' *Come on, you bastard, make an excuse. Then I'll know that I've always been right about you and that you're a traitorous douchebag.*

'Okay. Hell, no...'

There was a long silence that Ryan didn't interrupt. He tapped the fingers of his free hand against the steering wheel instead as he waited it out, confident now that Bill was running scared and had fallen into self-preservation mode.

'There's a co-agency briefing that I will have to attend,' Bill went on. 'The secretary of state's private secretary's in on it.' A smug note had entered Bill's voice but whether that was because he was now playing with the big boys or because he'd duped the boys in question for God alone knew how long and no one suspected a thing it was hard for Ryan to judge. 'Can't get out of it. I'll call you once I'm free. Hang fire and make yourself available.'

'Don't you want a précis of what I've learned in order to brief the agencies on the case?' Ryan forced an element of surprise into his tone. 'It's high-level stuff, Bill. Category One risk.'

'Who's the target?'

'POTUS,' Ryan replied, using the well-known acronym for the president.

'Holy fuck!'

'Quite.' Ryan had rarely heard Bill swear. He wondered if it was a genuine reaction. He must have already known from his paymasters who the target was but assumed that information was top secret. There again, if he knew that Amin was the leader's son, it was also reasonable to assume that he'd be in the know.

'When? Where?'

Ryan told him.

'Not likely.' Ryan imagined Bill shaking his head and could hear the scepticism in his tone. 'The chances of success are minimal. All signals will be jammed around Chequers the roads closed and the place tied down tighter than a nun's knickers. It would be suicidal.'

'But would also make a point insofar as it would tell the world that nowhere is impenetrable and that they can get to whoever they like, whenever they want to. They don't care about self-interest because they're willing to die for their cause.'

'Even so, if we let on that we know, then the head guy who we've been after for years will leg it.'

'Well, you're the boss. This is above my paygrade,' Ryan said, borrowing Josh's terminology. 'In your shoes I'd cover my own back by passing it on, but the decision is yours. We have camera footage of the meeting so you can hear it for yourself.'

'That'll work. I'll wait until I've seen it.'

'I can send it to you,' Ryan said, playing a hunch, hoping like hell that Bill wouldn't agree. If he did then Ryan was screwed.

'No time now. Get it to my encrypted inbox and I'll take a look after the meeting. Probably better if I don't announce to all and sundry that we think home-grown terrorists have plans to blow up the president but we don't actually know who's behind the plot. It could very well be a distraction. The bad guys know all our efforts will be concentrated on Chequers, leaving them free to cause mayhem somewhere else.'

'Possibly,' Ryan agreed, thinking that the UK would have been blown to smithereens long before now with a weak man like Bill at the helm of such a vital undercover agency. He also thought that the rigorous vetting process all applicants went through couldn't be that rigorous if Bill's true allegiances had slipped beneath the radar. There again, perhaps he was a recent recruit. If the bad guys had something to hold against him it was easy enough to see how he could have got in above his head, no way out possible. Ryan almost felt sorry for the prick.

Almost.

The line went dead and Ryan was about to pocket his phone when a WhatsApp pinged in from Sky. Curious, Ryan read it and his heart turned to stone.

'What the fuck...'

I'm here. Come and get me.

Followed by an address in Canning Town.

Ryan's mind raced with possibilities as he called Beth on her direct line and gave her the address.

'What do we know about it?' he asked. 'Anyone known to us living there?'

'Give me a moment.'

A sound of fingers tapping on keys echoed down the line.

'Just a seedy terrace converted into bedsits, as far as I can tell. We don't have any connections to it. Why?'

'Any idea of the names of tenants?'

'Unlikely. They're the sort of places rented out by the week. By the hour, possibly.'

Ryan nodded, even though Beth couldn't see the gesture. He'd been worried that would be the response.

'Check the electoral role anyway. You never know.'

'Will do.'

'Priority one.'

'Ok.'

He thanked Beth and cut the call, thinking that his earlier concerns about Sky had just been validated. Wondering what the hell had possessed her to traipse off to such a place. Feeling fear like he hadn't known it for decades, he fired up the engine, put the address in his satnav and set out to respond to her cry for help.

* * *

Sky had been expecting her uncle to use physical force and was prepared to meet it head on. She needed to give as good as she got if she was to stand any chance of exorcising her demons. She felt confident that the hours she'd spent perfecting her skill at martial arts would not only provide her with an element of surprise but also give her the edge. After she'd recovered from her feelings of self-loathing for allowing it to happen – Uncle Brian was right, she had examined her conduct and blamed herself – she had decided that no man would ever take advantage of her ever again.

And so she hadn't even told her parents that she'd enrolled in an Aikido class. She quickly become hooked on a Japanese art that teaches women to defend themselves without harming an opponent. That was the only element she disagreed with, since she trained so hard with just one opponent in mind. One who deserved everything he got, and more.

As Sky sweated to rise through the ranks, she also saw the increase in the sport's popularity as more and more women decided to stand up for themselves against hostile partners. Part of the attraction, she knew, was that the training was gentle on the body, could be taken up by women of all ages, and focused on a spiritual approach.

But spiritual wouldn't cut it against a man who always had to have the last word, which is why Sky had progressed to karate, focusing her aggression on images of her uncle, her dedication eventually earning her a black belt.

Which was a fat lot of good to her when she was pressed up against the wall, the pressure of her uncle's forearm on her throat cutting off her air supply as his free hand groped her body. The vile feel of his hand pawing at her breasts infuriated her but she knew better than to struggle. That would only increase the pressure of his arm and likely cause her to pass out. Besides, he liked it when she fought him and her unwillingness spurred him on to greater depths of depravity.

Her being unconscious wouldn't prevent him from throwing her on that stinking bed and taking what he wanted from her, she knew. Anyway, she wasn't about to be that predictable.

'Cameras,' she managed to gasp around the pressure on her throat momentarily eased and she greedily drank in a lungful of air.

'Cameras?' He leered at her. 'Want me to film us, darlin'?'

'There's camera footage of the meeting.'

She choked the words out, pretending to be weaker than she actually was. As she had hoped would be the case, the pressure eased a little more, presumably because he assumed she had no fight left in her. *Never assume, arsehole!* She dropped her hands to her thighs, leaned forward and gulped down more air. Aware of him watching her and glowering as he tried to decide if she was telling the truth.

'Show me!' he barked.

'Can't. You broke my phone.'

He turned the air blue with his language. 'Who else has it?' he asked, his tone a threatening rumble.

'The agency wanting to get to Amin's father.'

Her uncle slowly shook his head. 'No one knows anything about him. He's dead. You're having me over.'

'What? You think I had the time, knowledge and forethought to wire my own flat for vision and sound when I had virtually no notice that a meeting would take place there, much less what it would be about? Or that you would put in an appearance and boast about your vile misdeeds, come to that?'

She could see that her words had struck a chord but he wasn't ready to believe her quite yet, perhaps because he knew he'd screwed up and didn't want it to be true. She finally had the upper hand over a man who had featured in her worst nightmares these past fifteen years but knew he wouldn't give in without putting up a fight. Or doing something reckless if he thought she'd boxed him into a corner. She had always known that might be the case but also knew those nightmares would never go away, that she would never be able to get on with her life until she had evicted all traces of her uncle from it. And she could only do that by confronting him directly.

She had only been living a half-life since her uncle had taken advantage of her – scared of her own shadow, never putting herself forward. And not just because Nancy always eclipsed her. That's what people thought and, since it suited her purpose, she'd never bothered to put them straight.

The urge to one day exact revenge had kept her going, given her purpose. A reason to get out of bed in the morning. She had never told a living soul about what happened to her all those years ago, not even Nancy. But now, if she somehow came out of this alive, there was a possibility that she would be able to put the past behind her and start to live life to the full.

And if she did not... well, she would rather be dead than live with memories that refused to go away. That was why she had come here today. She had known that no one else would understand, especially not Ryan, which was why she hadn't attempted to explain. Besides, he had the small matter of the American president's life resting in his capable hands. He had no time to listen to her bleating on about historic events. Even if she'd attempted it, he would probably wonder why she hadn't simply relegated her memories to the past, where they belonged, and got on with life.

If only it were that easy, she thought, letting out a wistful sigh.

'Then why aren't the authorities knocking at my door?' Uncle Brian finally asked, grinning at her and displaying teeth yellow with nicotine. 'Sorry, love, but you're clutching at straws. You probably rigged up some sort of sound device but there's no way that you have pictures.'

'They will be here. They're on their way.' Well, she sincerely hoped that they were but had no way of knowing if Ryan had even read her message yet, much less responded to it. 'I wanted to confront you about the death of my father first. To tell you precisely what a scumbag you are.' She gave his living quarters a scathing glance. 'The lowest of the low. I need to understand why you felt that you had to do it.'

'Why the fuck do you think?' A plethora of resentment welled up in his expression; a spoilt child who'd finally been told 'no' and whose tantrums no longer had the power to influence. 'I was done out of my fair share of our parent's estate, that's why. It's no coincidence that your old man came sniffing round my sister's petticoats just as we were about to inherit.' His eyes had narrowed to slits of resentment and Sky could see that he'd managed to convince himself that he spoke the truth. 'Of course, as I'm a man, the lot should have come to me.'

Sky had managed to free one hand from her side, where it had been held in place by her uncle's body. She could do a lot of damage with that hand but desperately wanted to hear what he had to say in justification and so made do with massaging her sore neck with it. 'What century do you think we're living in?' she asked.

'I was given assurances,' he said, sounding as though he was attempting to convince himself. 'So I had expectations and had acted accordingly. If I'd known the truth. If I'd known that our old man would screw me over then I would have behaved very differently.'

'What? You'd have killed your own father as well as mine?' she goaded.

'Careful!'

'Or what?' Sky ignored the threat. 'As I understand it, everything was split down the middle. You have no reason to complain. My father invested wisely on my mother's behalf; you did not. Even though your constant need for handouts put pressure on her marriage, Mum never let her little brother down. I lost count of the number of times I heard her telling Dad she was only going to help you out one more time. She'd helped to raise her little brother, so had a soft spot for him and you played upon her emotions.' A soft spot, Sky reminded herself, that had prevented her from telling her mother the truth about what had happened to her, thereby forcing her to take sides.

'Throwing crumbs to a pigeon like a generous benefactor and expecting me to be grateful.' His expression turned sour, resentful. 'My sister and I agreed that if anything happened to one of us, the other would take over their share of the inheritance.'

Sky gave a bitter little laugh. 'Then it's fortunate that you didn't peg it, otherwise my mum would only have inherited debts.'

'We're not all the pipe and slippers type, old and stuck in our ways at forty. Some of us like to speculate in order to accumulate but that takes capital, and balls.'

'How's that going for you?'

Sky knew she shouldn't goad him but also knew that getting him to air his resentments had made him forget for the time being about his desire to kill her. She glanced at his shrine that depicted her, thinking he probably had other desires to satisfy first and shuddered. He was clearly besotted and she knew from bitter experience that rape was his favoured modus operandi.

'Temporary setbacks,' he replied, leaning his body weight into her and pinning her back against the wall.

Damn! She hoped he hadn't noticed the space that had grown between them. A space that was almost wide enough for her to be able to launch a surprise attack.

Almost.

But frustratingly not quite enough. He would be able to block her in a nanosecond. So, there was only one thing for it. She would have to go on the offensive still, but verbally. Not that she had much hope of defeating such a biased and resentful man with reasoned argument, but at least it would buy her some time.

'We can stand here, you bullying me with your superior strength as you whinge about how hard done by you are but it will change nothing. You've admitted to murder and I wasn't stupid enough to come here without first saving that recording to the cloud and sending it to a person whom I trust.' She paused, forcing herself to meet his repugnant gaze. 'You have limited options. Either help me to stop a terrorist attack by giving me the name of your boss or take the fall for killing my father. Your choice.'

He gave a harsh laugh. 'Little girl, if you were really working with the authorities they would be here now, blue lights flashing, in force.' He shook his head, causing greasy hair to flap repugnantly. 'Nah, you're having me on. I assume you came here because you can't resist my charms.'

Sky sent him a scathing look but remained silent. There was nothing she could possibly say to that since it would seem odd to him that she'd confronted him alone. Knowing how highly he thought of himself, he probably believed what he'd just said was the truth. He *had* been a handsome man thirteen years previously, a real Jack the lad. Women were drawn to him like bees to pollen, especially when he was in funds and flashing the cash, but he didn't seem to realise that the years hadn't been kind to him and any self-respecting woman would give him a wide berth nowadays.

'No one knows where you are, I'm thinking,' he said, smirking, 'and so I can do what the hell I like with you *and* ingratiate myself with my boss by tipping him the wink.'

'A ruthless man of that ilk who has gone to so much trouble to rise from the dead and remain anonymous didn't do so by giving men like you the benefit of the doubt.' Sky attempted to portray confidence even though she could tell from his manic expression that he was unlikely to see reason. 'He will wonder about your loyalties, especially since no one else has even guessed at his real identity all these years.' Uncle Brian looked pensive and Sky knew she'd struck a chord. 'He hasn't got as far as he has without cutting out loose ends,' she pushed ahead to say. 'Why do you think he recruited you; a non-believer? So that you can take all the risks, and the fall. That's why.'

A hefty fist, so swift that she didn't see it coming, struck the side of Sky's face. With a cry, she fell back on to the filthy bed, dazed and disorientated. She blinked to clear her vision but could still see two outlines of her uncle's vile person towering above her. One was more than enough and she closed her eyes to block out the image.

'You're getting above yourself, little girl, and need to be reminded who's the boss.'

'Not you,' Sky replied, her head clearing. Did he but know it, her uncle had done her a favour. He still didn't seem to have clocked her skills at martial arts and now that he wasn't on top of her, she had options. 'Don't make the mistake of assuming that you'll inherit if anything happens to me. Not only have I made a will that specifically excludes you but I really have also sent that recording to my solicitor, *with* pictures.' She smiled at him. 'Yeah, you're still not sure if there are pictures and it's killing you. I can see that.'

Well, she conceded, she would have done both things if time had permitted but her uncle wasn't to know that it hadn't. Only a crazy person would confront a rapist and confessed murderer without taking precautions, wouldn't they? She decided not to try and figure out what that said about the current state of her mental health.

Uncle Brian responded with a slow, ironic round of applause, but Sky could see that she'd finally got through to him and that he was rattled.

'I think we'd better see what your boyfriend has to say about the situation,' he said, reaching for his mobile.

Sky watched as he made the call, waiting for an opportunity. He stood frustratingly just out of her range as he barked orders to Karim into his phone.

'We have a situation,' he said curtly. 'Get here now!'

Sky decided to treat Karim's impending arrival as an opportunity to divide and conquer. One of them would put self-preservation first and sell out Karim's father in return for leniency. Her money was on her uncle. Karim would be aware that if he was in custody and was perceived to be a grass then his life expectancy would be zero.

Uncle Brian hung up, presumably before Karim could even respond, and smacked his lips together.

'Now,' he said, 'how are we gonna pass the time until lover boy gets here?'

18

The thought of dancing to such an insignificant man's tune infuriated Karim but he knew that he had little choice in the matter. How had it come to this? Greaves was not fit to polish Karim's shoes; nor the sort of person Karim would ordinarily spare the time of day for. Unfortunately, he was also a graduate of the street of hard knocks, grasped whatever opportunities came his way, didn't understand the meaning of loyalty and knew how to fight dirty. Karim felt intimidated by him, but would never make that admission. What was indisputable was the fact that Greaves had too much on Karim for him to lay down the law. Karim was his to control.

For now.

When he arrived at Greaves's insalubrious address – a place he'd never had the dubious pleasure of visiting before – he felt vulnerable and probably looked as out of place as he knew himself to be. Men had been knifed for less than a tenner in this part of London, which was why Karim had come prepared for trouble. He felt the reassuring presence of the knife in his pocket, took a deep breath and strode towards the house, giving every indication of a man confident in his own skin. Show the first signs of weakness and, he knew, the loitering gangs eyeing him speculatively would look upon him as easy prey.

'How the hell can anyone live like this?' he wondered aloud, ignoring barking dogs, couples yelling insults at one another, blaring music and babies screaming as he entered the building and rocked on his heels at the smells that assaulted his nostrils.

Two youths slouched across the access to the final flight of stairs, staring sullenly at Karim, making it obvious that they had no intention of letting him pass. Until Karim withdrew his knife and casually ran his fingers down the serrated blade.

'Evening lads,' he said affably.

Neither of them could be much over eighteen, Karim estimated, but despite their heavily tattooed arms, their attempts to intimidate fell woefully short of the mark. Karim's weapon wasn't all for show. He'd knifed a man before and a strong sense of self-preservation wouldn't prevent him from doing so again. Appearing to realise that they'd met their match, the pair shifted just enough to let Karim pass without completely losing face.

Karim reached the top floor, only slightly out of breath, pride partially restored because he'd won that particular encounter. He heard footsteps behind him and assumed that a less streetwise visitor was about to be on the receiving end of the lads' wounded dignity.

Dismissing the incident from his mind, he rapped at Greaves's door and waited, fingering his knife again as he wondered what surprises awaited him. Any number of possibilities ran through his head; any apart from the one that confronted him when Greaves wrenched the door open, dressed only in dirty boxers.

'What the fuck?'

'Just in time to join the fun,' Greaves said at the same time, grinning.

They were the last words to pass his lips before a whirlwind sprang up behind him, swivelled in a circle and expertly caught Greaves with the side of her foot just below his ear. He crumpled to the floor and lay there in a semi-conscious stupor.

* * *

Ryan drove like a bat out of hell towards Canning Town, trying to decide whether to call up reinforcements. He decided against it in the end, partly because he didn't know what he would find when he arrived but also because the call would have to go through official channels, meaning Bill would get to hear of it.

'What the hell have you gotten yourself into, Sky?' he asked aloud, blaring his horn as he went through an amber light just as it turned red. The responding horns coming from those in the opposite direction as he cut them off barely registered.

His phone rang just as he'd reached the point of maximum frustration with heavy traffic that seemed determined to slow his progress.

'What do you have for me, Beth?' he asked, pushing the button on his steering wheel to take the call.

'That address is used as a halfway house for prisoners out on licence,' she replied.

'Do we have the name for a caretaker who can give us a list of current residents?' he asked, already suspecting what answer she would give.

'Nope. These are guys who've finished their sentences but haven't bothered to move on. No close watch is being kept but I figure someone must know who resides there. They must pay rent. I'm on it, Ryan. Soon as I know, you'll know.'

'Okay, thanks. Keep this to yourself for now.'

'Don't I always?'

Ryan imagined her rolling her eyes as she hung up.

By the time he'd reached his destination and found a parking spot, Beth still hadn't gotten back to him but he couldn't afford to wait so he'd just have to wing it. He wished that Sky had had the foresight to tell him which room she was visiting and who occupied it. Presumably she'd been under pressure when she sent the message and had no time to go into detail, which in turn implied that she'd set out for this address with no intention of telling him where she'd gone or why.

Until she got in trouble and needed his help.

'Irresponsible, headstrong, impetuous...' Ryan continued to mutter to himself as he stood across the road from the depressing building, wondering what the hell was happening to Sky, always assuming she was still inside.

And still alive.

His presence drew a few curious glances from the constant mass of people stomping past him, all of them looking older than they probably were, and already defeated by life.

Aware that he would have to get inside and try to find her, his dilemma was resolved when he noticed a familiar and very out-of-place figure walking towards the door. With a glance over his shoulder, Amin pushed it open and went inside. Ryan didn't hesitate. Sprinting across the road, dodging oncoming cars and kamikaze bike couriers and receiving horn honks and verbal abuse by way of reward, he reached the opposite pavement intact. Close on Amin's heels, he entered the building.

The first thing that hit him was the stench – a combination of excrement and human misery. Ryan ignored it. He'd known worse but doubted that Sky had – his concern at her presence in this rathole intensifying. He heard Amin's feet on the stairs above him. He paused when he heard a brief conversation above the noise coming from behind various doors. Karim had obviously been confronted by more than one person but Ryan was damned if he'd go to his rescue.

In the event, intervention proved to be unnecessary and he heard Amin's feet thundering up the next flight. Ryan followed but his way was blocked by two youths brandishing knives that had clearly failed to halt Karim; unless he'd paid them to let him pass, of course. Ryan was in no mood to follow his example.

'Out the way, boys,' he said, putting emphasis on the final word.

'Give us yer wallet,' one of them said, his voice not even broken yet. Ryan supposed he shouldn't be surprised. What chance did kids brought up in this environment have of getting any sort of decent life?

'Stand aside,' Ryan said calmly, 'and no one need get hurt.'

The boys shared a look and Ryan could sense the desire to scarper warring with the need to save face. They lunged simultaneously and awkwardly, leading with their knife hands, telegraphing their moves to a man of Ryan's experience. Ryan ducked beneath one arm and grabbed hold of the other, twisting at the wrist until bones cracked. The kid screamed with pain and dropped his knife. Ryan, not even out of breath, turned to face the other, who now looked anything but sure of himself. The disturbance clearly hadn't registered on the Richter scale of noise coming from the various rooms and even if it had, Ryan assumed that the residents had learned to mind their own business since no one came to intervene.

'Don't be stupid,' he told the child.

But the kid seemed infuriated and lunged. Ryan timed it so that he'd ducked low when the boy reached him and simply toppled him by grabbing an ankle. Hard. And pulling. He screamed as he fell, cutting his arm on his own blade.

'Nice meeting you kids,' Ryan said. 'Have a good day now.'

So saying, he took the remaining stairs two at a time, praying that whatever was going down, he wouldn't be too late to save Sky from her own stupidity.

He paused at the top of the stairs to see Amin standing in an open doorway. He either didn't hear Ryan's footsteps or was too preoccupied to care about who was there because he didn't once look back. Ryan moved forward, close enough behind him to take him in a headlock, and could see now what had held Amin's attention so comprehensively. He himself was scarcely less surprised.

Sky stood over a prostrate, semi-conscious Greaves. Clearly, Sky was responsible for using such professionally and potentially lethal force against her uncle and her stance made it clear that it would be wiser if he didn't attempt to get up. How hadn't Ryan known that she could handle herself so efficiently? He scratched his head. Why hadn't she said? What other secrets had she kept from him?

'Sky!' Karim's mouth fell open. 'What the fuck?'

'Want some of the same?' she asked, her eyes gleaming with hostility as she turned to face him, still poised like a coiled spring, bouncing on the balls of her feet, hyped-up and limber. 'Or are you willing to see reason, you worthless waste of space?'

Ryan remained just out of sight, ready to intervene if necessary but beginning to suspect that his services would be surplus to requirements. Greaves was clearly the tougher of the two and if she'd taken him down then she would have little trouble handling Amin. In fact, she would probably welcome the opportunity to exorcise a few demons, the nature of which she hadn't bothered to share with Ryan.

He wouldn't deprive her of that opportunity.

'Sky, what is this? Did he hurt you?' Amin stepped forward, his oily attempt at sincerity making Ryan want to vomit.

'You have *no* idea. Or then again,' she added in a cold tone, 'perhaps you do, given that you're cut from the same cloth.'

'What the—'

'Keep yer mouth shut!' Greaves croaked from his prone position.

'Speak when spoken to,' Sky said, delivering a sharp kick to his ribs and another to his face. A gush of blood spurted from his nose as a rush of profanities fell from his lips. Even Ryan was surprised by the viciousness of the attack. He assumed that Sky had waited a long time to exact revenge, but even so...

Then he recalled what Greaves had said about Sky in her flat and how she had sobbed on his shoulder afterwards. She hadn't told him precisely what had happened to her. She had even denied being raped but Ryan could see now that she'd been economical with the truth. Perhaps because she felt ashamed. His heart went out to her as he stayed right where he was, watching and listening.

'You really think I fell for your bullshit, don't you, Karim,' she said in a sweetly sarcastic tone. 'Well of course you do. No woman can resist your charm, or so you like to believe.'

'Darling, I don't know...'

'Shut up! This is my party.' She smiled but there was no warmth behind the gesture. 'I was playing a part; I was in character. It was the only way I could bear to let you touch me.'

That's my girl. Ryan sensed that she was finally getting rid of the pent-up anger that she'd been holding back for too long. He was also filled with relief because he could tell that she'd told the truth. She really had seen through Amin all along and *she* had been playing *him*; not the other way around. Shame she hadn't let him in on her secret but she'd obviously wanted to handle things her way. Good on her. She'd waited long enough.

Something fundamental changed within Ryan at that moment. He'd been holding back because he wasn't prepared to compete for Sky's affections, especially not against that arsehole. Now he was seeing a side of her that he hadn't even suspected she possessed.

A side that no one else had ever seen. And a whole world of possibilities, previously unthinkable, opened up to him.

'Sky, darling, I have absolutely no idea what this is all about but I'm sure we can sort it all out if you'll just let me...'

She swivelled on her heel and brought a roundhouse kick to rest in the centre of Amin's belly. He gasped and deflated like a forlorn balloon left waving in the breeze at the end of a raucous children's party.

'You really think you'll get away with trying to assassinate the president of the United States?' she asked in a scathing tone. 'We've been ahead of you and your *dead* father every step of the way.'

'We? Who are you?' Still clutching his stomach, Amin stood upright, looking deathly pale and shocked. 'Who are you working for? Which agency?'

'I get to ask the questions. You answer them. That's how this works.'

Ryan admired the manner in which she positioned herself so that she could see both men and would be ready to counter any attack they launched. Whoever had instructed her in the art of self-defence had done a bang-up job.

'What do you want?' Amin asked.

'For you to give up your father. I gave this scum the chance,' she said, directing another kick at Greaves, 'but he declined to take me seriously. *Big* mistake, as he's now learned to his cost. I'm no longer a star-struck teenager subjected to multiple rapes.'

'How did you... know—'

'That you were targeting me for my money?' Sky sent Amin a scathing look that didn't entirely disguise her hurt feelings. It wasn't lost on Ryan that the allegation of rape hadn't warranted even a word of sympathy from Amin. 'You're not quite as clever as you think you are. Or there again, perhaps you underestimated my intelligence, or overestimated my supposed infatuation with you. It was all an act, every second of every minute I spent with you, in case you are still in any doubt. I couldn't abide your touch, or anything else you did to me but you're too far up yourself to even suppose that a woman would find you repulsive.' She sent him a sweetly sarcastic smile, clearly enjoying Amin's look of shocked incomprehension. 'Yeah, I can see that I got that much about you right.'

'Then why...'

'Why did I endure your less than welcome advances?' She gave a casual shrug. 'A means to an end; nothing more. Once I got my hands on communications between you and this rat,' she poked at Greaves, still on the floor, with her toe, 'discussing getting your grubby hands on my funds I knew I'd got it right. You might be careful what you commit to email but not nearly careful enough. I've known where this idiot hangs out for a while, you see, guessed he'd come looking for me so decided to find out what he intended. I had a friend hack into his email for me and imagine my surprise when your name came up, closely followed by free tickets to your club. I saw an opportunity to use you and finally have him admit to killing my father. Of course, I didn't imagine that I'd get the entire thing on video and audio. That was an added bonus which served to validate my patience.'

'What the fuck...' Amin's jaw fell open and he seemed incapable of saying anything more. But it was clear to Ryan that he believed every word and had gone into self-preservation mode.

'No escape fund coming from my hands, I'm afraid,' Sky said sweetly. 'And this bastard is going down for double murder.' She rested a foot in the centre of Greaves's chest, rather like a poacher posing proudly over an animal's carcass for the camera.

'Double?' Greaves gasped.

'Oh yes,' Sky said. 'I suppose you didn't realise when you punched me so violently in the stomach the last time we were alone together, that you not only killed my baby but also made it impossible for me ever to bear a child again.'

Oh shit!

Her tough façade crumpled and tears rolled down her face, which is when everything went to hell in a handcart. Amin saw his opportunity and leapt forward at the same time as Greaves pushed himself violently back to his feet, sending Sky tumbling backwards.

* * *

Sky berated herself for allowing emotion to get the better of her. She had sworn to herself that if this moment ever came she wouldn't do so. She knew it had cost her the advantage she had so painstakingly made for herself. She would never be able to fight them both off so she had to make a lightning-quick decision. Glancing at her uncle, she could see that he was still dazed, and hurting.

Not nearly enough.

She shouldn't have held back, she realised, but it was too late to worry about that now. Karim was approaching her with a vicious knife in his hand and a rictus smile creasing his face. She fell back on her training, her heart palpitating despite the fact that an icy calm had slowed her breathing and sharpened her reflexes. He was no longer underestimating her but she could still get the better of him, if she kept her nerve.

She sprang at exactly the right moment, a split second before he was on her, and would have disarmed him but for the fact that her uncle grabbed her from behind, pulling her to the floor. She cried out, waiting for the inevitable slice of the knife. It would almost be welcome. She had failed to get the better of Uncle Brian and would for ever have to live with what he'd done to her. Revenge, what little she'd managed to exact in the past few minutes, wasn't all it was cracked up to be. He would escape unpunished and she would be left blaming herself for that as well.

The cry, when it came, wasn't from her but from Karim when he tumbled to the ground, disarmed, blood pouring from his mouth.

'Ryan!' she breathed, as she turned and delivered a vicious blow with the side of her hand to her uncle's throat, knocking him out cold.

'Hey,' Ryan replied, crouching down to help her gently to her feet. 'Thought you might need some help but you seemed to be doing pretty good all on your own.'

The fight had drained out of her and she fell into his arms, more than willing to lean on his broad shoulder now that she'd made her point. 'You got my message. You came.'

'Always for you,' he said, folding her in his arms and kissing her. 'Will you be okay for a moment? I need to make a few calls and have this garbage carried out.' He indicated the two prostrate men as he spoke.

'Sure. You make your calls and I'll make sure these two don't go anywhere.'

'I need medical help,' Karim said, screaming as he clutched his bleeding face.

'Not yet you don't,' Sky told him with a sweet smile. 'But it could be arranged.'

Karim had the good sense to remain quiet after that. Sky filled her gaze with the sight of Ryan's musculature as he paced the tiny room, answering a few questions put to him by whoever he was speaking to and then issuing orders.

'Right, all in hand,' he said, pocketing his phone and smiling at Sky. 'You all right?'

'Never better,' she replied, because it was true. It already felt as though a huge weight had been lifted from her shoulders and she was ready to embrace life again.

19

A week later Ryan and Sky sat together in the hospital's cafe, still dithering between flowers and grapes, both available from the gift shop in the foyer.

'Is Steve a flowers sort of guy?' Sky asked.

Ryan grinned. 'He'll hate them, which is why I made the suggestion.'

'That's mean.'

'He will know we still love him if we're mean to him.' Ryan rubbed his jaw. 'Still can't believe that he's made such a rapid recovery. I knew he was tough but I didn't realise he was quite that tough. He's astonished all his doctors, apparently, and is now complaining about the food, which is an excellent sign.'

'And I can't believe you're taking me to meet him. I'm highly honoured.'

'He wants to thank you in person for what you did. Your actions helped to save his agency's future. Of course, I'd prefer to tan your backside for being so irresponsible but even I can understand why you had to do it.' He thought back to the heart to heart he'd had with Sky soon after the dust had settled and Karim's father had been arrested.

'I'd been carrying the guilt and sorrow around with me all those years,' Sky said, with a sad little shake of her head. 'I worshipped the ground that my uncle walked on and really did believe him when he said I was responsible for what had happened between us. That I'd led him on.' Ryan curled his upper lip but said nothing. Now that the floodgates had finally opened, Sky seemed to want to talk about the events that had marred her life; events that she'd not spoken about ever before, apparently. Even Nancy hadn't known. 'I saw a glimpse of his real self when I told him I was pregnant. He calmly told me to get rid of it. When I suggested otherwise he completely lost it, punched me and... well, you know the rest.'

'And now you can't have children.' Ryan shook his head. 'I'm sorry. I talked to you about them once and should have noticed the pathos in your expression.'

'I've already told you: I'm good at disguising my feelings. I worked with the school theatre group. Not on stage, of course, I was far too shy for that. But I studied the actors, saw how they got into character and that's what I did when my uncle first... well, you know. I pretended to be playing a part. It was happening to someone else. Once I started seeing Karim and knew why he'd singled me out I remained in character the entire time, convincing my alter ego that I was in love with him. Otherwise I would have lost my nerve.'

Ryan shook his head. 'You are remarkable.'

'Hardly.'

'So anyway, your despair at losing your baby inspired you to learn to defend yourself.' Ryan touched her hand. 'You didn't feel able to tell your parents?'

'God, no! But I think Dad knew, or suspected. I changed after losing the baby. Anyone would and he noticed the differences in me. Mum not so much. She was wrapped up in her charity work and her first bout of chemo, so she was distracted. I was glad about that. Not about her cancer but about her priorities changing. I was so damned ashamed of myself, Ryan. You can have no idea. Besides, once she got ill there was no way I could tell her what her brother had done to me. It would have destroyed her even quicker than the cancer did and made her final days a torment.'

'And yet you let Amin touch you.'

'I did.' She hung her head. 'I finally saw an opportunity when I made the connection between him and my uncle to get closure, so I was prepared to do pretty much anything. I've known where my uncle was living for a while but it would have been pointless to confront him about the rape. He would never take responsibility for that, but I hoped somehow to get him to admit to killing my father.' She shrugged. 'I didn't really have a definite plan but also knew I'd never get another shot at it. Then when you came along, it all fell into place. It was meant to be.'

'I feel used,' he quipped.

She playfully punched his arm and Ryan was glad to see that her smile was now genuine and uncontrived; the shadows that had always lurked just beneath the surface no longer in evidence. 'Get over yourself! Not everything's about you.'

'It's not?' Ryan affected surprise. 'I've been seriously misled.'

'Well anyway, you've got Karim's father somewhere secure and the US president's visit went off without a hitch.'

It did and they had. Ryan called in the cavalry, Amin and Greaves were taken to an unpleasant location and soon both were singing like canaries in a misguided attempt to save their own hides. Too little too late. No way was Greaves getting out of a murder charge; Ryan would personally make sure of that. But Sky had balked at the idea of him being charged with her rape. She knew he would deny it and she would be obliged to give evidence, reliving a nightmare that she finally stood a chance of putting behind her, or so she insisted. Ryan thought it a very great pity that victims of rape had their entire lives put under a microscope and were themselves often made to feel like the guilty party. Something had to change.

Ryan had called up a contact in MI5, keeping Bill in the dark, and the remaining men who'd met at Sky's flat had been arrested and charged. So too had Amin's father. His influential friends had deserted him like the proverbial rats and he was no longer quite so smugly self-assured, especially since his worldwide assets had been frozen and no one was willing to bail him out.

Bill had been hauled in by MI5 and the evidence was stacking up against him. He'd been seen at Amin's club in a cinch with another guy – a stooge employed to entrap him. That evidence had been used to force him to work for the dark side. Ryan thought he was an idiot to have allowed it to happen. No one batted an eyelid nowadays at another person's sexual tendencies but it seemed that Bill was still in denial, felt it made him less than a man, and got sucked in so far with Amin senior's organisation that there was no way out for him.

Ryan would have felt sorry for him, but for the fact that he'd tried to blame Beth for the leaks emanating from their agency and for the fact that his intel was responsible for the attack on Steve. As things stood, as far as Ryan was concerned, he could rot in hell.

'You've been very open with me,' Ryan said. 'I hope it feels better to talk about it.'

'Much better,' Sky assured him, reaching across the table and touching his hand. 'Which is why I think you should do the same thing.'

Ryan didn't pretend not to understand her. 'You think that my dislike of Amin is personal?' He nodded in response to his own question. 'Very astute of you.'

'Tell me,' she said softly.

'I was engaged to a lady called Sarah,' he replied, his voice sounding hollow and distant even to his own ears. 'She worked at MI5 and so did I at the time, which is why I have so many connections there. Technically, it's against the rules for two agents to become romantically involved and so we'd decided that Sarah would give up her career and go into private security instead. But she had one last assignment to carry out before we announced our engagement; one that she desperately wanted to see through because she had already invested so much time and effort into the job.' Ryan paused to rub at his chin, feeling haunted by the past. 'If I'd insisted that we make our announcement immediately then perhaps she'd still be alive. I will always blame myself.'

'Your line of work is dangerous. I'm sure she understood that.'

'Even so. It was a joint agency assignment but MI5 were running the show. Just as always, the people I now work for were acting as bag-carriers, doing their dirty work, their actions deniable. Anyway, they'd got a bead on Amin, knew he was involved with an active terrorist cell and Sarah's brief was to get close to him, see what she could uncover.' Ryan looked away from Sky, unable to face the sympathy in her expression.

'Suffice it to say, Amin cottoned on and... well, Sarah's body has never been found. We couldn't even have a funeral. I went off the rails a bit but was offered a position with Steve that gave me more leeway and I jumped at the chance.' He spread his hands. 'You know the rest.'

'Now I understand why you kicked Karim's face so hard after you'd disarmed him,' Sky said. 'In your place I don't think I would have been quite so restrained. Still, I don't suppose they'll bother to set his broken nose properly where he's living right now and we both know how proud he was of his pretty-boy looks.'

'Well, wherever Sarah is, she can rest in peace now. Her death has been avenged and it feels good to finally let go.'

Sky nodded. 'I know,' she said.

Ryan smiled at her, aware of the failure, the regret, leaving his expression. 'Well,' he said, standing. 'We'd best go and see the boss man so I can give him this.' He pulled an envelope from his pocket.

'What is it?' she asked, standing to join him.

'My resignation.'

'Your resignation.' She shook her head in obvious bewilderment. 'But why? You love what you do and your star is now very much in the ascendence since you've been credited with breaking the single most wanted terrorist cell in this country.'

'Best to leave on a high. And don't delude yourself. Where one cell folds, another springs up to take its place. The war on terror will never end.'

'Then you are needed more than ever.'

'Perhaps I want to live a normal life.' He fixed her with a probing look, hoping he'd gauged her feelings right and wasn't about to make an almighty fool of himself. All he knew from bitter experience was that the chance for lasting happiness was fleeting. He had thrown it away once and wasn't about to make the same mistake again. 'Live like normal people, not always looking over my shoulder, thinking the worst of everyone, looking for hidden agendas.'

'I see your point but still don't get why. You thrive on the danger and will be bored witless within a month if you give it all up.'

'I intend to be a consultant, if they want me. Fall back on my experience and educate the new guys in a classroom. This is a young man's game.'

'And you're decrepit,' she replied, grinning. 'Past it. I can quite see that.'

'Watch it, woman!' He grasped her hand and ran his fingers down the length of hers, oblivious to the hustle and bustle of the café, its occupants going about their daily business around them, blithely unaware of the drama being played out in front of their eyes. 'I have another pressing reason for giving it up.'

'Which is?' She tilted her head and regarded him closely from beneath curling lashes.

'The discouragement of relationships. Perhaps I want one.' He paused. 'With you.'

'You do?' She bit her lower lip in that entrancing way of hers and her smile widened. 'Do you think that's wise? I'm not exactly the domesti-cated type. Besides,' she added, focusing her gaze on the floor and biting her lip, 'I can't have...'

'Children?' He placed a finger beneath her chin and forced her to meet his gaze. 'You're more than enough for me, darling. Never doubt it. So, what do you say? Quite apart from anything else, someone has to save you from your own impetuosity.'

'Well, in that case, I guess I'll consider myself saved,' she replied, falling into his arms and tilting her head back, making the process of kissing her that much easier to achieve.

ACKNOWLEDGMENTS

My thanks to all the wonderful Boldwood team and in particular to my talented editor, Emily Ruston.

MORE FROM EVIE HUNTER

We hope you enjoyed reading *The Scam*. If you did, please leave a review.

If you'd like to gift a copy, this book is also available as an ebook, digital audio download and audiobook CD.

Sign up to Evie Hunter's mailing list for news, competitions and updates on future books.

https://bit.ly/EvieHunterNewsletter

The Fall, another nail-biting revenge thriller from Evie Hunter, is available to order now.

ABOUT THE AUTHOR

Evie Hunter has written a great many successful regency romances as Wendy Soliman and is now redirecting her talents to produce dark gritty thrillers for Boldwood. For the past twenty years she has lived the life of a nomad, roaming the world on interesting forms of transport, but has now settled back in the UK.

Follow Evie on social media:

 twitter.com/wendyswriter

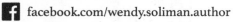 facebook.com/wendy.soliman.author

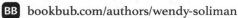 bookbub.com/authors/wendy-soliman

Boldwood

Boldwood Books is an award-winning fiction publishing company seeking out the best stories from around the world.

Find out more at www.boldwoodbooks.com

Join our reader community for brilliant books, competitions and offers!

Follow us
@BoldwoodBooks
@BookandTonic

Sign up to our weekly deals newsletter

https://bit.ly/BoldwoodBNewsletter